Heartless, lungless, he could neither groan nor scream. A dozen times, the monitors in the form-change unit flared their warning signs. Chemical concentrations were wildly far from equilibrium, ion balances at fatal levels, synapses firing spastically out of sequence. The semiconscious body in the tank shuddered and writhed, enduring rates of adaptation beyond all rational limits.

Every organ, every cell screamed for relief. The fear was no longer deep in his brain. It was rampant surges of pain and terror, invading every hiding place of will and resolve.

And then it was over. He had the right final form; he knew it without looking. His tortured body had been cast up, twisted and misshapen, on a strange shore.

Bey Wolf had crossed the form-change ocean.

By Charles Sheffield
Published by Ballantine Books:

SIGHT OF PROTEUS

TRADER'S WORLD

THE WEB BETWEEN THE WORLDS

PROTEUS UNBOUND

Charles Sheffield

A Del Rey Book

BALLANTINE BOOKS • NEW YORK

To Emma

Acknowledgments: My special thanks to Drs. David Brin and Robert Forward, who made many valuable suggestions and even seem to agree with me that entropy can be interesting.

PART ONE

"S = k.log W"

Epitaph of Ludwig Boltzmann (1844–1906),
carved on his tombstone in Vienna

CHAPTER 1

"When change itself can give no more
'Tis easy to be true."
                                —Sir Charles Sedley

They found Behrooz Wolf on the lowest levels of Old City, in a filthy room whose better days were far in the past.

In the doorway, Leo Manx paused. He looked at the sweating, moldy walls and cobwebbed ceiling, gagged at the rank smell, and retreated a step. The floor of the room was covered with old wrappers and scraps of food. The man behind pushed on through. He was grinning for the first time since they had met. "There's a breath of Old Earth for you. Still sure you want him?"

"I have to have him, Colonel. Orders from the top." Manx tried to breathe shallowly as he moved forward. He knew Hamming was goading him, as everyone had done since he had arrived on Earth and explained what he wanted. Manx ignored Hamming; the mission was too important to let small issues get in the way.

The furnishings were minimal: a single bed, a food tap, a sanitary unit, and one padded chair. As Manx moved farther inside, the stink became stronger; it was definitely coming from the man slumped in that chair. Bald, sunken-eyed, and

3

filthy, he stared straight ahead at the life-size holograph of a smiling blond woman that covered most of one spotted and water-stained wall. The lower part of the holograph displayed a verse of poetry in letters three inches high.

Ignoring both the man and the 'graph, Colonel Hamming crouched to inspect a little metal box on the floor next to the chair. Plaited braids of multicolored wires ran from the box to the electrodes on the seated man's scalp. Hamming peered at the settings, his nose just a couple of inches away from the control knobs.

"You're in luck. It's so-so, a medium setting."

Manx stared at the seated man's lined, grimy neck. "Meaning what?"

"Meaning he's been emptying his bladder and his bowels when he needs to, and maybe he ate something now and again, so he shouldn't need surgery or emergency care. But he won't have bothered with much else."

"So I see." Leo Manx examined the man with more disgust than curiosity, knowing that in a few more minutes he might have to touch that greasy, mottled skin. "I thought Dream Machines were illegal."

"Yeah. So's cheating on taxes. All right, Doc, tell me when you're ready. When I turn this off, he may get nasty. Violent. Losing all his nice dream reinforcement. I've got a shot ready."

"Don't you want to check that we have the right man before we begin? I mean, I've seen pictures of Behrooz Wolf, and this—he's—well . . ."

The security man was grinning again. "Not quite up to your expectations? Don't forget Wolf is seventy-three years old. You've probably only seen pictures when he's on a conditioning program. We'll check the chromosome ID if you like, but I'll vouch for him without that. It's not the first time, you know. He did this three other times, before he was kicked out as head of the Office of Form Control. He always comes here, and he always looks pretty much like this. Never quite so far gone before. When he still had his official position, we came and got him earlier. Can't let a government bureaucrat die on the job."

"You mean this time, if I hadn't asked to find him . . ."

"You, or someone else." Hamming shrugged. "I don't know how you Cloudlanders do it," he said, contempt in his voice, "but here on Earth a free citizen can die any damn way he chooses. Get ready, now—I'm pulling the plug. We'll go cold turkey."

Manx hovered impotently near as the security officer flipped four switches in quick succession, then ripped taped electrodes from the bald scalp. There was no sound from the biofeedback unit, but the man in the chair shivered, gasped, and suddenly sat upright. He stared wildly around him.

"Wolf. Behrooz Wolf," Manx said urgently. "I must talk—"

"Grab his other arm," Hamming ordered. "He's going to pop."

The man was already on his feet, glaring about with blood-shot eyes. Before Leo Manx could act, Behrooz Wolf had spun around to pull free and was feebly reaching for him with scrawny, taloned hands. The security officer was ready. He fired the injection instantly into Wolf's neck and watched calmly as the scarecrow figure froze in its tracks. Hamming waved a hand in front of Wolf's face and nodded as the eyes moved to follow it.

"Good enough. He's still conscious. But he has no volition; he'll do what we tell him." Hamming was already turning to pack away the cables in the compact biofeedback kit. "Let's get him aloft and dump him into his own form-control unit before he starts to get lively again."

Manx could not take his eyes away from the frozen tormented face. Behrooz Wolf was still glaring at the hologram, not interested in anything else. "Do you think that the form-control unit will work? He has to *want* it to. He seems to want to die."

"We'll have to wait and see. Hell, you can't *make* somebody want to live. You'll know in a few hours. Carry the feedback unit, would you?" Hamming took Wolf's arm and began to walk him toward the door. "Oops. Mustn't forget her. It's the first thing he'll want if he makes it through the form-control operation." He detoured to the wall and pointed to the verse. "That's the way Wolf was feeling. And here—" He poked the projection of the woman in her bare navel. "—is the reason for it."

Manx read the verse below the picture.

My thoughts hold mortal strife; I do detest my life,
And with lamenting cries, peace to my soul to bring,
Oft call that prince which here doth monarchize,
But he, grim-grinning king,
Who caitiffs scorns, and doth the blest surprise,
Late having decked with beauty's rose his tomb,
Disdains to crop a weed, and will not come.

"Gloomy thoughts. What does it mean?"

"Damned if I know. Wolf was always a nut for old-fashioned things—poetry, plays, history, useless crap like that. He must have thought the poem applied to him."

"That's terrible. He must have loved her very much to break down like this when he lost her."

"Yeah." Hamming had switched off the projection unit and put the cube into his pocket. He shrugged. "It's odd. I knew her, and she wasn't much of a looker. Good in bed, I guess."

"How long ago did she die?"

"Die? You mean Mary there?" Hamming had taken hold of Wolf's arm again and was leading him firmly out of the room. He gave a coarse, loud laugh. "Who mentioned *dying*? Mary Walton is alive and well. Didn't you know? She dumped him! Buggered off to Cloudland with one of your lot, some guy she met on a lunar cruise. Me, I'd have said good riddance to her, but he took it different. Come on, let's get Wolf up to his tank. I've had enough stink for today."

CHAPTER 2

"A message is not a message until the rules for interpreting it are in the hands of the receiver."

—Apollo Belvedere Smith

They would not go away. There was nothing to see, nothing to hear, nothing to taste, to touch, or to feel. Nothing. And yet there were the voices, whispering, prompting, nudging, cajoling, commanding.

That way. It was a generalized murmur. *That's where you are going.*

"No. I don't want to change." He struggled, unable to move or speak as he tried to identify the source of the sounds. The argument had been going on inside him forever, and he was losing. The voices were invading him micrometer by micrometer.

This way. This way. Change. They were ignoring his wish to rest, pulling him, pushing him, twisting him, turning him inside out. He could feel them in every cell, growing stronger and more confident. *Change.* A trillion voices merged. Blood rushed through clogged arteries, organic detergents washing the dry, inelastic skin, the weak, flabby muscles, and the old, tired sinews. *Change.* Liver and spleen and kidneys and testicles, ion balances on a roller coaster, local temperatures

7

anomalously high or low—*too high, too low. He was dying
...Change.* The delicate balance of endocrine glands: testes
and thyroid and adrenals and pancreas and pituitary. All dis-
turbed, homeostasis lost, desperately seeking a new equilibrium. *Change. Change. CHANGE.*

He cried out, a silent scream. *"Leave me alone."* The in-
truders ran wild in every cell. He was helpless, fainting, fading before the assault of a chemical army.

CHANGE. All over his body: fluctuations in thermodynamic potentials, in kinetic reaction rates, hormonal levels;
energy rushing to dormant follicles, sloughing old tissues, re-
defining organic functions, thrusting along capillaries. A fer-
ment of cellular renewal boiled within the changing skin.
CHANGE. Solvents along sluggish veins and arteries, the
sluice of plaquey deposits, the whirl of fats and cholesterol
...*CHANGE.* Liver, spleen, kidneys, prostate, heart, lungs,
brain...*CHANGE.* Fires along nerves, synapses sparking er-
ratically, spasms of motor control, floods of neurotransmitters,
flickering lightnings of pain, crashing thunderstorms of sensation, signals flying from reticular network to cerebral cortex to
hypothalamus to dorsal ganglia. A clash of arms at the blood-
brain barrier...*CHANGE. SYNTHESIZE. ACCOMMODATE.*

And then, suddenly, all voices merged to one voice and
faded, weakening, withdrawing, drifting down in volume. He
could hear it clearly. He listened to the murmur of that dying
voice and at last recognized it. Knew it. Knew it exactly. It
was the mechanical echo of his own soul, whispering final
commands through the computer link: his physical profile,
amplified a billionfold, transformed in the biofeedback equipment to a set of chemical and physiological instructions, and
fed back as final commands.

The tide was ebbing. The changes shivered to a halt. In
that moment, senses returned. He heard the surge of external
pumps and felt the wash of amniotic fluids as they drained
from his naked body. The tank tilted, and the front cracked
open, exposing his skin to cold air. There was a sting of with-
drawn catheters at groin and nape of neck and a slackening of
retaining straps.

He felt a growing pain in his chest and a terrible need for air. As the pertussive reflex took over, he coughed violently, expelling gelatinous fluid from his lungs and taking in a first ecstatic, agonizing breath. Its cold burn inside him was simultaneous with the sudden full opening of the tank. Harsh white light hit his unready retinas.

He shivered, threw up his forearm to protect his eyes, and sagged back in the padded seat. For five minutes he moved only to lean forward and cough up residual sputum. Finally he summoned his strength, stood up, and stepped out of the tank. He staggered forward two steps, caught his balance, and stood swaying. As soon as he was sure of his own stability he reached for the towel that hung ready by the tank, wrapped it around his waist, and turned back to the form-change tank itself. Another moment to gather his will, then he gripped the door and swung it firmly closed.

It was a final, ritual step, his first choice after the unspoken decision to live. He was rejecting the idea of tranquilizing drugs to ease the rigors of transition. Instead he walked across the room to a full-length mirror and stared hard at his own reflection.

The glass showed a nearly naked man about thirty years old, dark-haired and dark-eyed, of medium height and build. The new skin on his body still bore a babyish sheen, though it was pale and wrinkled from long immersion. Soon it would smooth and mature to deep ivory. The face that peered back at him was thin-nosed and thin-mouthed, with a cynical downward turn to the red lips and thoughtful, cautious eyes.

He examined himself critically, working his jaw, lifting an eyelid with a forefinger to inspect the clear, healthy white around the brown iris, peering inside his mouth at his teeth and tongue, and finally rubbing his fingers along his renewed hairline. He flexed his shoulders, inflated his chest to the full, moved his neck in an experimental roll back and forth, and sighed.

"And here we are again. But why bother?" He spoke very softly to his reflection. "'What a piece of work is a man. How noble in reason, how infinite in faculty. In form, in moving, how express and admirable. In action, how like an angel, in apprehension how like a god. The beauty of the world, the paragon of animals.'"

"Very good, Mr. Wolf," said a silky and precise voice from the communications device in the corner of the room. "The Bard wrote it, and perhaps he believed it. But do you?"

Bey Wolf turned slowly and cautiously. The unit was showing no visual signal. He stepped across and turned on its video and recorder. "You did not let me finish that quotation. It goes on, 'Man delights me not, no, nor woman neither.' And let me point out that this is my private apartment. Who are you, and how the devil did you get my personal com-code?"

"I brought you there." The voice was unembarrassed. "I helped to carry you up out of Old City—for that, you may thank me or curse me. I set you up in that form-change tank. And I stayed, long enough to turn on your communications unit and note its access code." The screen flickered, and a man's image appeared. "I do not want to intrude on your privacy, and you will note that I was not receiving visual signals until you just activated that channel. I am sure you are still feeling fragile, but I must talk with you as soon as you are recovered. My name is Leo Manx. I am a member of the Outer System Federation."

"I can tell that much by looking at you. What do you want?"

"That cannot be discussed over public channels. If I could return to your apartment, or if you would agree to visit me at the embassy—my time is yours. I came all the way from the Outer Cloud, specifically to seek you. Perhaps you could join me for dinner—if you feel able to eat, so soon after so full a treatment."

Behrooz Wolf stared at the other man. Leo Manx had the piebald look of the fourth-generation Cloudlander, brown freckles on a chalk-white hairless skin. His build was thin and angular, with overlong arms and bowed, skinny legs. "I can eat," he said at last. "Provided it's Earth food—none of your rotten Cloud synthetics."

"Very well," Manx replied without hesitation, but there was a sudden half-humorous twist of the mouth and the flicker of an eyelid. Like any Cloudlander, Manx would be disgusted by the thought of food made from anything beyond single-celled organisms. Bey Wolf had insisted on an Earth meal more to gauge Manx's seriousness of purpose than anything else. But now, on the basis of the flimsiest of evidence, he decided that he rather liked Leo Manx. Nobody could be all bad who recognized Shakespeare.

"Why not?" he said. "I'll come and see you. I've nothing better to do, and I haven't been outside for a long time."

"Then I await your convenience." Manx nodded and disappeared from the screen.

Wolf consulted his internal clock. Until that moment he had had no idea what time it was—or what day or month it was. Midafternoon. If he left in the next half hour he could be at the embassy before the evening shower. He skimmed his accumulated mail and messages but found nothing worth worrying about. Better face it: since he had been fired by Form Control, he had become a nonentity. He dressed quickly and dropped ten floors to street level. There he worked his way over to the fastest slideway, threading his way easily through the crowds and staring around him as he went.

A BEC catalog must have been issued since he had fled underground in Old City. The new forms were already appearing on the streets: squarer shoulders, more prominent genitals, and deeper-set eyes for the men; a fuller-bosomed, long-waisted look in the women. As usual, BEC had chosen the styles with great care. They were different enough to be noticeable but close enough to the previous year's fashions for the form-change programs to be just within the average person's price range.

As head of the Office of Form Control—*former* head, he reminded himself—Bey Wolf considered himself above the whims of fashion. He wore his natural form, with minor remedial changes. That made him a rarity. More and more, the people on the slideways all looked the same as one another. It was—soothing? No. Boring. After a few minutes he keyed in his implant to receive the communication channels.

He had a lot of news to catch up on. With his retreat to Old City and his subsequent spell in the form-change tank, he had missed a minor political battle over optimal population levels, the BEC release of a spectacular new avian form, a revised species preservation act that applied to all of Earth, impeachment of the head of the United Space Federation on charges of corruption, and a heated new exchange of insults between the governments of the Inner System and the Outer System concerning energy rights in the Kernel Ring.

He had also, though this was not news, missed seventy-five days of a perfect summer. But why count time when he no longer had a job? The purposive feedback process could do no more than respond to his will, so there was no doubt that he *wanted* to live, deep inside. But for what?

"How weary, stale, flat, and unprofitable . . . "And at that very moment, before the familiar words could complete themselves in his mind, the madness began again. The slideways and the scene from the news broadcasts darkened as another image was overlaid on them.

The Dancing Man. He was back. Dressed in a scarlet, skintight suit, he came capering across Bey's field of vision. He danced backward with jerky, doll-like movements of his arms and legs. There was curious music in the background, atonal yet tonal, and the man was singing in a tuneful, alien manner that sounded like Chinese. In the middle of the overlain field of view, he paused and grinned out directly at Bey. His teeth were black and filed to points, and his face was as red as his suit. He spoke again, seeming to ask a question, then waved, turned, and danced backward out of the field of view.

Bey shivered and put his hand to his head. He had heard Hamming's words underneath Old City, but the colonel had been wrong. Mary's loss had been desperately painful; he thought of her every day, and he would carry her holograph with him always. But something else had driven him over the edge to seek the solace of the Dream Machine: conviction of his own growing insanity.

Since the Dancing Man had first appeared, he had checked every possible source of the signal. No one else could see it—even when he or she was viewing the same channel as Bey. Every test for outside signal had proved negative. He had mimicked the Dancing Man's speech, all that he could remember of it, and had been told by specialists in linguistics and semiotics that it corresponded to no known language. Worst of all, when Wolf went into recording mode, the signal vanished. It was never there to be played back. Physicians and psychiatrists were unanimous: the signal was generated within Bey's own head. He was suffering "perceptual disturbance" of a "severe and progressive form, intractable and with a strong negative prognosis."

In other words, he was going crazy. And no one could do a damned thing about it. And it was getting worse. At first no more than a scarlet spot on the scene's horizon, the Dancing Man was getting steadily closer.

And the ultimate irony: as long as he and Mary had lived together, he had been concerned with *her* sanity, *her* mental stability! He had been the impervious rock against which the tides of insanity would break in vain.

Wolf saw that he had reached his destination, the deep-delved embassy of the Outer System. He fled for the express elevators—". . . then will I headlong run into the Earth; Earth gape. Oh, no, it will not harbor me . . ."—and plunged down, down, down, rejecting his own frantic thoughts and seeking the cool caverns of underground sanctuary.

CHAPTER 3

"I fled him down the nights and down the days,
I fled him down the arches of the years.
I fled him down the labyrinthine ways
Of my own mind..."

—Francis Thompson

The average surface temperature of real estate in the Outer System was minus two hundred and fourteen degrees Celsius: fifty-nine degrees above absolute zero, where oxygen was a liquid and nitrogen a solid. The mean surface gravity of that same real estate was one four-hundredth of a g. Mean solar radiation was 1.2 microwatts per square meter, weaker than starlight, a billionth as intense as the Sun's energy received by the Earth.

Faced with those facts, the designers of the Earth Embassy for the Outer System had a choice: Should they locate the embassy off-Earth and face extensive transportation costs to and from the surface for all embassy interactions? Or should they accept an Earth environment uncomfortable and highly unnatural to the ambassador and staff? Since the designers were unlikely to visit Earth themselves, they naturally took the cheaper option. The embassy that Bey Wolf was visiting sat five hundred feet underground, where temperature, noise, and radiation could all be controlled.

Gravity was another matter. He dropped with stomach-wrenching suddenness through the upper levels. As he did so his surroundings became darker, quieter, and colder. Every surface was soundproofed. At four hundred feet the hush became so unnatural and disturbing that Bey found himself listening hard to nothing. He decided he did not like it. Humans made noise; humans clattered and banged and yelled. Total silence was inhuman.

Leo Manx was waiting for him in a room so cold that Bey could see his own breath in the air. The Cloudlander remained upright long enough to shake Bey's hand and gesture him to a seat, then sank with a sigh of relief into the depths of a water chair that folded itself around his thin body. The head that was left sticking out smiled apologetically. "I used a form-change program to adapt me to Earth gravity before I left the Outer System." His shrug emerged as a ripple of the chair's black outer plastic. "I don't think it was quite right."

A piece of your lousy software, by the sound of it, Bey thought. But he merely nodded and waited.

Manx sat silent for a few moments and then said abruptly, "My visit to Earth, you know, is for a very specific reason. To see you and to ask for your help—as the head of the Office of Form Control and Earth's leading expert on form-change theory and practice."

"You're a bit late. I'm not with that office anymore."

"I know that is the case. I heard that you had . . . resigned your position."

"No need to be diplomatic. I was fired."

The pale head bobbed. "In truth, I knew that also. You may be surprised to learn that from our point of view, your dismissal offers advantages."

"None from my point of view."

"It is my task to convince you otherwise." Leo Manx stretched upward, his thin neck and hairless head craning like a turtle from the black supporting oval of the chair. "To do so,

I must request your silence about what I am to tell you."

"Suppose I refuse to go along with that?" Wolf saw the other man's discomfort. "Oh, hell, get on with it. I've spent my whole career not talking about things. I can do it for a while longer."

"Thank you. You will not regret it." Manx subsided in the chair. "Mr. Wolf, there has arisen in the Outer System a problem so serious that all knowledge of it is given only on a need-to-know basis. In a few words, there has been a widespread breakdown in the performance of form-change equipment, to the point where the process is being undertaken only in cases of emergency, such as my own visit to Earth."

"Widespread? Not just a machine or two?"

"Hundreds of machines, with rates of malfunction that have been growing rapidly. A year ago, we could point to two or three cases of gross error in results. Today, we have case histories of thousands."

"Then it has to be a general software problem. You don't want me for that. There are others who know more and can give you better guidance."

Manx's eyes, startlingly round and hollow in the absence of eyebrows, looked away. "If you are perhaps thinking of Robert Capman . . ."

"I would, but he's on a long-term stellar mission. My suggestion is BEC themselves. Why not call them in? They'll be as keen to sort this out as you are." Bey tried for an innocent expression. It was as good a way as any of testing the honesty of the Cloudlander.

Manx looked pained. "We already approached the Biological Equipment Corporation. They sent a team of experts, who reviewed everything we could show them and declared that they could find no evidence of any problem. Unfortunately, we are not convinced that they conducted as thorough a review as one might wish. There has been a long-term disagreement with BEC as to the proper amount of royalties the Outer System is accruing for the use of BEC's form-change hardware and software systems—"

"They say you stole their ideas, ignored their patents, and infringed their copyrights."

"Well, that is a little crudely put—but, yes, you have the gist of their argument." Manx smiled ruefully. "I see that our own security is less than we are inclined to believe."

"In a case like that it is. BEC will tell anyone on Earth who'll listen that the Outer System is robbing them blind."

"Which is certainly a—a—"

"Lie?"

"Exaggeration. A misrepresentation."

"You don't need to persuade me. I don't like monopolies, either, and BEC has one for the Inner System. But you said they did a review of 'everything we could show them.' Like to be more explicit?"

There was a raising of nonexistent eyebrows. "You are a very perceptive man. There were a number of units that we could not and did not show to the BEC team."

"Pirated designs?"

"The Outer System prefers to think of them as independent developments. However, I believe it would have made little difference. The anomalous behavior occurs with rather greater frequency in BEC's own equipment. Yet they insist that everything is working perfectly."

"Did your own engineers watch the BEC tests?"

"Yes. As BEC said, no anomalies were observed. As soon as they left, new peculiar forms were again produced." Manx began to push away the enfolding arms of the chair. "If you would be interested to see some of those forms, I have images here with me."

"No. You'd be wasting your time."

"These forms are extremely strange."

"Dr. Manx, odd forms don't do anything for me. I've seen so many of those over the years, I doubt if you could surprise me." Bey stood up. "I accept that you have a nasty problem, but it's not one that would justify dragging me partway to Alpha Centauri. I lost my job, but I still like Earth. And I doubt if I could do anything to help you."

"How do you know that without personal observation?"

"I've been around form control for a long time. As I said at the beginning, you have a software problem. The fact that BEC's team couldn't find it—or chose not to—makes no difference. Call 'em again, ask for Maria Sun. If anyone can solve it for you, she can."

Manx stood up, too. "Mr. Wolf, it is my opinion that you underestimate both yourself and the difficulty of this problem. But I cannot change your mind about that, here on Earth. Rather, allow me to introduce a new variable into the equation. While you were on the way here I asked for and read a copy of your dossier from the Office of Form Control. It is something that I ought to have done earlier. I learned more of your personal circumstances."

"You found out I'm going crazy."

"You are sick. If you know anything of the Outer System, you may know that we are advanced in the treatment of mental illness. That happens to be my own field. If you would agree to travel back with me—merely to observe the phenomena for yourself, for no more than a few days—I will devote my best efforts to your personal problem."

"Sorry. It's still negative." Bey headed for the door, but Leo Manx made a great effort and was there first.

"One more point, Mr. Wolf. And please excuse this importuning. You lived with Mary Walton for seven years. Is it possible that your reluctance to visit the Outer System arises from a fear that you may be obliged to interact with her there?"

Bey eased past the other man, trying not to touch him. "You're a conscientious and persistent man, Dr. Manx. I don't resent that—I respect you for it. I can't answer your question. Maybe I'm afraid I would meet Mary again. But in any case, I still refuse. Tell your superiors that I am honored to be considered."

"Yes, of course. But if by chance you should change your mind," Manx called after Bey as he headed for the elevator, "I will be here on Earth for two more days! Call me, at any hour."

But Wolf was already out of earshot. The final question

about Mary had gotten to him more than it should have. Was he over her or wasn't he? Would he turn down a potentially fascinating problem simply because he might be forced to see Mary with the man she had chosen over him?

He was oblivious to the high-acceleration ride to the surface, oblivious to the evening crowds that pushed at him on the slideways. Manx's offer of dinner had never been realized, but in any case Bey had lost his appetite. He skipped dangerously across from high-speed to low-speed track, exited the slideway, and hurried up to his apartment. He grabbed a projection cube at random from the file—they were all of Mary, it made little difference—and sat down to view it.

Predictably, it was one he hated to watch but also one he had viewed again and again. Mary in an amateur musical, dressed in a long gown, bonnet, and parasol, singing in the sweet, artificial little voice of a young girl. "Let him go, let him tarry, let him sink or let him swim. He doesn't care for me, and I don't care for him. He can go and find another, that I hope he will enjoy, for I'm going to marry a far nicer boy."

Bey felt his heart wither inside him as he watched. Nothing of her had faded; it hurt as much as ever. He was reaching to cut the cube when Mary Walton's demure figure rippled and darkened. A new scene was overlaid on the old and familiar one.

The Dancing Man, twisting and tumbling across the image, red-clad limbs akimbo. He paused in the middle, nodded at Bey, and made a singsong questioning little speech that could almost be understood. Then he was away, skating backward into the distance, head bobbing and hands waving cheerfully.

The Dancing Man—even here! In the middle of a sequence that Bey had recorded personally four years earlier. How could anyone possibly change that recording? Bey set the projection again to the beginning and forced himself to watch it through again. This time there was no Dancing Man. It was Mary all the way, to that intolerable final line when she set her parasol over her shoulder and waved good-bye.

Bey watched to the bitter end. Then he went across to the communications unit and called Leo Manx.

CHAPTER 4

"All isolated systems become less orderly when left to themselves."
(This version of the Second Law of Thermodynamics was offered by Apollo Belvedere Smith, age five, to explain why his room was in such a mess.)

"There is one other thing you ought to decide before we embark." Leo Manx was inspecting both his traveling companion and Bey Wolf's luggage.

"Namely?"

"Do you want to spend time in a form-change tank on the way out to the Cloud? If so, we must make sure that the programs are available."

"You mean, switch to something more like your own form, for physical comfort?" Wolf shook his head. "I like this form, and I know it tolerates low gravity and cold pretty well."

"That was not the reason for my suggestion." Manx took Bey Wolf's little traveling case and floated it one-handed across the cabin to secure it in the cargo hold. "My concern is with the response you may receive from Outer System citizens. It will be apparent to them that you are from Earth, or at least from the Inner System. The two federations are not at war—"

"Yet."

"But we are certainly locked in an economic struggle over rights to the Kernel Ring. There have been skirmishes in the Halo. If you remain in your present form, I foresee some unpleasantness and rudeness when we arrive. You will hear yourself called a Snugger—a Sunhugger Imperialist; there will undoubtedly be sly remarks about your hairy skin."

"Same as you've been getting when people here call you a bare-faced Cloudlander?" The other man's reaction was no more than a moment's twitch of the lip, but Bey was used to reading subtle signals. "Dr. Manx, if you got by on Earth without any major form-change, I can do the same in the Outer System. I'm used to criticism and sneaky comments."

"It was quite different in my case. I knew I would be here only for a little while, until you accepted or rejected our plea." Manx caught Wolf's expression and realized he had made a mistake. "Of course, you have agreed to stay with us only long enough for a preliminary evaluation of the problem. I realize that. But I was hoping, if you find the situation intriguing enough, that you might prolong your stay. Not only for our sakes; for yours. If one has never visited the Outer System, there are many things to see and do."

"No sales pitch. If you're wrong, it's not worth it. If you're right, I can use a program when we get there."

"That is true."

"So what are we waiting for?"

Manx gestured out the port. Bey suddenly realized that they were not waiting. Earth had disappeared, and they were already passing the Moon. The McAndrew inertialess drive had been switched on while they were talking, and they were accelerating away from the Sun at more than a hundred g's.

"Twelve days to crossover point, then another twelve to the Opik Harvester," Manx said. "It is not the nearest harvester to Sol, but it has a large number of form-change units on it. I have discussed our destination with my superiors, and we agree that it is a good place to begin."

"How far out?"

"Twenty-six thousand a.u.—about four trillion kilometers."

Manx called a stylized three-dimensional figure onto the display screen. It was a representation of Sol-space geometry. Even with a logarithmic radial scale, the graphic occupied one full wall of the cabin. The Inner System, comprising everything out to Persephone, was crowded within a Sun-centered sphere of ten billion kilometers radius. The Halo reached out two hundred times as far, a diffuse torus within which the Kernel Ring sat as a well-defined narrow annulus. The Oort Cloud, home for the Outer System, was a vast sprawling spherical region, approaching the Halo on its inner limit but seven times as large as its outer edge, stretching a third of the way to the nearest star.

Manx pointed to a cluster of color-coded habitats in the Outer System and to the arrowed flight path that extended to them from the Earth-Moon environment. "The Opik Harvester is fairly near the inner edge of the Cloud, but a safe distance from the Kernel Ring. No danger of trouble from there. As you can see from our trajectory, we'll be flying rather close to the Ring itself in about nine days." He gave Bey a sideways glance. "I thought you might be personally interested in taking a look at that."

Bey was learning. Leo Manx's omissions—rarely accidental—were more informative than his speeches. Manx was too self-conscious or diplomatic to say some things himself. He preferred to leave logical loopholes, then answer questions.

"I have never been near the Kernel Ring," Bey said. "I assume you know that."

"Your background summary says as much."

"Then it should also show that I know little about Kerr-Newman black holes and even less about how we use the kernels themselves as energy sources."

"That is indeed the case." The reply was polite and noncommittal. Bey would have to dig deeper.

"So what makes you think I have any personal interest at all in looking at the Kernel Ring? Do you think you see a connection with my—other problems?" Damn it, the habit was catching. He was getting as indirect as Manx. "I mean, with my hallucinations."

Instead of answering at once, Manx sat for a few moments, thinking. "That depends on the cause of those hallucinations," he said at last. "I hope that we will explore that subject together on this journey, when we have plenty of time. But answer me one question, if you will. When did your problems begin? Was it before or after Mary Walton left you."

"Long after. Four months after."

"In that case, I do not believe that the Kernel Ring is connected with your hallucinations."

It was like pulling teeth. "But the Ring *is* connected with Mary?"

"Possibly. Probably." Manx was getting there; Bey could see the decision reflected in the expression on the other man's face. "Mr. Wolf, I deduce that in addition to knowing little about the Kernel Ring, you also are unfamiliar with customs in the Outer System. According to Colonel Hamming, whom I did not find to be a particularly sensitive person—"

"He's an asshole."

"A felicitous description. He told me Mary Walton left to 'run off to Cloudland with one of you guys,' and the inference was that he was referring to a person from the Outer System, one that she met on a lunar cruise. Is that your own understanding of the situation?"

"It is."

"Did you ever meet this person?"

"Not a person. A man. No, I didn't meet him. If I had, I'd probably have tried to cut him in two."

"So you are unfamiliar with his appearance? Now, if you will permit me a more personal question. You knew Mary Walton better than anyone else. Was she a woman impressed by appearances? How a person looked? Whether he was handsome?"

"I guess so." More stalling! Bey cursed his own reluctance to give straight answers. "Yes, she was. Too impressed. Looks mattered to Mary."

"Very well. You know what men from the Outer System

look like. I suspect that I am a fairly typical example, and although I am quite happy with my own appearance—" Manx looked admiringly at his skinny body and bowed legs. "—I know that I am far from the standards of beauty currently popular on Earth."

"That's irrelevant. Handsomeness is easy; all it takes is a little while in a form-change tank."

"Very true. *If* a person wishes to make such a change. I certainly did not, and you had a similar reaction when it came to modifying your own appearance to match an Outer System form. However, there is a more important point here. Although the man Mary Walton ran off with *could* have picked an appearance that appealed to her, he would have had to do so *in advance* of meeting with her on that lunar cruise."

"I see where you're heading. You are questioning that he was from the Outer System?"

"More than that. Mr. Wolf, our citizens do not indulge in lunar cruises. To us, it would have as much attraction as a tour of Old City would offer the average Earth person."

"But some people might do it. Just to be different."

"They might." Manx looked away, refusing to meet Bey's eyes again. "But they did not. I have rather more information than I have so far revealed to you. Before I left our Earth Embassy, I checked all our visitors to Earth-Moon space for the previous four years. There was no one from the Outer System who went on a lunar cruise. Whoever Mary Walton met, he was not from our federation."

"So where does that leave us?"

"With no more than a speculation. I have of course no direct evidence—"

"Talk, man! I can stand it."

"I do not think you will find your Mary in the Cloud, even if you plan to look for her there. The most likely person to have offered a false identification and to be interested in Earth-Moon space as a possible source of energy needs would be a renegade."

"You mean a rebel? An inhabitant of the Kernel Ring?"

"Precisely. The inhabitants of the Ring practice a curious

coexistence. Rebel outposts are scattered here and there through its whole volume, side by side with peaceful settlers, energy prospectors, and free-space Podder colonies. The Ring admits every form of oddity, every human shape attainable by the form-change equipment. You should look there."

"For someone who works in the high-gravity environment around shielded kernels. Someone whose unmodified appearance is more like mine than yours."

"You follow my thoughts admirably." Manx moved the cursor on the display to delineate the annulus of the Kernel Ring. "Here. To conclude, it is my opinion that Mary Walton is not to be found anywhere in the Outer System. She is *here*. In the Halo, almost certainly somewhere in the Kernel Ring itself."

"Shacked up with a damned outlaw."

"I'm afraid so. A dangerous man, Mr. Wolf, who recognizes the sovereignty of neither my federation nor your own. A man who would not hesitate to kill either of us. Mr. Wolf! Do you hear me?"

Bey was no longer listening. As Manx moved the cursor across the display, a familiar figure had appeared on top of it. He was sitting cross-legged, riding the little blue arrow and waving jauntily out at the two men. His song sounded a little different but was still just beyond comprehension.

The scarlet suit was brighter than ever. The expression on his grinning face was more than usually smug. Forget that hope, it said. It takes a lot more than a move to the Outer System to get rid of the Dancing Man.

CHAPTER 5

Kernel (def.): A Kerr-Newman black hole, i.e., a black hole that is both rotating and electrically charged. Kernels are found in nature only in the *Kernel Ring* (q.v.) between the Inner and Outer Systems. They range in mass from a hundred million to ten billion tons.

—Webster's New World Dictionary

At the end of the seventh day Manx began to push for a different approach. He had switched off his recorder and was glaring impatiently at Bey Wolf.

"I suppose you imagine that you are cooperating with me? You are not. I ask you for a full, detailed account of your relationship with Mary Walton, something I must have if I am to help you end your hallucinations. What do I get?" He tapped the recorder. "Monosyllables. Two- or three-sentence descriptions of complex interactions. Evasion. Obfuscation. Equivocation. Deliberately or not, you are prevaricating."

"I'm sorry. I don't like to talk about emotional matters. Particularly *those* emotional matters."

"Of course you don't. No one does, unless they have quite different mental problems. But if there's to be any progress you have to give me information. *Detail*. As much of it as you can. I perceive that you will not do so with simple question-and-answer techniques."

"So we're stuck?" Bey sounded more relieved than upset.

"No, we are not. With your permission, I want to put you into an enhanced recall status."

"That's illegal."

"Not in the Outer System. We have no statutes against self-incrimination."

"Barbaric."

"Perhaps we have less need of them. Stop trying to change the subject by inciting an argument. Will you allow me to induce an enhanced recall state, or will you not?"

Wolf looked at him warily. "For how long?"

"If I could tell you that, I might find it unnecessary. A couple of days, maybe more."

"Then I'll miss the transit of the Kernel Ring you want me to see." It was a weak argument, and Bey knew it. Leo Manx was slow but persistent, like the turtle he sometimes resembled, and he would not give up easily.

"That crossing will occur tomorrow. Is it agreed, then? After we complete the transit, we will move to enhanced recall technique. If the idea still makes you uncomfortable, we can begin with direct reporting, then proceed to stimulated and dream sequences."

Bey nodded. At best it felt like a stay of execution.

The transit of the Kernel Ring was an anticlimax. Even with the highest magnification the ship's sensors could provide, the Halo was no more than a scattering of misty dots of light. The unshielded kernels themselves gave off large amounts of energy, gigawatts for even the most massive and least active, but they radiated at wavelengths too short for the human eye to see. The shielded kernels were, by design, invisible. It was difficult to imagine people living in that emptiness, still less that it was the home of ruthless pirates, savages who might come boiling up from the darkness to take over cargo or passenger ships as they made their out-of-ecliptic transit from the Inner System to Cloudland. Least of all could Bey imagine Mary, his lively, cosmopolitan Mary, enduring that waste of nothingness.

"You see with an Earthman's distorting perspective," Manx said in answer to Bey's skeptical reaction. "To you, the Halo is nearly empty. To me, or to anyone from the Outer System, it is packed with life and energy."

"You use an odd definition of 'packed.'"

"Do the calculation for yourself. There are millions or billions of people living in the Halo—we have no idea how many, since there is no central government there. Compare it with the Outer System. We are about fifty million people, and we know that we are grossly underpopulated. We will be for centuries. Naturally, we crowd together, most of us close to the harvesters, but were it not for the help of our self-reproducing machines, we could not exist. If we spread out evenly, each person in the Outer System would have a region sixty times as big as the whole of your Inner System to move around in. By comparison, the Halo is packed. It teems with life. Much too crowded for us."

Current accommodation allotment on Earth: one hundred cubic meters per person. Bey thought of that and wondered why the Outer and Inner Systems were arguing over rights to the Kernel Ring. From what Manx was saying, there was no way that the average Cloudlander would ever be comfortable with the "cramped" life-style in the Ring and no way that the average Earth dweller would be able to accept so much empty, frightening space.

"The argument is over energy, but surely there are more than enough kernels for everyone?"

"I wonder about that myself," Manx said. "And there is an element of presumption that leaves me uncomfortable. Both the Inner System and the Outer System governments assume that they could, if they wished, displace the present rulers of the Kernel Ring. I am not sure that is the case. Have you heard of a leader called Ransome, and of Ransome's Hole?"

"Black Ransome? According to Earth's newscasts, he's just fiction."

"If they believe that, they have never left Earth. I know of a half dozen prospectors working the Halo who have lost cargo to Black Ransome. Some have lost ships, also. It is a reasonable speculation that some have lost their lives, too, and are in no position to report anything. At any rate, true or not, the Outer System seethes with rumors about Ransome. Ships found empty and gutted, cargoes taken, crew and passengers ejected to empty space."

"If he's such a problem, why don't you send a force in to take care of him?"

Manx waved at the displays. "Find him, and maybe we could do it. His base is as much a mystery as he is. Ransome's Hole—or maybe it's really Ransome's *Hold*; everything about him is hearsay—is supposed to be somewhere in the Kernel Ring. But where? You're talking a volume of space thousands of times as big as the whole Inner System. And if we found him, I'm not sure any force that we sent in would win. Ransome's Hole is supposed to have its own defense system, able to handle anything we could throw at it. And he might have allies. The whole Halo is a melting pot, the place that anyone can flee to if they find civilization intolerable."

"Or we find *them* intolerable." Bey bent to the high-resolution sensors with new interest. Was one of those spots of light, disappearing fast behind the speeding ship, some huge, well-armed base of rebel operations? And what else was down there, hidden in the darkness? Perhaps some lost colony of ancient doctrines, vanished from the rest of the system. "Home of lost causes, and forsaken beliefs, and unpopular names, and impossible loyalties." Who had said that? One of the Victorians.

"Black Ransome," Bey said, looking up. "Where did he come from, the Inner or the Outer System?"

"We don't even know that much. He must have plenty of energy, because he never takes the kernels from the ships. But where does he get his food supplies, or his other equipment? We just don't have answers to those questions."

The Kernel Ring was fading behind them. Leo Manx turned off the displays. Bey saw that he was holding the polished black cylinder of an enhancement recall unit and smiling in what looked like anticipation.

"And we will find nothing about Ransome here, Mr. Wolf. We are past the region where the ship is in danger of attack. So we can now proceed to possibly more productive work. When you are ready..."

I met her at an open-air historical event, seven years and four months ago, when there was an exhibit of Old Earth animals. It was the first time they showed results of breeding back successfully beyond the Cretaceous, and the big extinct forms had attracted a lot of interest.

I say I met her, but that is at first an overstatement. I was in an overview booth, with half an eye open for illegal forms— not much chance of that; I hadn't seen one for years—when I saw her, though she was too far away for me to speak to her. But my eye picked her out at once.

No, it's not that I was attracted to Mary Walton at that point, not at all. I was *puzzled* by her. I had been in the Office of Form Control for more than half my life, and one thing that I had learned to do, whether I wanted to or not, was to monitor for anomalies. It was an unconscious act with me, and it's more than half the trick to spotting an illegal form.

In Mary's case, I knew there was something peculiar, though it certainly wasn't something illegal.

It was this. As you can see, I choose to hold my own appearance to about age thirty, but that's unusual on Earth. Most people like to look between twenty and twenty-five, with twenty-two the most popular age. Now, sometimes you will get older people who don't like that idea. They want to separate themselves from the real youngsters for some activities, and they spend at least part of their time in a form corresponding to age forty or fifty—even more, though people over sixty are very uncommon, unless they have other problems and drop the use of form-change treatments altogether. You saw the results of that when you picked me up in Old City.

Mary Walton was wearing the form of a woman between

forty-five and fifty and dressed in the clothing style of a woman of that age, but I could tell from other indicators—eye movement, laughter, body posture—that she was actually a lot *younger* than she looked. It intrigued me. Why would anyone deliberately choose a form older than her true age?

While I was watching her, we had a minor problem with staffing, and I had to look elsewhere. But as soon as I could, I went to the place where I had last seen her, next to the big enclosure with the gorgosaurus in it. She was still there—trying to climb into the enclosure. If she had succeeded . . . The animal was carnivorous, four meters tall, two tons in weight.

I arrived just in time to drag her clear. And to arrest her. And then to introduce myself.

She told me she was an actress; she was doing it for publicity. I suppose I knew, right from the first moment, that she was crazy. Insane, hopelessly unaware of reality.

It made no difference. Others will say that Mary was not conventionally attractive, that she deliberately chose to look exotic and a little peculiar. When she was living a part—she didn't act parts, she lived them—she might form-change to any age and do anything she felt fit the character. Some of them were strange, sometimes disgusting.

As I say, to me it made no difference. From the first moment she looked down at me from the fence, when I had hold of her leg and I was pulling her back by her long gray skirt, I was lost. I was spoiling her publicity plan, but she didn't look annoyed. She grinned down at me, with her head on one side and that ridiculous round gray hat with a feather in the side of it, and the blond curly hair pushing out underneath it—she was naturally fair, though she preferred parts that made her a brunette. And then she let herself go limp, and she came rolling off the fence in that old-fashioned gray cloth dress and knocked me flat to the ground.

I was smitten even before I got up, and I knew it, but I wouldn't have done one thing about it. I have never been able to let people know how I feel. I have rationalized that, to the point where it does not usually bother me. Often, I insist it is a virtue. But not this time. I wanted Mary, but Mary was an unattainable prospect.

It wasn't just my inability to speak. I knew, even if she didn't, that I was three times her age. That alone should have made the whole thing impossible. Not for Mary. I didn't realize it at the time, but things like that made no difference at all to her. She was so much in her own world, and that world was so far from reality, that age wasn't even a variable. When she did find out how old I was, she just said, "Well, that means I'll have at most fifty years of you, instead of a hundred."

How do you reply to something like that?

If you are a wise man, you don't even try. You grab the chance—it only comes once—and make the most of it.

That first day, I began to arrest her. She talked me out of it in about two minutes and took me home to her apartment. I never left.

I had no idea at the time how sick in the head she was. That emerged little by little, as we came closer. Maybe it was a lot more obvious to others than to me. I always had the blinders on—I still do. When an old friend of mine, Park Green, came to visit from the Moon, we went to see one of Mary's performances. I asked him what he thought of it, and he shook his head and said she was good but he could see the skull beneath the skin. I hated him for that, and I never told Mary; but he was right.

That might have been the thing that limited her as an actress. She could play high drama, or artificial, mannered comedy, or broad farce—she was a wonderful comedienne, but she didn't much care for those parts. What she could not portray were simple people, because there was nothing simple inside her that she could build on. It limited her. She was always busy, always working, but in the end I know that she was disappointed with her reputation.

You know, I honestly believe that I was good for Mary. In our years together she never had to go for official treatment. There'd be times when she went nonlinear, and when that happened I'd drop everything I was doing and stay with her constantly. And she'd come out of it. But those times became more and more frequent, and more and more severe.

When she suddenly told me, without a day's notice, that she was going off for a lunar cruise, I was delighted. Mary was always at her best when she had a new environment to learn, something fresh to challenge her. She was becoming more and more upset by crowds—an odd omen for an actress, but I didn't read it. The Moon would offer plenty of peace and a change of pace.

She went. She called once—to say that she was not coming back; she was heading for the Outer System. And that was all.

I just about came apart.

Four months later the Dancing Man appeared for the first time. And I came apart completely.

Bey lay back in his chair and looked up at Leo Manx. "Well?"

"Good." Manx was examining his records. "Very good."

"You have enough?"

"Goodness, no." Manx was incredulous. "This is a *start*— the first iteration. Now we can perhaps begin to learn something about you and your relationship with Mary. Give me another couple of days. Then it may be time to worry about your little dancing friend."

CHAPTER 6

> "Entropy is missing information."
> —Ludwig Boltzmann

> "Entropy is information."
> —Norbert Wiener

> "Entropy is leftovers."
> —Apollo Belvedere Smith

One quarter of the way to the edge of the Oort Cloud; that did not sound too far. Call it twenty-six thousand astronomical units and it became more substantial. Call it four trillion kilometers; it was then an inconceivable number, but no more than a number.

To appreciate the distance from Earth to the Opik Harvester, it was necessary to have direct sensory inputs. Bey Wolf looked back the way they had come and searched for the Sun.

There it was. But it was the Sun diminished, Sol with no discernible disk, Sol dwindled to the bright, brittle point of Venus on a frosty Earth night.

"The element of fire is quite put out. The sun is lost, and earth, and no man's wit, can well direct him where to look for it." Bey, still staring back the way they had come, took no comfort from the old words and longed for the cozy familiarity of the Inner System. At his side, Leo Manx was looking the other way, scanning the starfield ahead.

"Eh-hey! There we are! Ten more minutes, we'll be home." The Cloudlander had already shed his loose travel suit in favor of a pale yellow one-piece. His hairless arms and legs stuck out from it like the limbs of a gigantic and excited cricket. "There, Mr. Wolf. See it now? The harvester!"

He spoke as of a first sighting, but he had already pointed out the Opik Harvester to Bey an hour before, as a dark spot occulting a tiny patch of stars. But as the clumsy bulk drifted closer, glimmering with feeble surface lights, his excitement was increasing.

Bey followed the pointing finger. For eyes conditioned by the constraints of gravity, the shape of the harvester was difficult to comprehend. A dozen spheres clustered loosely to form a central grouping, but their coupling was done by the invisible bonds of electromagnetic fields, and the configuration constantly changed. Long, curving arms cantilevered away from the central nexus, reaching out to bridge a gulf that had no end. The final silver girders and antennae of those arms grew gradually thinner and less substantial, fading so slowly into void that their terminal points could not be seen.

According to Leo Manx, the big middle sphere was roughly twenty miles across. Bey could not verify that. It was impossible to gain any sense of scale from the harvester's main features. The whole structure had been built by self-replicating machines of widely differing sizes and had been designed to be run by them. Humans had been late arrivals, occupying the harvesters only when the final step of life-support systems had been added.

The ship's McAndrew drive had been switched off two hours earlier, ending the signal silence introduced by the ionized plasma that propelled it. The communications unit had at once begun to scroll and chatter, urging Wolf and Manx to join a meeting that was already in progress.

Manx, happy to be back in "decent" gravity, watched

Wolf's clumsy movements for a few seconds as they disembarked, then grabbed him by the arm. "Hold tight. You can practice later." He towed a weightless Bey along a succession of identical corridors, all unoccupied and showing no signs of human presence.

"Almost ninety thousand people," Manx said in reply to Wolf's question. "The harvester is a major population center of the Outer System. About ten million service machines, I imagine, though no one keeps count. They make whatever new ones they decide they need; it has been that way since the first ones were sent here from the Inner System. I've sometimes wondered what the machines would have done if people had never arrived in the Cloud. Would they have eventually downed tools and quit, or would they have found some other justification for continuing to modify the Cloud? If there were no humans to use the biological products of the harvesters, would the machines have found it necessary to invent us?"

To Bey's relief, they had reached a region of noticeable gravity. He was not too keen on the other implications of that—a shielded kernel had to be somewhere near, and that much pent energy made him uncomfortable. But it was nice to have an up and a down again, even if it was only a twentieth of a g. He followed Leo Manx through a final door and into a long room with a curved floor.

Three Cloudlanders were sitting at a little round table, each dressed uniformly in a lemon-colored one-piece suit.

Wolf at once recognized the woman facing him. Given the frequency with which she appeared on Earth newscasts, it would be hard not to do so. Cinnabar Baker was one of the three most powerful people in the Outer System and a scathing critic of everything that happened closer to the Sun than the inner edge of the Cloud. Her cheerful appearance belied her reputation. There was presumably the thin, gravity-intolerant skeleton of the Cloudlander within her, but in Baker's case it was well covered. She was a vast, smiling woman, maybe two hundred kilos in mass, with flawless, pale skin. Her hair was thin and close-cropped, revealing the contours of a well-shaped and delicate-looking skull. The clear eyes and fine skin tone gave evidence of regular use of form-change equipment.

She stood up and held out a chubby, dimpled hand. "Welcome to the Outer System. I am Cinnabar Baker. I'm responsible for the operation of all the harvesters, including this one. Let me express my appreciation that you agreed to come here, and allow me to introduce you to some of my staff. Sylvia Fernald." She gestured at the woman on her left. "In charge of all software development and control theory in the Outer System. Next to her, Apollo Belvedere Smith—Aybee for short and for preference—my top science adviser and general gadfly. Leo Manx, senior psych administrator and Inner System specialist, you know already—probably all too well after your trip together from the Inner System."

"Behrooz Wolf," Bey muttered. It hardly seemed necessary. They knew who he was. How many hairy strangers were there on the harvester, a foot and a half shorter than everyone else and with four times the muscles? Bey greeted the others, making his instinctive and immediate assessment of their ages, original appearance, and major form-changes. There were anomalies, points to be thought about later, particularly in the case of Apollo Belvedere Smith, who was extra-tall, rail-thin, and glowering angrily at Wolf for no discernible reason. But for the moment Bey was pondering a more substantial question.

Cinnabar Baker was there with three of the Cloud's scientists, technicians, and administrators, all apparently tops in their fields. They had been summoned to worry a technical problem of malfunctioning form-change equipment. Wolf had come to know and like Leo Manx, with his quirky sense of humor and his shared interest in Earth history and literature. He felt that a perfect choice had been made: Manx was just the right combination of seniority, experience, and intellect to work with Bey on form-change questions. But the others? It made more sense for Bey and Leo Manx to go straight to work. Why a top science adviser? Most of all, why Cinnabar Baker? She was far more senior than the problem justified.

Bey felt the stir of an old feeling, something that had been dormant for too long within him: suspicion, and with it, the frisson of powerful curiosity.

"Sylvia Fernald and Leo Manx will be your principal day-to-day contacts," Baker was saying. "If you find it necessary to travel through the system, one or both of them will accompany you. Aybee usually travels with me, and I have to be all over the place, but you will have first call. Any time you require him, he's at your service. That's enough, Aybee," she put in as the man across the table grunted his disapproval. "I told you the rules." She turned back to Wolf. "Tell us what you need to know about our form-change programs, Mr. Wolf, and we will do our best to provide it."

Wolf sat down between Leo Manx and Aybee Smith. He wanted to see more of the harvester, but that could wait. It was time for a direct approach. "Naturally, I would like an overview of the problem you've been having with form-change equipment and programs. But that's not my first priority."

They were staring at him in surprise.

"I'd like to know what's going on here," he continued. "I don't think I have been given the full story. There are factors that have not been described to me." He caught Cinnabar Baker's quick look at Leo Manx and the other's tiny shake of the head. "I must know what they are."

Apollo Belvedere Smith gave a grunt of approval. "Hey. I didn't want to bring you here, but mebbe you can do something useful, after all." He turned to Baker. "Was I right, or was I right? He cottoned. I guess I should brief the Wolfman."

Cinnabar Baker shook her head. "You'll go too fast and leave too much out."

"Naw. If he's smart as he needs to be, he'll follow."

"Maybe. But it's still no. You can impress him with your brilliance later. I want Fernald to brief him. But before we begin—" She stared straight at Bey, and he saw past the fat, friendly exterior. Cinnabar Baker was a person with drive to match her bulk, a woman who made up her mind in a hurry. "I won't ask you to pledge secrecy when you go back home, Behrooz Wolf," she went on. "Just don't talk about this while you're around here. We want to minimize alarm—panic, if you prefer that word. Now I'm starting to sound mysterious. Go on, Fernald, let's have it. Tell him what's been happening."

"Everything?"

"The whole story."

While they were talking, Bey had taken a closer look at Aybee Smith. His appearance suggested a man in his early twenties, but that of course meant little. Bey listened, looked, integrated posture, speech style, and the exchange between Aybee and Cinnabar Baker, and came up with a surprising conclusion: Apollo Belvedere Smith was a teenager, still under twenty. Yet he was Baker's top science adviser. Which meant he had to be at least half as smart as he seemed to think he was.

"Background first." Sylvia Fernald had moved around to face Bey. She was a good and logical briefer, and she began with a summary of what Bey had already heard in fair detail from Leo Manx. Three years earlier there had been problems with form-change processes. Humans emerged from the tanks either with an incorrect final form or in just the same state as when they went in. The problem had not attracted much interest at first, since a repeat of the form-change process would always lead to the desired result.

That had become less true in the past two years. Deviations became more pronounced, and repeat treatments often led to new anomalies. One year earlier the first deaths had occurred in the form-change tanks. Every attempt to trace the problem had failed. And the numbers of deaths and abnormalities were growing exponentially.

Wolf was hearing little that was a surprise, and his main attention was concentrated on the speaker. Sylvia Fernald had chosen neither the walking skeleton of Leo Manx nor the roly-poly bulk of Cinnabar Baker. She was slim but not skinny, and incredibly ugly by Earth standards. She towered over Bey by a foot or more, with a gawky, angular build that seemed all spidery arms and legs. Like Baker, she wore her carroty-red hair short, swept way back from a high, pale forehead. But unlike the others at the table, she had eyebrows, pale sandy arches that emphasized the size and brightness of her deep-set gray eyes and the sharp angle of her thin, jutting nose. Bey ignored the overall unpleasant impression, did his usual summation of variables, and decided she was on the young side of early middle age.

"How many cases, total?" he asked when she paused.

She hesitated and looked at Baker, who nodded. "Tell him."

"Nearly eighty thousand."

"My God. That's more than we've had on Earth in a century and a half."

"I know. And remember, that's out of a total population of fifty million, not your fifteen billion."

"And getting worse. Can you provide me with the rates of change?"

Sylvia Fernald nodded after another quick look at Cinnabar Baker. "That's not the end of it, Mr. Wolf. I'm not an expert on the technology of the Inner System, but here our form-change systems, hardware and software, are the most delicate devices we have. They have to be shielded against interference, and there's triple redundancy and error checking in every electronic signal."

Bey nodded. "Same on Earth. I'd be amazed if the procedures and the error-correcting codes are any different. I don't see how they could be. Form-change won't tolerate transmission errors. It's so delicate that an error rate of one bit in ten to the twelfth is enough to show. Nothing else comes close in sensitivity."

"Not on Earth, perhaps," Cinnabar Baker said. "But remember, here in the Outer System we are far more dependent on all kinds of feedback control systems. Go on, Fernald. The whole story."

"Three years ago we had our first problems with form-change processes. That was bad. But two years ago, other things began to go wrong. On a big scale. There are now billions of tons of hydrogen cyanide floating free near the edge of the Halo. The whole product line from the Kuiper Harvester went sour on us. It was supposed to produce aldehydes and alcohols from prebiotic bodies in the Cloud, but the program went wrong, the automatic checks didn't work, and the first thing we knew was when a crewed surveyor reported anomalous spectral signatures."

"A year's production down the drain," Baker added. "And five years more work before we'll be able to clean it up."

"Another harvester is producing the wrong materials," Sylvia Fernald said. "We caught that early, with no damage. We're busy now, checking the other thirty. We've also had signs of instability in a kernel control system; gigawatts of raw radiation if one of those got away. And oddest of all, nonsense reports have been coming in from our remote monitoring systems. They're scattered all over the system. Either our communications are generating batches of spurious signals, or space in the Outer System is filled with bizarre . . . things."

"Things?"

Aybee Smith produced a humorless laugh. "Yeah. Things. Tell him, Sylv."

"Visual phenomena." Sylvia Fernald was clearly uncomfortable with her own words. "Impossible events. I don't believe in them myself, but the people who report them do."

"Come on, Sylv—you're stalling." Aybee Smith grinned fiercely at Wolf. "How about a space dog—a blood-red hound running across Sagittarius, filling five degrees of the sky? It was reported from Spanish Station, on the other side of the Sun. Would you believe that?"

"No, I wouldn't." Wolf looked at Cinnabar Baker, but her face was serious, and she showed no sign of interrupting. "It's ridiculous."

"Right. So how about a flaming blue sword, down near the edge of the Halo? Or a rain of blood, sleeting across Orion. Or a great snake, wrapped around the Kernel Ring and swallowing its own tail?"

"How many people reported seeing these?"

"People?" Aybee Smith shook his head in disgust. "Wolfman, people are flaky. They'll see anything, or say they do. Look at you; you prove my point. You've been having visions, but they're right there inside your skull—no one else sees 'em, right? Right. So if it was just *people*, I'd say the hell with it, they're all crazy—no offense—and who cares what they say they see. But this is different. These were *instrument* readings, not people babble. Sensors *recorded* this stuff. People only saw it later, when they looked at the files. We're talking serious here, not just crazy. You know what a lot of the people who've heard about this say? They don't say phenomena, they say *portents*. How do you like that?"

Bey was listening, but half his attention was elsewhere. Again, something was not adding up. It took a few seconds to recognize what it was and turn again to Cinnabar Baker. "This has been going on for years?"

"More than two years. But getting worse, bit by bit. It sounds like nonsense, I know, but with everything else going on, I have to take it seriously." She paused. "You're skeptical. I'm not surprised. But believe me, neither Sylvia Fernald nor Aybee is exaggerating or inventing."

"I do believe you. But I think we're still both playing games. Let me tell you something you may not care to hear." Wolf nodded at Leo Manx. "When he asked me to take a look at your form-change problems, I refused. Then an hour later I called him up and agreed. So why did I change my mind? I'm not an idiot, even though you may think I act like one. Well, I left Earth because I knew if I didn't, I'd be back in Old City in less than a week. I came to a place where I couldn't do that, even if I wanted to. I was going crazy there—maybe I'm still going crazy."

"I do not agree." Leo Manx sounded comfortingly confident.

"We'll see. Either way, I didn't feel I was cheating you. Crazy or not, I know form-change theory and practice as well as anyone. So I would get away from Earth, and maybe lose my hallucinations—you can dismiss them as nothing, but I couldn't. And maybe you would get help with your problem.

That would be a fair exchange. Except that you haven't been honest with me. You're having trouble with form-change, sure, but now you're admitting your problem is much more general. *All* your signals and communications are screwed up. Form-change just happens to be unusually sensitive; signal distortions show up there first."

"That is probably correct." Cinnabar Baker was not embarrassed.

"So now let's look at things from your point of view. I know form-change, but I sure as hell won't solve your other problems. You ought to have experts in bifurcation theory, in optimal control theory, in signal encoding and error correction, in catastrophe theory. Those are not my fields."

"I agree."

"So why don't you get the right people, people who already know the Outer System?"

"For this reason." Cinnabar Baker gestured to Aybee Smith, who took a thin card from his pocket and passed it to Bey. "Do you recognize any of those names, Mr. Wolf?"

Bey scanned it briefly, noting his own name halfway down. "I know two-thirds of them. You're certainly on the right track. The ones from the Inner System are top people. If the ones from here are comparable, you've got the best systems talent of the Solar System on that list."

"I'm glad you agree with Aybee's judgment. He made the list; it's good to know he gets something right." Baker waited for Apollo Smith's indignant snort, then continued. "We tried to obtain the services of all those people. Every one."

"And they refused to help? I'm surprised, if you told them what you've just told me."

"No, Mr. Wolf." The real Cinnabar Baker was showing through, powerful and deadly serious. "They did not refuse. They had no opportunity to do so, because we had no chance to tell them. Of the twenty-seven names on that list, twelve are dead. Seven are hopelessly insane. And seven have disappeared. Our attempts to trace them, assisted when appropriate by officials of the Inner System, have all failed. That makes twenty-six. You, Mr. Wolf, are the twenty-seventh."

She stood up slowly, a massive and massively determined woman. "And now I am holding nothing back from you. You know what we know, except for the details. Do you agree with my view—that you have special motivation to work on and solve this problem?"

CHAPTER 7

"The emitted particles have a thermal spectrum corresponding to a temperature that increases rapidly as the mass of the black hole decreases. For a black hole with the mass of the Sun the temperature is only about a ten-millionth of a degree above absolute zero. The thermal radiation leaving a black hole with that temperature would be completely swamped by the general background level of radiation in the universe. On the other hand, a black hole with a mass of a billion tons would release energy at the rate of 6,000 megawatts, equivalent to the output of six large nuclear power plants."

—Stephen Hawking

The builders, caretakers, and first inhabitants of the harvesters worked around the clock, without thought of rest. Bey Wolf was beginning to wonder if the human occupants were expected to follow the same schedule.

When the conference with Cinnabar Baker was over, he had been settled into a huge but pleasant set of rooms complete with form-change unit and extended library access. Leo Manx, who had taken him there, pointed out that the quarters provided a fortieth of a g sleeping environment. He obviously expected Wolf to be delighted. Bey, knowing that the source of the local gravitational field could only be a power kernel no more than thirty meters below his feet, was not pleased. The triple shielding on a Kerr-Newman black hole had never failed—yet—but according to Sylvia Fernald, several in Cloudland had recently come close. At thirty meters, a few gigawatts of hard radiation would not just kill him, it would dissolve him, melt his flesh from his bones before he knew what was happening.

Bey was tired by the journey and the novelty of the harvester, and glutted with new information. He wanted to lie down for a while and digest what he had learned, but Leo Manx showed no signs of leaving.

"Sylvia Fernald and Aybee Smith will both be excellent colleagues," he said. He had stretched himself out on Bey's bed, just lengthy enough for him, and closed his eyes. "But there are things about them that you should know before we begin. Aybee is extremely able but a little immature."

The bed was apparently very comfortable. Bey coveted it. "He's just a kid."

"Exactly. Nineteen years old, but more knowledgeable and scientifically creative than anyone else in the Outer System. You may rely on him for science, but not for judgment."

"I'll remember. What about Sylvia Fernald?"

"She is more mature and also more complex. Her judgment on some of the subjects we discussed today may not be sound."

"Fifty-five years old?"

Manx lifted his head from the bed to stare at Wolf. "Fifty-six, as I recall. Are you able to do that with anyone?"

"I don't know. Probably. I've had lots of form-change experience. Why is she suspect?"

"You saw the list of names of people who died or disappeared. One of them, Paul Chu, was Sylvia's consort for many years. I believe they planned to become parents. But he vanished without a trace six months ago on a routine trip to the edge of the Halo."

"The Halo again."

"I know. I have had the same thought. But without evidence . . ."

"We'll have to look for evidence."

"Certainly." Manx lay silent, eyes closed, for another minute or two. He sighed. "You know, I was originally very doubtful about my trip to Earth, but it was a very good idea. Before I went, I always suspected that deep inside I was by nature an Earthman. Your history is so fascinating, and Earth is the origin of all the worthwhile cultures and arts. But not until I had made a journey there for myself did I realize that it was not for me. It was not home. *This* is home." He patted the bed and lapsed into another and longer silence.

"I think I'll have a sign made for that far wall," Bey said at last.

"Indeed?"

"Yes. It will say, 'If you have nothing to do, please don't do it here.'"

Manx frowned and opened his eyes. "You wish for privacy?"

"I wish for sleep."

Manx sat up reluctantly. "Very well. Then I will leave. But I must mention one other matter of importance to you. I have completed my analysis of your own difficulties."

Fatigue changed to a tingle of anticipation. "The hallucinations? You think you can stop them?"

"No. On the contrary, I am sure I cannot. Because I am convinced that what you have been seeing are not the distorted constructs of your brain. They have been imposed from *without*."

"That's impossible. I've been in situations where I saw that Red Man, and there were other people watching the same broadcast. They saw nothing. I've seen him on a recorded program, too, then played the same program through a second time. He didn't reappear. And anyway, why would anyone *want* to make me crazy?"

"I don't know. However, I believe that if we can answer the first problem, of *method*, we will have gone far toward answering the second one, of intention. And an induced effect is a *technological* problem, not a psychological one. That offers us recourse. I propose to present the idea at once to Apollo Smith. If I know Aybee, it will intrigue him." He levered himself off the bed, sighed, and nodded to Bey. "And so to bed. Sleep well."

Which, of course, Leo Manx had now made out of the question. Bey turned off the light and lay on the bed, but he no longer felt sleepy. Induced effects, he thought. He had considered that idea when the Dancing Man had first appeared, but he had dropped it for two good reasons: he could not see how it might be done, and he could not imagine why anyone would want to do it.

After five useless minutes, during which he again concluded that he knew of no way to turn Leo Manx's opinions to useful facts, Bey rose, dumped his clothes into the service hopper, and went through to the shower room. It was sinfully big, the size of a five-person apartment on Earth; no wonder Leo Manx had been crowded there. After a minute of juggling with unfamiliar controls, Bey ran the water as hot as he could stand, then accidentally switched it to an icy downpour. He jumped out of the spray with a scream and turned on the hot air.

As soon as he was dry he realized he had made another mistake. The only clothes offered by the dispenser were more of the pale yellow one-piece suits, too long and too narrow for his body. His own clothes had been eaten by the service hopper, and he could find no sign of shoes anywhere.

Finally he stuffed himself into one of the suits and managed to engage the fasteners. Looking at himself in the mirror was an unwise decision, but he suspected he was already as ugly as he could get by Cloudland standards. Bey left his quarters barefoot and headed along a corridor that spiraled slowly away from the kernel. He had no idea where he was going, but he felt confident that he could find his way home. There was not likely to be another kernel in the interior of the harvester, and as long as he followed the kernel's gravity gradients "up" and "down," he could not get lost.

After a few minutes of wandering he found himself in a

broad accordian-pleated passage that was pouched and folded like the alimentary canal of some giant beast. That similarity went beyond appearances. Bey knew that the harvesters prowled the Oort Cloud, seeking bodies high in volatiles and complex organic materials. Once found, they were ingested by the comet-sized maw of the harvester for transfer to the interior. They were heated with energy extracted from the power kernel, thawed, and dropped into the internal lake-sized vats, to be stirred and aerated by jets of carbon dioxide and oxygen. In that enzyme-seeded brew, the prebiotic molecules of the fragments—porphyrins, carotenoids, polypeptides, and cellulose—were converted to edible fats, starches, sugars, and proteins.

Bey stood by a viewing port and peered into a bubbling sea of pale yellow-green. Close by him, there was a shudder of moving machinery. A great valve had opened. Hundreds of thousands of tons of broth went streaming along helical cooling tubes, on the way to extraction of water, chlorophylls, and yeasts. This batch was near its final stages. Most of the final product would be compressed, packaged into spaceproof containers, and launched on the long journey to the Inner System. The harvesters fed the population of the Cloud itself, but more important, their products were essential to the survival of everyone closer to the Sun. The same food products were the working capital that funded the outflow of technology and finished goods from the teeming Inner System.

And if there were a war or an embargo? As Bey left that enormous production plant, he could not help wondering what would happen if the supply line failed.

At first, nothing would be noticed at the destination. The payloads were transported to the Inner System at only a fraction of a g acceleration, so they took a long time to get there. There would be food in the pipeline of the delivery system for at least ten years, even if the supply from the harvesters were cut off at once. But then the Inner System would be in real trouble—as much trouble as the Cloud would suffer if the Inner System were one day to cut off the supply of power kernels or refuse to ship out manufactured goods. With such total interdependency of the two groups, any talk of war or of breakdown of commerce between them seemed ludicrous. And yet Bey knew that such talk was growing more and more common, more and more strident.

He had followed the local gravity vector downward and was almost back at his quarters. But the thought of the Kernel Ring led him to keep going, descending a steep staircase that dropped toward the kernel itself. Within fifteen meters he found himself on a black, seamless sphere with no visible entry points. He was standing in a thirtieth of a g field on the first of the three kernel shields. Nothing organic would survive for a millisecond on the other side of it. Twenty meters or less beneath his feet was the kernel itself, a rapidly rotating black hole held in position by its own electric charge. This one would mass a couple of billion tons. It served as the power source for one whole sphere of the harvester. Streams of subnuclear particles passed through the kernel's ergosphere, slightly slowed the kernel's rotation, and emerged with their own energy vastly increased.

The power provided by a kernel was large but finite. After maybe twenty years, its angular momentum and rotational energy would be depleted. A "spun-down" black hole with no rotation would continue to radiate according to the Hawking evaporative process, but that energy was far less controlled and useful. It was even a nuisance, since the monitor sensors within the shield needed multiple signal redundancy to assure error-free messages to the outside. A spent kernel was a useless kernel. It had to be "spun up" again to high angular momentum from some other source, or replaced by a new one from the Kernel Ring.

And if the Kernel Ring became inaccessible? Then the Cloudlanders would starve for energy, as surely as the Inner System would starve for lack of Cloudland food supplies. And yet the Kernel Ring was the least controlled part of the whole system, and it was not clear who had the most rights to it. Was it the Podders, the Halo's migrant spacefarers who lived within their spacesuits? Or maybe it was Black Ransome, waging war against both Cloudlanders and Sunhuggers from the mystery hideaway of Ransome's Hole.

Bey found the train of thought leading him again to Mary. Was she in the Kernel Ring, as Leo Manx insisted? Or was she to be found somewhere *here*, in the unthinkably big volume of the Cloud? If so, the Cloud's central library system might help him locate her. Assuming that he wanted to.

"Since there's no help, come let us kiss and part. Nay, I have done, you get no more of me." Mary's last message had asked him not to look for her, but in typically Mary terms. She had left an opening for ambiguity. Bey turned to head back for the stairs, thinking that if he started to learn the library access system, he would never get to sleep.

He was so preoccupied with his thoughts that he almost walked into the three strangers.

There were two men and a woman. Wolf had time for no more than a quick look at them—again, no eyebrows, and suddenly that made sense; perspiration would not trickle down foreheads in zero g—then they were advancing on him.

"What the devil are you doing here?" The shorter of the men spoke loudly and angrily. He came close and glared down from his superior height.

"I'm sorry," Bey began. "I didn't know the kernel level was restricted territory. I was about to—"

"The kernel level!" The man turned to his companions. "Just like a Snugger, he doesn't understand what you say to him."

The woman stepped forward. "We're not talking about the kernel. You don't belong on the harvester—or anywhere in our system. You get back to your own stinking kind."

The other man did not speak, but he stepped to Wolf's side and jabbed him painfully in the ribs with a bony elbow. At the same moment the woman trod on Bey's bare instep with a hard-soled shoe.

"Hold it, now—" Bey took a step backward. They were in a low-g field, which favored the Cloudlanders, but Bey was sure that if he had to defend himself he could do it very well. He could break any of those thin limbs between his hands, and

their feeble muscles had probably done as much as they could
to hurt him. But he did not want to fight back—not when he
had no idea who or why. He lifted his arm as though to strike
at the man in front of him, then lunged for the staircase instead.

He was all the way up before they had even turned to
pursue. At the top he slammed the door in position and raced
off along the corridor. On the threshold of his own quarters,
he ran into a tall figure coming out. Bey braked as hard as he
could, but there was still contact. The man gave a grunt of
surprise and went sailing away through the air, bouncing off
the wall and then falling face down across the bed.

"Hey! What the hell!"

Bey recognized the complaining voice. It was Apollo Belvedere Smith. He went across and helped him sit up.

Aybee rubbed his midriff. "What's all that about?"

"I was going to ask you the same. I was running away from
three of your people. I've no idea who they are, but they tried
to start a fight."

"Oh, yeah. I came here to warn you not to leave your
quarters. Close the door, Wolfman, and lock it."

"Why? What the devil's going on here?"

"You're the man they love to hate." Aybee stood up and
began to wander around the room. "You didn't hear the news-
cast, right?"

"I've been looking at the inside of the harvester."

"Yeah." Aybee was still scowling, but that was apparently
his natural expression. "You know something? Most people
are real idiots."

"Not true. By definition, most people are average."

That earned a quick grin. "Y'know what I mean. They're
animals. Last few days there's been more growling and
scowling between government here and government in the
Inner System than you'd believe. So in comes news a couple
of hours ago from the far side of the Cloud. Bad deal. A
whole harvester destroyed, blown apart, thirty thousand people dead. Power plant went blooey. And newsword is that you
Sunhuggers did it."

"Nonsense. The Inner System would never destroy a harvester. We need that food."

"Hey, I never said I believed it, did I? It's like I said—people here are dumb. They see somebody looks like you—" Aybee paused to give Bey a detailed inspection, then shook his head and went on "—they hate him. You're not safe here now."

"That's Cinnabar Baker's problem. If she wants me to be useful, she'll have to find a way to give me working space."

The answering grin was even less pleasant than usual. "No worries. You'll get work space, Wolfman. The other thing on the news is just your line. Form-change foul-ups on the Sagdeyev space farm, a day from here. You and Sylv'll be heading there, see what you can sort out."

"You won't be going?" Bey wanted to know how important the problem was in Cinnabar Baker's mind.

"Don't think so. Not 'less you need me. Sylv can handle it. She's no dummy, and she's reliable. You'll like working with her."

It was probably the highest level of praise that Aybee offered to anyone. Bey nodded. "I have the same feeling. We'll get on together."

"Mind you, she's no good at *real* science. She comes to me for that."

"You're too modest."

"Mebbe I am." Aybee was examining Bey with a look of clinical curiosity. "Mind if I ask you a personal question?"

"Probably."

"Do you have hair like that all over? I mean, it must drive you crazy."

Bey held up his hand to show Aybee the open palm.

"Okay you know what I meant." Aybee grinned. "You think I'm a smart-ass, don't you?"

"Not at all. Fifty years ago, I was just like you. Brighter than fusion. I'm amazed how much smarter other people are these days."

"Senile decay?"

"Hang in for a little while. Your turn will come."

Aybee scowled. "Hey, Wolfman, don't say that. That's too true to be funny. Top mathematicians and physicists do their real stuff before they're twenty-five. After that they're just hacking. I've only got six years left, then it's all downhill for the next hundred years. How's it feel to be real old?"

"I'll let you know when I am."

"Sylv says you're pretty well along—after the meeting she got Manx to let her peek at your personal records. She's nosy. She tells me you been seeing things, and you don't know how you could have been fed 'em. And the Manxman thinks I could help. Tell me more."

"Not tonight, Josephine."

"Who?"

"Somebody even older than me." Bey advanced slowly on Aybee. "Shoo. You're leaving now. I'm going to throw you out—literally, if I have to. Catch me in the morning; I'll tell you all you want to know about me. Even how I grow hair."

"Sure." Aybee headed for the doorway. "I guess old people need lots of sleep."

"I guess we do." Wolf closed and locked the door after him. If any more visitors were on their way tonight, they would have to break it down. He sat on the bed and considered Apollo Belvedere Smith.

Aybee was young, arrogant, opinionated, brash, and insensitive.

Bey liked him very much.

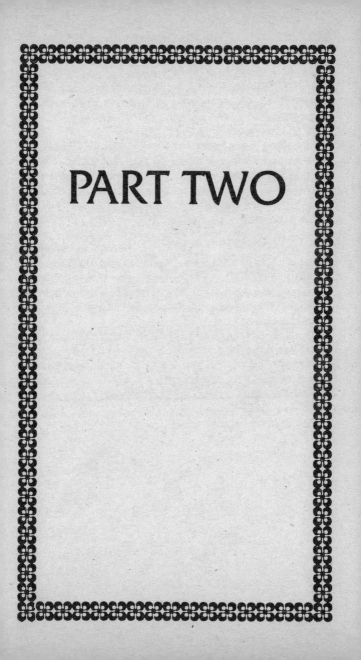

PART TWO

CHAPTER 8

Cinnabar Baker had no home, or perhaps she had thirty. Apartments were maintained for her use on every harvester, identical in size, gravity, and furnishings. She traveled constantly and spent at most ten days a year in each one.

She was said to have neither human intimates nor personal belongings. Turpin went with her everywhere, but he was not a possession. He was an old, cross-eyed crow with a big vocabulary and an absence of tail feathers. When he was in a bad mood, which was often, he had the habit of tugging plumage out with his bill.

He was doing that now, and it was an unpleasant sight. Sylvia Fernald found it hard to take her eyes off him. The crow would pause occasionally to glare at her with rheumy, droop-lidded eyes, then go back to his self-destructive preening. He made no attempt to fly; instead, he went waddling back and forth in a piratical roll all over the little round table in front of Sylvia, wings half-open and muttering a bad-tempered parody of human speech. Sylvia tried to ignore Turpin and keep her attention on what Cinnabar Baker was saying. It was not easy. Sylvia had been asleep when the call had come. She bit back a yawn, wondering how it was possible to be so nervous and yet so sleepy.

The latest summons had caught her by surprise, as had the

57

earlier order, a week before, to attend the meeting with Wolf
and help to brief him. She worked for Baker, that was undeni-
able, but the boss of the harvesters had reached down past two
intermediate levels of command to get to Fernald and had
never offered an explanation.

This new call had been equally casual, as if there were
nothing unusual in asking a junior staff member to come to a
one-on-one meeting well after midnight. The big woman had
been sitting cross-legged in the low-g apartment when Sylvia
arrived. She had exchanged the yellow uniform for a billow-
ing cloud of pale-green spun material that left only her head
and hands uncovered, and she seemed as fresh and alert as
ever.

"Now let's think a bit more about Behrooz Wolf," she said,
as though continuing a conversation already in progress. "We
have Leo Manx's impressions, of course, and I have now
heard from Aybee. But neither one is a close observer of what
I might call inner states. You saw as much of Wolf as I did.
What sort of man did you find in there?"

Sylvia had expected a discussion of harvester control systems or perhaps of form-change procedures. Her job did not
include character assessments, but she could not tell that to
Cinnabar Baker. And she was fairly sure that Baker could not
be stalled with platitudes.

"Competent but complicated. I don't think I was ever sure
what he was thinking."

"Nor did I." Baker smiled like the Gautama and waited.

"He's obviously intelligent, but we knew that from his reputation. And I don't just mean for form-change theory. He saw
that there were other matters involved here very quickly."

"Almost too quickly." Cinnabar Baker did not elaborate.
Again she sat and waited.

"And he's obviously a sensitive type, too. I saw Leo
Manx's reports on Wolf and his relationship to Mary Walton."
(And I can imagine how he felt when she left, Sylvia thought,
but I won't say that to Cinnabar Baker.) "That means he's still
very miserable and thinks he's not getting much out of life.
But he took a lot of interest in what we told him, so I suspect

that although he *believes* he feels things strongly, his intellectual drives are more powerful than his emotional ones. He's like Aybee; he lives in a thought world more than a sense world. He wouldn't admit that; maybe he doesn't even know it. As for his other interests, it's hard to say anything. How does he spend his time when he's not at work?"

While she was speaking, Sylvia found herself asking the same question about Cinnabar Baker. The apartment was tiny by Cloud standards, and minimally furnished. The walls were a uniform beige, unrelieved by pictures or other decorations, and there were no personal bits and pieces like the ones that filled Sylvia's own apartment to overflowing. Cinnabar Baker had a reputation for hard work. On the basis of the evidence, work was all she had.

"Did you find him attractive?" The question was so unexpected that Sylvia was not sure she had heard correctly.

"You mean *physically* attractive?"

"Exactly."

"My God, no. He's absolutely *hideous*." Sylvia let that answer sit for a couple of seconds, then felt obliged to add, "I mean, I suppose it's not his fault. Lots of people from the Inner System probably look like that. And he has an interesting mind, and I think he has a good sense of humor. But he's revolting-looking, and of course he's very little, with those short stubby arms. And worst of all, he's—he's too—"

"Too?"

"Too *hairy*. I wouldn't be surprised if he's covered with hair all over him, like an ape, everywhere. Even on—" Sylvia suddenly became aware of how extreme she must sound. "Of course, I suppose he can't *help* any of that. Though with form-change equipment available . . ."

"I'm sorry you find him a little unattractive." Cinnabar Baker apparently had a great gift for understatement. Reaching out to stroke the back of the crow standing in front of her, she looked down so that her eyes were hidden from Sylvia. "You see, I wish to make an unusual request of you. And since it's outside the usual range of duties, it has to be no more than an informal request."

"If I can do anything to help you, naturally I will." The day has been crazy so far, she reflected. Let's see if it can get any stranger.

"Good. You know that you will be working closely with Behrooz Wolf, and traveling with him?"

"That's the plan."

"I want you to seek a relationship with him. A very close relationship."

"You mean—you want me to—Surely you don't want me to—" Turpin chose that moment to give a long, gurgling laugh like water flowing away down a drain, and Sylvia could not finish the sentence.

"I mean a psychological attachment," Baker said calmly. "And, if possible, even a physical attachment. And I'll tell you why. Wolf was one of twenty-seven people we considered contacting to help us. He's the only one left, so we tend to say to ourselves, hey, he was really lucky. Maybe he *was* lucky. But maybe there's more than luck involved. Maybe Wolf knows more than he admits, and maybe there's a good reason why he didn't get wiped out with the rest. And some reason why he agreed to come here, after first refusing. If so, I need to know all that. Pillow talk is better than truth drugs. If you could get close to him, persuade him to confide in you—"

"I can't do it!" Sylvia had not listened to anything past Baker's first sentence. "It's totally out of the question. I'm willing to do most things, but that's too much to ask *anybody*. And anyway," she added, reaching for a second reason, "I'm sure it's mutual. He'd never want to look twice at me."

"Maybe." Baker stopped stroking Turpin's back and fixed cool blue eyes on Sylvia. "But maybe not."

"You've seen what Snugger women are like. Short and brown, all fat and hips and breasts. He must think we're hideous. My God, I'm a foot taller than he is, if I'm an inch. And miles too skinny for Earth taste. And anyway—"

"Anyway," Turpin said suddenly. "Anyway, anyway, in for a penny-way." He took off with an excited flapping of black wings, flew up and around in a lurching spiral, and landed leering on Cinnabar Baker's shoulder.

"You underestimate the effects of prolonged personal interaction," Baker was saying. She smiled. "In other words, talking leads to touching. And beauty is easy. A few hours in a form-change tank—not that I'm suggesting this, you understand—and you could be Wolf's ideal of beauty."

"Never. I'm sorry, but I won't even consider it. That's final." Sylvia stood up. She had to leave as soon as possible, before Cinnabar Baker could try again to talk her into something.

And so much for her own career as a control specialist—her now-blighted career. It had been ruined in the past five minutes.

The last thought was the bitterest of all. When the original summons had come from Cinnabar Baker, Sylvia had been flattered and excited. The quality of her work must have singled her out for special attention. She would be assigned to the visitor from the Inner System because she had unusual competence in form-change and systems work.

Now it was clear that her professional skills had nothing to do with it. Her role was that of convenient female, a lure set out to catch Bey Wolf. And now that she had refused? Cinnabar Baker might say she did not hold it against her, but she would. Sylvia's career was in tatters.

"Please excuse me now." She looked at Baker, found no words, and headed blindly for the door.

Cinnabar Baker watched her leave. As expected, Sylvia Fernald had refused—vehemently. But the idea had been planted. Now Sylvia would be unable to meet and work with Behrooz Wolf, without also evaluating him at some level as a prospective partner. And that was all Baker had hoped to achieve.

"Hormones are everything, Turpin," she said to the bird on her shoulder. "Brains are nice, and looks are nice, and logic's even nicer; but hormones run the show. For everyone, even for me and you. But we never know it. I hope I wasn't too hard on Sylvia. Let's see if she'll change her mind when she knows him better."

The night's work was far from over. Humming softly to

herself, Cinnabar Baker bent over the desktop communications unit and reviewed the official statement she had prepared warning the Inner System about their interference in Outer System affairs. It would do. There were a couple of key words that could have been stronger—"demand" instead of "request," and "intolerable" was better than "impermissible"— but they were easily fixed.

She approved the statement for release. Then she entered coded mode and requested a dedicated circuit for new, real-time communication. There was a moment's delay pending approval of heliocentric coordinates outside the usual network. That was cleared, using Baker's own authorization. The scrambling codes were assigned. Finally, on the outermost structures of the harvester, the half-kilometer antenna turned its focused hyperbeam toward a destination deep in the Halo.

CHAPTER 9

"You can run, you can run, just as fast as you can,
You'll never get away from the Negentropic Man."
—crèche song of the Hoyle Harvester

Cloudland ships were easy to recognize: hydrocarbon hulls, bracing struts of carbon fiber, transparent polymer ports.

Necessity and nature had set the rules. The bodies of the Oort Cloud provided a limited construction kit, little but the first eight elements of the periodic table. Metals were in particularly short supply. Rather than dragging them up the gravity gradient from the Inner System, the Cloudlander fabricating machines had learned to improvise. Less than one-tenth of a percent of the ship that would carry Bey Wolf and Sylvia Fernald to the Sagdeyev space farm was metal, and that fraction would be reduced again in the new models.

Wolf was trying to hold a conversation with Sylvia Fernald as they prepared to leave, but it was difficult going. Two days earlier she had been friendly and at ease with him. He had known it, and so had she. They were strangers, but they had hit it off together in the first few minutes, comfortable with each other's work style and attitude. He had been pleased at the prospect of working with Fernald—Sylvia, she had asked him to call her that before the first informal planning meeting ended. But today. . .

Today he had been wringing words out of her, one by one. "This looks as though it will only hold two people. What about Leo Manx, Sylvia? I thought he was planning to come with us."

"He changed his mind." Her voice was expressionless. She was staring at the fine black hairs on his forearms and refusing to look him in the eye.

Was *that* it? His appearance? When he had arrived at the Opik Harvester, Bey had been wearing the long-sleeved, long-legged style of the Inner System. Today he had adopted the scanty uniform of the Cloudlanders, and his physical differences were more apparent. The widespread use of form-change equipment had allowed Earth people to get used to pretty much anything. But the people he had seen on the harvester were all very similar, limited thin or fat variations on a single body type.

She had turned to check fuel and supply status and was bending low over the panel. He moved closer to her, reaching out a muscular arm and stealthily comparing it with her pale, smooth limb. She sensed he was near her and spun around.

"What are you doing?"

"Nothing." Bey wondered why he sounded guilty and why her cheeks were flushed. If she stayed that jumpy for the whole trip, it was going to be an unpleasant twenty-four hours. The one accommodation shortage in Cloudland was found in their transit vessels. The McAndrew drive was fine, but the inertial and gravitational forces were balanced only in a small region on the ship's main axis. Bey and Sylvia would share that space, a cylindrical cabin about seven feet across. Standoffishness would be hard. Sylvia herself was close to seven feet tall.

They were making final preparations for departure, running a countdown together with awkward formality, when Aybee hurried in.

"Good. Thought mebbe I'd missed you."

"Four minutes more, you would have." Sylvia did a poor job of hiding her relief. "Are you coming with us?"

"No way." Aybee looked around the little cabin in disgust. "I need *space*, room to shine. You'd have to fold me double to get me in here. It'll be cozy enough with just you and the Wolfman."

The tense atmosphere went right by him. He was swinging a square satchel up from his side and opening the clasps. "Talked to old Leo again, and this time we got the problem right. First time, he asked me, How can you track down an input video signal that nobody else can see? I said, Hey, I'll tell you five ways to do that, but I can't tell you which one's being used without more information."

"Three minutes," Bey said. "Or we'll have to start over with a new countdown."

"Loads of time." Aybee pulled from the satchel a thin rectangular box, a head-covering helmet, and a whole snake's nest of wires and electrodes. "Today, the Leo-man tells me we had the problem wrong. He don't care *how* the signal gets in your head, he just wants to *see* it, know what it is drives you crazy. Different deal, right? Lot easier, because who cares if the signal came from outside or if you made up the whole thing? The *memory* of it's tucked away somewhere in there." He gestured at Bey's head. "So this gadget can pull it out for us."

Bey eyed the device without enthusiasm. It had a random and unfinished look. "You want me to put that thing over my head? How am I supposed to breathe?"

"Same as usual, in an' then out. There's air passages fkr that. Hey, loosen up. If I wanted to kill you, there's easier ways."

"Two minutes," Sylvia Fernald cut in. "Aybee, we should be in our chairs. You have to leave."

"Lots of time. Wolfman, don't you *want* to know how this works? It's dead good. See, you start thinking about what you saw—little red bogeymen, whatever. Those memories are stored away somewhere inside your head, scene-perfect. You never forget anything you experience, no one does, you just can't get at it, not in detail. So this takes your first-cut memory output, feeds it back to you, and asks if it's a perfect match. If not, it iterates the presentation until there *is* a match. My algorithm guarantees convergence. And all the time we're recording what we get. So at the end of a session, we've caught whatever you saw—even what you *thought* you saw, provided there's detail to it." He glared at Wolf, who was packing the flexible helmet away into its case. "Hey, what kind of ungrateful bozo are you? I put a lot of work in that. Aren't you going to try it?"

"Are you saying it may not work?"

"Sure it'll work, sure as my name's Apollo Belvedere Smith."

"Then I'll use it when we're on the way to the farm." Bey pointed at the countdown indicator. "See that? You can look at the results of your work in real time if you don't get out of here in the next forty seconds. The hatch secures automatically thirty seconds before the drive comes on. You coming with us?"

"No way!" Aybee was jumping for the cabin exit. "Call back and tell us what you get. Leo Manx is itchy, too." He was gone, but as the other two were moving to the bunks he poked his head back in. "Hey, Wolfman. Did you really rough up those three people last night before you ran into me?"

Bey was strapped in, clutching Aybee's satchel to his chest. "Just the opposite. I didn't touch them, but one had a go at my ribs; another trod on my foot. I could show you the bruise."

"Don't bother. You see one hairy leg, you've seen 'em all. But take a look at the news. They say you attacked them, without any warning. You're getting out of here just in time."

And so was Aybee. The two passengers heard the outer hatch close no more than two seconds before the siren announced that the drive was being engaged.

• • •

Aybee's last-minute delivery proved a blessing. Bey had attempted conversation with Sylvia again once they were on the way, but she was so obviously upset about something that after a few minutes he took out the flexible helmet, attached the electrodes, and placed the set over his head.

Aybee had not bothered with such details as operating instructions. Bey sat in darkness for a while, wondering if he had omitted to switch it on. He was ready to remove the helmet, but he did not want to confront Sylvia's anxious face. If the device operated as advertised, he should be concentrating on the clearest memory he had of the Dancing Man. It was easy to bring into mind that tiny figure, coming into view from the left of the screen . . .

It was like form-change, but with one difference. The compulsion came from outside, not from within his own will. Bey was still conscious, but he had no control over anything. In his mind, the Dancing Man moved across the screen, paused, and moved again. *Dance, pause, adjust, reset, dance. Dance, pause, reset, dance.* On it went, again and again, each time so little different from the last that Bey could detect no change. *Dance, pause, adjust, reset.* He tried to count while the act repeated forever, scores of times, hundreds of times, thousands of times. But he could not hold the number in his head. *Dance, pause, adjust, reset.* An endless, invariant procession of dancing men capering one by one across his field of view, twisting, turning, shuffling backward out of view. They sawed deeper and deeper into his skull, through the protective meningeal sheath, carving into the tender folds of his brain while he was screaming silently for release.

At last it came. The cycle was broken—with stunning abruptness—and the helmet was removed. Bey shuddered back to consciousness and found himself staring up at the frightened eyes of Sylvia Fernald.

"I'm sorry." She reached out to touch his forehead, then instantly jerked her hand back. "I felt sure you were in trouble. You lay there for so long, and then you started to groan. I was afraid you might be in pain. Were things going wrong?"

Bey put up his hands to cover his eyes. The light had become much too bright, and he had a terrible headache. "I'd say they were, but Aybee might not agree. I think he set the tolerances for convergence of his program too tight. I might have been days trying to reconstruct what I saw. Maybe I never would have gotten there. I could have been in that damned loop forever. Anyway, I'm all right now." He reached out and took her left hand in his, holding it tightly enough that her reflexive jerk did not free it. "I appreciate what you did, Sylvia. I could never have broken out of that on my own."

It was done on impulse, but suddenly it became an experiment. How would she react?

She allowed the contact for maybe half a second. Then she firmly pulled away and with her right hand reached across to press a switch on the side of the instrument. There was a click, and a brief buzz of sound. She waited a moment, then touched the front panel.

Bey stared at her. "You know how it works!"

"I looked at it long enough, while you were lying there. And I knew Aybee would keep it simple—he says he wants his work to be like the Cloudland Navy, designed by a genius to be run by idiots. I know which buttons to press, if that makes me an expert." She paused, her hand still before the flat front panel. "Would you like to see if you got anything? There's a playback feature; we could put it up on the display screen."

It was Bey's turn for anxiety. He wanted to know, didn't he? Surely he did, after all those months of worry. But he also felt uneasy, the same subliminal discomfort he had experienced when he learned that Mary was sending him a message from beyond the Moon.

"Well?" Sylvia Fernald was waiting, her long, slender finger poised above a point on the panel.

The moving finger writes, and having writ, moves on, nor

all thy piety nor wit, shall lure it back to cancel half a line . . .
Bey sensed himself on the brink of irreversible change, with
that waiting finger as its agent. Old Omar the Tentmaker
might be warning him. After months of accepting the Dancing
Man as a harbinger of madness, perhaps Bey was about to
discover darker possibilities. Knowledge might be more
dreadful than ignorance.

He was very tired. His head was aching, worse than ever.
His mind had turned to mush. And still he sat, unable to
speak, unable to nod, and watched that poised digit.

"*Well*?" Sylvia was becoming impatient. And no wonder.
What was wrong with him? He had to understand. Yet he
found himself drifting off again into a half-trance, turning his
thoughts away from the present . . .

Bey roused himself. Bad news or not, he *had* to know.

He sat up, shivered, and nodded. "Run it."

The screen flickered, went dark, and slowly brightened.
There was a splash of sharp images: red men running, dancing, leaping, sitting cross-legged, diving away, all overlaid
one on another. Then the multiple exposures faded, and one
picture emerged. It was as Bey remembered it, but in terrify-
ing detail. The little man, the sharp-toothed grin, the strutting
walk, the backward somersault, the jerky twitch of agile
limbs. The voice. It was the same singsong voice, rising at the
end of the sentence to frame a not-quite-intelligible question.
Bey watched, listened, and was carried away into a dizzying
resumption of the past. He reached out to play the sequence
again. And again. The fourth time, Sylvia's hand was there
first, pushing him away.

"No more. Not now." She had seen the expression in his
eyes. Bey was far gone in his own fugue.

He sighed. "Aybee did it. He said he would. That was it,
you know. Exactly."

"I know."

"I have to see it again." His hand was moving to hers,
trying to push her aside. He had no strength in his arm.

"No. Later." She touched his forehead. As she had suspected, it was hot and sweaty. "Bey, you have to sleep. It's been too much."

"I have to see it again. I have to *understand* it. You see, Sylvia, even now I don't understand." His voice was puzzled, a lost voice, but even as he spoke his eyes were closing. In less than thirty seconds he was sound asleep.

He was no threat now. Sylvia watched him for a few minutes. His face was the countenance of the Inner System itself: dark, older, guarded. She reached out and moved him so that he could not see the display. He sighed in his sleep but did not move from his new position.

She reset the audio input so that she alone would receive it and settled down to play the image sequence over and over. It had meant something personal and disturbing to Bey Wolf, but to her it offered different and more practical mysteries. There had been hints to grasp at even in the first viewing.

She solved the first problem after four runs through Bey's reconstructed memory sequence. After another look at the controls, she made one adjustment and watched with satisfaction what came onto the screen.

The second problem was not so easy. It depended on a dubious recollection from more than a year ago. Sylvia finally asked for help from the data base on the space farm, seven hours travel ahead of them. They sent an image that confirmed her hunch. Then she settled down to wait for Bey to waken, watching his dark-complexioned face, wanting him to rest but willing him to wake. She was itching to tell him.

He slept for almost six hours. As he woke, he at once turned and reached to turn on the display. She gripped his hand in both of hers.

"No. Bey, you don't need to."

He stared at her uncomprehendingly, still dazed with sleep.

"Watch," she said. She made the adjustment to Aybee's equipment and started the playback.

The Red Man appeared, and still he was speaking. But his singsong words were clear. *"You can run, you can run, just as fast as you can, but you'll never get away from the Negentropic Man."* And then, just before he danced away, off at the right side of the screen, he spoke again. *"Don't you worry, don't you fear, the Negentropic Man is here!"*

Bey sat openmouthed. "What did you do?"

"Time reversal, and slowed it down." She set out to play it through again. "It was obvious. You'd have seen it, once you'd watched it right through—objectively—a few times. The movements didn't look right, too jerky, and the intonation was wrong for normal speech. Playing it backward, that's all it took to make the message clear." She saw Bey's shake of the head. "What's wrong?"

"It's *not* clear. Not to me. I understand what he's saying, and maybe Aybee knows how the trick was worked to send me that signal. But what does it *mean*?"

"Negentropic?"

"That will do for a start. Negentropic. Negative entropy? But that's just a word." Bey stood up. He wanted to pace about, but there was not enough space in the cabin to take more than two steps each way. After a moment he sat down again and slapped at his knee in frustration. *"Negentropic.* Why should somebody say he's the Negentropic Man? Better yet, why would anybody send a message like that to *me*? I don't see how a person can have negative entropy—I'm not even sure I understand what entropy is. And I certainly have no idea who's behind it all."

"But I do."

Sylvia's quiet answer caught Bey off balance. He stared at her. "How can you?"

"I recognized your Dancing Man. I had a suspicion when I first saw him, but I wasn't sure. While you were asleep I called ahead to tap into the space farm's data base. And I found I was right."

"You mean he's somebody from the Outer System rather

than the Inner System? He doesn't look anything like a Cloudlander."

"He's not. And he's not a Sunhugger, either." Sylvia was so caught up in her discovery that she forgot to be cautious. She leaned across and gripped Bey's hands excitedly in hers. "Your Dancing Man isn't one of us. He lives in the Halo. He's famous, he's a rebel, and his name is Black Ransome."

CHAPTER 10

"**M**anx is on the way." Sylvia floated into the open bubble that looked out to the stars and secured herself next to Bey. "Flying a high-acceleration probe. He'll be here in twelve hours."

"He must be keen." Bey thought for a moment. "And cramped. The hi-probes are emergency equipment—the cabin's less than six feet across. He won't have room to turn."

"He'd better not try—it's a one-person ship, and Aybee says he's coming with him." Sylvia sounded quite cheerful at the thought. If she could survive the forced intimacy of her trip with Bey, she was prepared to let Aybee and Leo Manx suffer through their shorter travel time. "I told him what we found," she went on. "He can't wait to see it for himself."

They were at the space farm and ready to disembark. Bey, accustomed to the formal—and protective—procedures for entry to Inner System ports, was baffled by the absence of quarantine. They had flown to a point near the central hub of the farm and been docked automatically without passing a checkpoint.

"Of course we were checked," Sylvia said when Bey expressed his surprise. "The computer checked our ship's ID when we were still hours away."

"But if the wrong people were inside it—" Bey began. He

stopped. Cloudland was so far from the Inner System in awareness of security measures; he could talk to Sylvia forever, but he doubted if she would fully understand him. Was that why a handful of rebels from the Kernel Ring could cause such chaos in the Cloud?

The failure to understand went both ways. Bey had been briefed on the Sagdeyev space farm, but somehow he had reduced it in his mind to a size that he could comprehend. A farm suggested solidity, intensive activity, compact production. The reality was so insubstantial that he felt they had arrived nowhere.

The farm was a monomolecular collection layer two billion kilometers across. Its crop had been seeded hundreds of parsecs away and thousands of years earlier, conceived in the fiery heart of supernovas and blown free by the same explosions. The harvest had drifted through space for millennia, borne on the winds of light pressure, until random galactic airs carried the precious atoms to the Cloud. Most of them would drift on until the end of the universe, but a few would encounter and be held by the electrostatic charge of the collection layer. For them, aggregation could finally begin.

It was slow and selective work. The farm was interested only in the heavy elements, metals and rare earths and noble gases. It winnowed billions of cubic miles of space to find their invisible traces.

The machines that monitored the farms needed no central processing facility. They could carry hundreds of tons of material with them, accumulating steadily until there was enough to ship to the harvesters. The humans, frailer creatures, needed more. At the center of the collection layer sat the habitation bubble, three hundred meters across. In it dwelt the score of people who had made the farm their home. Two of them were dead.

"Don't expect them to meet us," Sylvia said as their ship docked at the outer edge of the bubble. "In fact, don't be surprised if we don't meet anyone in all our stay here. The farmers avoid strangers, and that includes me as well as you.

They know we're here, and they appreciate our help. They just don't want to see us."

"Suppose we need to talk with them about the form-change problems?"

"We'll probably do what they do themselves—use a communications link." Sylvia led the way to the bubble interior, meandering along silent corridors that spiraled down through the concentric shells of the bubble. Everywhere was deserted, without even maintenance equipment. If Sylvia had not told Bey that there were people there, he would have believed the farm to be derelict.

Sylvia was heading for the kernel at the center of the bubble, but on their way they passed an area that was clearly an automated kitchen. Bey realized that he had not eaten since they left the harvester. During the whole trip to the farm he had been either unconscious or too preoccupied to consider food. He paused.

"Once we get to the form-change tanks we'll be in for a long session. Can we grab something here?"

He was starving. He headed for the dispensing equipment without waiting for her answer and placed an order. He did not bother to study the menu. Food in the Cloud was nothing like Earth fare, and he did not much care what he was given. When his dishes appeared, he went across to the seating area and waited for Sylvia.

She was a long time coming. When she finally arrived, she sat angled away from him. Her tray held a modest amount of food and a large beaker of straw-colored fluid. She stared at the liquid for a long time, then finally took a little sip, grimaced, and swallowed.

"Is it bad?" Bey lifted up a piece of food and sniffed it suspiciously. It looked like bread and smelled like bread. "Maybe we worked the machine wrong."

"No." Sylvia turned and gave an apologetic shake of her head. "The food is fine. The drink, too. But I've not eaten a meal with someone else for years. It's not a law or anything, but we don't do it, you know, except with a partner. Go ahead and eat, and please excuse my rudeness. I'll be used to this in a minute."

Not just hairy and unpopular; his habits were disgusting, too. Bey put down the bread he was holding. "I'm the one who should apologize. I knew Cloudland customs, but Leo Manx and I ate together all the time on the way to the Outer System. I didn't even think of it here."

"Leo was specially conditioned for the assignment. But really, it will be all right. It will. Watch me." She speared a yellow cube on her fork, squinted down at it in front of her nose, and put it stoically into her mouth. She chewed for a long time before she finally swallowed. "See! I did it."

After a moment Bey began to eat his own food. "Is it all right if we talk while we eat? Or would that be too much?"

"Of course. I would prefer it."

Bey nodded. So would he. The food was pretty terrible, bland and flavorless. Good thing I couldn't order the meal I'd really have enjoyed, he thought to himself. Come to Earth, Sylvia, and let me introduce you to a broiled lobster. "I wanted to ask you about Ransome," he said after a minute of silent chewing.

"I don't know all that much."

"But you knew enough to recognize him. Back in the Inner System, most people don't even believe there is a Black Ransome. And Leo Manx told me that he's a mystery figure. If he's such an unknown quantity, I don't see how you could possibly have recognized him."

"Ah." Sylvia stopped eating and laid down her fork. She had managed only three small mouthfuls. "I wondered when you would get around to that. Did Leo tell you about my background?"

"A little."

"Paul Chu?"

"He did mention that. But only to say that you and Chu used to be partners, and he disappeared on a trip to the Kernel Ring. His ship was attacked, and he was taken prisoner."

"That's the official version, and I don't dispute it. But I don't believe it." Sylvia paused. She was not sure she wanted to talk about her personal history with Bey Wolf. She would rather talk than eat, but he might misunderstand her reasons.

"Paul and I lived together for nearly three years," she went on. "Most people who knew us thought it was permanent—I'm sure Leo thought that. But it wasn't. We argued like hell, all the time. If Paul were around now, I don't think we would be together."

"I heard from Leo Manx that you were planning to have children."

"No. That's Leo's wishful thinking. He's such a sympathetic type, he likes to think the best of people. He may have heard Paul and me talk about having children, a long time ago—but even when we were splitting up, we never disagreed in public."

"Why did you fight?"

"Not what you might think. Not sex. Politics. I'm sure you suspect I'm not friendly to Earth and the Inner System. I'm not. I believe that you are like parasites—and not even smart ones. You've failed the first test of a successful parasite: moderation. You wiped out parts of your own habitat—the passenger pigeon and the dodo and the whale and the gorilla and the elephant. Thanks to you, half the species on Earth have become extinct in less than a thousand years. Humans may be next."

"I agree, and I'm as sorry about it as you are." Bey looked at her earnest face. She was angry, but that made her an easier companion. The cold, wary Sylvia was more difficult to deal with. "You sound pretty extreme about it."

"Extreme! Me? Bey Wolf, you don't understand. I'm a *moderate*. Everyone in the Cloud feels the way I do about Earth and the Inner System. We learn it when we're little children. But most of us would never do anything to harm the people of the Inner System. It's just a few fanatics who want to go a lot further than general dislike. Paul was one. He *hated* the Inner System and everything you stand for. One year before he disappeared, he joined an extremist group that talked seriously about starting a war between the Inner and Outer

Systems. Paul told me their ideas and asked me to join. I told him they were all crazy."

"We have people back on Earth who feel the same, but the other way around. They hate the idea that the Cloud controls food supplies. They want to crush Cloudland and control the Outer System. But they're all mad, both sides. If we went to war with you or cut off communications, it would be like men and women refusing to have anything to do with each other. We could do it, but our species would die out in a generation."

"Paul said it wouldn't work like that. After the collapse of the Inner System, there could be a new start for everyone. But it would need a group that was all ready for the takeover, with its own strong leader. He showed me a secret piece of recruiting material. I decided that the whole thing was crazy, and the leader—Ransome—was craziest of all. But apparently he's terribly plausible and charismatic. Paul thought Ransome was wonderful. He said that Black Ransome had a secret weapon, something that made sure he would win, even if he didn't have many followers. I could see that people were following Ransome's ideas, even though they were wild."

Sylvia had pushed her own plate away from her, but she was watching intensely as Bey continued eating. He found it disconcerting. There were odd undercurrents flowing beneath the conversation, a sense that he was performing some old, disgusting, and perversely erotic rite, when all he was doing was eating a dreary piece of synthetic protein.

"But then Paul disappeared," Sylvia added at last. "And I feel sure he didn't die, and he wasn't captured. He's somewhere in the Halo. Probably in the Kernel Ring—he's an energy specialist. I think he's working for Ransome. But I never found out what that 'secret weapon' might be."

"Did you actually meet Ransome?"

"Not in person. But I saw his video image when he called with a message for Paul. He's your Dancing Man, I'm quite sure of it."

"If he's the Dancing Man, I'll never forget him. It's burned into my brain, exactly what he looks like and sounds like. Do you know a way to reach him?"

"Not directly. He hides away in the Halo, but he has more and more influence all through the Outer System." Sylvia had taken another sip from her beaker. She was peering at Bey's moving jaws, her gray eyes glistening.

He stopped eating. "I believe what you've told me, Sylvia, but it doesn't explain anything. I can accept the idea of Ransome as the leader of an organized terrorist group. I can even see how influential he might become in the Cloud. But I can't see why he would appear on a crazy message to *me*."

"Maybe he hopes to recruit you, too."

"That's ridiculous. For one thing, you don't recruit people by sending messages that drive them crazy and that they can't understand. For another, he has no idea who I am."

"Cinnabar Baker told me you are very famous—the top form-change theorist in the Inner and Outer Systems."

"That isn't enough to make anyone *famous*. Sylvia, Earth has lots of form-change specialists. I'm just one of them. You have to remember there are five hundred times as many people in the Inner System as there are out here."

"I know. If I had my way, we'd stay like that. Paul and I argued about this, too. He said the Cloud is underpopulated. I feel it's just right. We don't *need* more people. I don't think I could stand to live in the Inner System.

"Ransome probably feels the same way. Out here, he's a big bogeyman who's trying to start a war. He steals ships, he has a secret weapon, he kills people.

"But to some, like Paul Chu, he's a hero. Paul says Ransome started out as a Podder. He tried to do development deals with the Inner and Outer Systems, and he only became a renegade when he was betrayed by both."

"Maybe he's good, and maybe he's bad. He's certainly famous here. But back on Earth he's just a bedtime story that people tell to their children. A lonely, mysterious outlaw, Captain Black Ransome, flying the Halo in a creaking, battered ship, solar sails tattered and decaying. He drifts silent and powers down whenever there's a danger of discovery. He steals power, supplies, and volatiles wherever he can find them. He's the space version of the Flying Dutchman."

"Who is that?"

"An Earth legend. A man who sails Earth's oceans, endlessly seeking redemption. Deep water is his home. He never finds a landfall. He's not quite real, but he's very romantic. That's the way we think of Ransome, a combined myth and outlaw. If you suggested to someone from Earth that Ransome was trying to recruit me—a Sunhugger, a planet man who's only happy at the bottom of twenty miles of atmosphere— they'd say, well, they'd say that you were losing it. Crazy."

"*You're* from Earth. Are you saying I'm crazy?"

Bey sighed. "Not crazy. Maybe a little strange and unpredictable. Come on, Sylvia, let's get moving. I want to see the farm's form-change systems before Aybee and Leo arrive."

"I hope you'll find something. You know, Aybee looked at the failed form-changes on the harvesters. He got nowhere, and he's awful smart."

"He certainly is."

"And he'll see this as a sort of contest, just the two of you. Do you think you can handle him?"

"I'll bet on it." Bey had finished eating. "I learned something a long time ago. My first boss wasn't a good scientist, and he had dozens of political fights with bright young people from the general coordinators' office. They were mostly right, but he won, every time. I asked him how he did it. He pointed out the sign on his office wall." Bey allowed Sylvia to steer him out of the galley. "'Old age and treachery will defeat youth and skill,' he told me. It's one of the world's great truths. Aybee happens to be on the wrong side of the inequality."

CHAPTER 11

"Those are pearls that were his eyes:
   Nothing of him that doth fade,
   But doth suffer a sea-change
   Into something rich and strange."
      —William Shakespeare: Ariel's song, *The Tempest*

Behrooz Wolf was four trillion kilometers from home, floating uncomfortably in free-fall in the territory of people who hated him, surrounded by a silence so total that it hurt his ears. In that environment, the familiar technology of form-change was his lifeline.

Sylvia had led him to a chamber containing four change tanks. Two of them were empty. The others contained the bodies of two dead farmers. At Wolf's request, they had been left untouched by their fellows until he arrived at the farm. He and Sylvia went at once to the transparent ports and peered in.

She took one look and turned away. Bey heard the sound of retching. He ignored it. He had seen too many illegal and unsuccessful form-change experiments to allow them to affect his stomach. He had work to do.

He rotated the two bodies using remote-handling equipment and examined their anomalies with the tank's internal sensors. Both had originally been male, and according to the tanks' settings both had been using the same program. The intended end point was a form with thickened epidermis, lowered metabolic rate, and eyes protected by translucent nictitating membranes. The men had been preparing for an extended mission outside, away from the farm's main bubble. According to Sylvia, such missions were absolutely routine, and the form-change program that went with them had been used a thousand times.

Bey would not take her word for it. He intended to go over that program instruction by instruction. But first he wanted to localize the problem area, and the only evidence for that was the end products in the tanks.

He studied the two corpses. Both men had experienced significant mass reduction—not called for by the program. The limbs had atrophied to stumps, and each torso had curled forward to leave the overgrown head close to the swollen abdomen. Death had come when cramped and shrunken lungs would no longer permit breathing.

"Did you ever see forms like that before?" Sylvia asked softly. She had herself under control and was hovering just behind him.

He shook his head but did not speak. It would take a long time to explain that the final form was close to irrelevant. His diagnosis of program malfunctions was based on more subtle pointers: the presence of hypertrophied fingernails and toenails on the flipperlike appendages, the disappearance of eyelids, the milky, pearl-like luster of the membrane-covered eyes, the severe scoliosis of the spinal column. To someone familiar with form-change, they were signposts pointing to certain sections of program code.

Bey began to call program sections for review. His task was in principle very simple. The BEC computers used in purposive form-change converted a human's intended form to a series of biofeedback commands that the brain would employ to direct change at the cellular level. Human and computer, working interactively, remolded the body until the intended form and actual form were identical, and then the process ended. The chemical and physiological changes were continuously monitored, and any malfunction would halt the process and set emergency flags. The process could fail catastrophically in two ways: if the human in the tank did not wish to live, or if there were a major software problem.

Bey could rule out the idea of suicide—it always resulted in death without any physical change except biological aging. That seemed to leave nothing but software failure, but he could see one other complication: the equipment had not been provided by BEC. It was a hardware clone, and the programs that went with it were pirated versions. There could be hardware/software mismatches, something that only BEC guaranteed against. His job with this setup would be ten times as hard.

He began to examine a new section of code. Behind him, he was vaguely aware that Sylvia was leaving the room. That was a relief. She could not help, and she was a potential distraction.

Line by line he followed the programed interaction, tracking physical parameters (temperature, pulse rate, skin conductivity) and system variables (nutrient rates, ambient gas profile, electrical stimuli). He did not check those parameters against any equipment performance specifications. He did not need to. The region of stability was well mapped, and over the years he had learned the limits of tolerable excursion from standard values. All the programs in use as they were swapped in and out of the computer provided their own audit trail, together with chemical readings and brain activity indexes. Reading and interpreting them was somewhere between an art and a science. It was something he had been doing for two-thirds of his life.

He sat there for six hours in a total trance. If anyone had asked him if he were enjoying himself, he could not have given a truthful answer. He was not happy, he was not sad. All he knew was that there was nothing in life that he would rather be doing. And when he found the first anomalies and began to piece together a picture, he could not have described the thrill. He had been provided with a precious broken ornament shattered into a thousand pieces. He had to recreate it. As he fitted those fragments together, one by one, tentatively and pains-takingly, he sensed the skeletal outline of a total pattern. That was exhilarating. But no matter what he did, the picture remained tantalizingly incomplete. And that was unbearably frustrating. Not all of the pieces had been provided. Parts of the code were not in the system at all.

He was roused by the sound of Sylvia Fernald's voice. She had entered the room with Aybee Smith and Leo Manx in tow. Bey turned and addressed his question to all three of them. "These form-change tanks aren't completely self-contained, the way the BEC units would be and should be. Where's the rest of the computation done?"

"That must be in the main computer system for the farm," said Aybee at once. "It's a lot less expensive to do some of the analysis there. BEC and the other manufacturers rip you off bad. They overcharge you ten times for storage in their units. Is there a problem to use distributed computing? We do it a lot."

"It *shouldn't* be a problem. On the other hand . . ." Bey gestured into the port of the form-change tank. Aybee came close and stared in, frowning, for thirty seconds. Leo Manx could not take more than one horrified glance.

"I've checked the code, line by line," Bey went on. "And I'm convinced that the local programs here are working fine. It means that the problem has to be over in the main computer."

"Or in the communications lines," Aybee said.

"No." Bey shook his head, and suddenly felt his exhaustion. "Redundant transmission should correct for electronic noise in the signal. Even if that somehow weren't working, thermal noise or outside interference would give *random* errors. What we're seeing here is definitely not random change. It was closely calculated."

"But that makes it murder," Leo Manx protested.

Aybee gave him a fierce grin. "I guess that's exactly what the Wolfman is saying. And in that case, we'll have to meet with the farmers." He waved aside Sylvia's objection. "Don't tell me, Fern; I know they won't want to do it. But for murder, they don't have a choice. You real sure about this, Wolf?"

"Positive."

"I mean, you wouldn't like me to check your results?"

"I'd love you to—or at least, I'd like to see you try. If you were really lucky and smart, that would take you about a month." Bey shook his head. "Aybee, it's not a question of your ability—but I *know* this stuff, inside and out. Believe me, it would take you a week just to rule out impossible combinations of the main variables. We don't have time for that. I'll take your first suggestion. Let's go meet with the farmers. Right now."

"Hey, what about your Negentropic Man? That's what me and Leo came here for, not to look at dead things that make you puke."

"Plenty of time to look at that, too. We can do it while Sylvia talks to the farmers." The interaction with Aybee was a fight with sharp weapons. The other was aggressive—and *smart*.

"More time than you think," Leo added. "The farmers may not agree to meet with you, Mr. Wolf."

"They have to," Aybee insisted.

"With *us*, they have to," Sylvia said. "They might be able to refuse to meet somebody from the Inner System, and get away with it."

"Then don't tell 'em where he's from." Aybee sounded impatient. "You and Leo can sort that out. The Wolfman and me need to see the stuff from inside his skull. Right? Let's get at it."

CHAPTER 12

"I know more than Apollo
For oft when he lies sleeping,
I see the stars at bloody wars,
In the wounded welkin weeping."
—Tom o' Bedlam's song

"The Neg-en-trop-ic Man." Aybee dissected the word, saying it slowly and thoughtfully. "And there he goes."

He pressed the button. For the tenth time, the grinning figure in red danced away across the screen and waved his good-bye.

"Any ideas?" When it was not form-change theory, Bey was ready to admit that Aybee had the better chance of deciding what was going on. Sylvia might return at any moment, and Bey wanted to have a lot of his thinking done before he encountered a farmer.

"Too many ideas." Aybee scowled at him. "It's not a well-posed problem."

"You don't think he means what he says? That he's a man with negative entropy."

"I'm sure he isn't. For a start, negative entropy has no physical meaning." Aybee made a rude noise at the display and turned it off. "'Negentropic' just refers to something that decreases the entropy of a system. So a Negentropic Man ought to be a man who reduces entropy."

"But what exactly *is* entropy?" Leo Manx had been listening carefully while the conversation made less and less sense to him. "Remember, I'm supposed to send a report back to Cinnabar Baker. I can't send her your gibberish about negentropy. She'd jump all over us."

"Hey, is it my fault if you're a dummy?" Aybee looked down his nose at Leo. "I'll give you a bunch of entropy definitions. You can pick any one you like. And don't blame me if you're wrong, because I sure as hell don't know how the word is being used here. Oldest use: entropy in *thermodynamics*. Entropy change was defined as the change in the heat in a system, divided by its temperature. Can a process involving heat transfer be run backward? If not, the entropy of the system must increase. Rudolph Clausius knew that nearly four hundred years ago. He pointed out that entropy tends to go on increasing in any closed system. If the universe is a closed system, its entropy must increase. So then the universe is running down to a state of maximum disorganization, and we'll all end up in uniform-temperature soup."

"But we're talking about a *man* here, not a universe."

"I know that, Leo. Hold on a minute, I'm getting there. Remember, this is complicated stuff. We don't want to make it so easy it's meaningless. Einstein said it right: Things should be as simple as possible—but not simpler. Maybe our Negentropic Man has something to do with thermodynamic entropy, maybe not. Entropy number two: Ludwig Boltzmann found a *statistical* definition of entropy in terms of the number of possible states of the atoms and molecules of a system. He showed that it produced the same value as the thermodynamic one, provided the system has a whole lot of possible states."

"How do we decide which definition we want?"

"We can't—not yet. We keep going, then we'll play pick and choose. Entropy number three: in *information theory*. Fifty years after Boltzmann, Claude Shannon wanted to know how much information a message channel could carry. He found it depended on a particular mathematical expression. The formula was the same as Boltzmann's entropy formula, except for a sign change, so Shannon called the thing he calculated the *entropy* of the transmitted signal. That confused the hell out of people. The information-theory entropy is a maximum when the information carried is as much as you can get with a given channel."

"Aybee, you're not helping. Three forms of entropy—and not one of them intelligible. Why don't people use clearly defined terms?"

"Hey, I understand them fine. We're lucky there's only four to pick from. Do you have any idea how many different things the word 'conjugate' can mean in mathematics? One more to go. *Kernels* have entropy. Even a nonrotating kernel—a Schwarzschild black hole—has an entropy. Two hundred and fifty years ago, Jakob Bekenstein pointed out that the area of a kernel's event horizon can be *exactly* equated to an entropy for the black hole."

"But we have to pick one of your four definitions! Aybee, how can we possibly do it? They're all totally different."

"No. They sound it, but they all tie together through the right mathematics. The mathematics of ensembles, it's called. As for deciding which one we ought to be thinking about . . . don't ask me. Spin a coin. Thermodynamic entropy, statistical mechanics entropy, information theory entropy, kernel horizon entropy—which one is Wolfman's buddy talking about? We don't know. But there's more. Before you spin that coin, let me give you the other half of it. You see, the universe moves to higher values of thermodynamic entropy—that's Clausius, and the Second Law of Thermodynamics. But *life*—any life, from us to bacteria and single-celled plants—is different—"

Aybee was interrupted as Sylvia Fernald hurried into the room, grabbed his arm, and began to pull him at once toward the door. "They'll meet with us," she said. "But we have to do it right this minute, before they change their minds. Come on."

She led the way for Aybee and Leo, leaving Bey floundering along behind. The others were expert at moving in low gravity. He still rolled and yawed and missed handholds. He reached the chamber half a minute after the others and looked around for the elusive farmers.

The room was dark and divided in two by a wall of ribbed black glass. As Bey stepped forward, dim ceiling lights came on and the glass wall lightened to full transparency. On the other side of the partition, shrouded in white garments that left only dark pairs of eyes, two human figures became visible.

"Five minutes," a deep, whispering voice said. Cowls were pushed back to reveal smooth skulls and nervous skeletal faces. "We promised at most five minutes."

"Did you see your people in the form-change tanks?" Bey asked at once.

"I did," the taller figure said. The deep voice was expressionless. "I found them."

"Were they alive?"

"Already dead. According to the temperature monitors, already cold. They must have been dead for at least a day."

"And no emergency signal was sent from the tanks?"

"Nothing. All indicators showed normal."

"Has anything like this happened before? Something maybe less extreme?"

There was a pause while the two farmers turned to look at each other. "Tell them," the second figure said. It was a woman.

"I think we must." The man turned back to Bey. "We had noticed some peculiarities. Nothing serious, nothing that was not corrected on a second attempt with the form-change equipment. We considered calling for help, but after a vote we decided against the intrusion. Our colleagues who died took part in and approved of the decision."

"You know when the problem began," Bey said rapidly. The two farmers were beginning to move about uneasily. "Can you relate it to anything else that happened here on the farm? Any visitor? Any change in procedures?"

There was another pause—precious seconds of interview time slipping away. "The problems began six months ago," the woman said. "There have been no visitors to the farm in more than a year. New form-change equipment was delivered to us at that time, but it performed perfectly for many months."

"How about unusual events? Did anything odd happen six months ago?"

"Nothing," the man answered. "There were automated deliveries to us, but that is usual. There were cargo shipments from here to the harvester, as always."

"And there were—" the woman began.

"No," the man interrupted. He reached out a hand, shielding the woman's eyes from the four visitors but being careful not to touch her.

"I must tell. Two of us are dead because we valued privacy above their lives. It must not happen again." The woman moved so that she could see Bey. Her voice was shaking. "Six months ago, some of us began to see things when we were out on the farm. Apparitions. Things that could not be real."

The glass partition was beginning to darken, the lights to fade. "What were they?" Bey asked.

"Many things. Five days ago I saw a woman, many kilometers high and dressed all in red. She had long brown hair. Her clothes were the clothes of Old Earth, and she carried a basket. She was striding across the collection layer in ten-kilometer paces. She wore a white peaked bonnet, and beneath it her face was the face of a madwoman."

"A white bonnet and scarlet dress?" Wolf jerked upright and reached out a hand. The partition was almost black. The ceiling lights were dim glows of red.

"No more," the white-garbed man said. His voice had risen in pitch and volume. "Our records will be available to you. You can see what came to the farm during the last year, what was sent from it. You can read what our people saw. But there can be no more direct contact. Good luck."

"One more question," Bey said. He was moving urgently toward the black glass. "It's terribly important."

But the room was dark again. There was no sound from the other side of the wall.

When the deadly strike came, each visitor to the Sagdeyev farm was in a different part of the habitation bubble. Officially, it was to allow them to eat alone. In practice, each had deliberately sought privacy.

Bey had been dumbstruck by the farmer's last words, to the point where he was hardly thinking at all. A brown-haired female, dressed in scarlet, carrying a basket and with a white bonnet on her head—that was his Mary, Mary Walton, exactly as she had looked in the *The Duchess of Malfi*. Bey had seen it in live performance five times and in recording another dozen.

A coincidence of dress? If so, it was too improbable a coincidence for him to accept. But if *anyone* were to see such visions of Mary, it surely ought to have been Bey himself— not some reclusive farmer, someone who had no idea what she was looking at. Bey sat with his head buzzing, too perplexed to feel hungry or thirsty. Somewhere on the periphery of his mind he knew that one of Aybee's comments on entropy was vitally important. Those ideas had to be integrated with the appearance of the Negentropic Man and with elements of Bey's own knowledge of form-change theory. But that synthesis had to wait until thoughts of Mary no longer obsessed him. The temptation to seek her was growing, even though his idea that she was tied to events on the farm was probably self-deluding.

Aybee Smith had not noticed that Bey was off in his own world, but it did not take him long to realize that talking to Bey at the moment was a waste of time. Aybee went off to a terminal and tested the farmer's offer. The final promise had been genuine; all the farm records had been made available to the visitors. Aybee set out to make a chronology of every external interaction recorded in the previous year and then to correlate that with the hallucinations and the anomalies in form-change performance. There were many hundreds of entries, but Aybee had lots of time. He never slept much, and if necessary he would plug along at the job for the next twenty-four hours. Like Bey, he relished intellectual challenge more than anything else in the world. He felt alert, fresh, excited, and confident.

Leo Manx felt none of those things. He had been awake for two full days. He had hoped to sleep on the trip to the farm, but Aybee had insisted on coming along, and then had hardly stopped talking through the whole journey. The hi-probe quarters were too cramped to hide away in, and Aybee had been too loud to ignore. He had gone on and on about signal processing and signal encoding until Leo was mentally numb. Bey's hallucinations, according to Aybee, must have been single-frame inserts, patched into a general signal but coded specifically to Wolf's personal psychological profile and comlink. No one else would notice the signal, even if he or she was watching the same channel as Bey. And it would be simple to make the single-frame inserts self-erasing, so even if Wolf tried to play them back on a recording, there would be no sign of them.

Now, at a time when Leo would have welcomed a nap, he could not get Aybee's latest comments out of his head. He rubbed at his aching temples and stared at the notes he had made.

"The entropy of the whole universe is increasing," Aybee had said. "But that doesn't mean that the entropy of everything in it must be increasing. In fact, life has the opposite effect. It increases regular structure—nonrandom phenomena —at the expense of disorder. Life is *always* negentropic. It reduces the entropy of everything that it comes into contact with. So *everybody*, and everything living, is negentropic in that sense."

"But the Second Law of Thermodynamics, the one you were quoting earlier—"

"Says that entropy tends to a maximum in a *closed, isolated* system. It tells you nothing about open systems, ones that exchange energy with others. That's us. We don't live in isolation. The Sun and the stars are constant sources of energy, and every living thing in the Solar System uses energy to create order at the expense of disorder. In the thermodynamic sense, you and me and the Wolfman and Fern are all negentropic."

"How about the other meanings of entropy? Do they make more sense for a Negentropic Man?"

"Considered in terms of information theory, the information in a message decreases when the entropy of the signal becomes less. A noisy communications channel is negentropic so far as the signal is concerned. If that's what the Negentropic Man does, we're not seeing signs of it. The reported random error rate for signals received in the Inner and Outer Systems doesn't seem to have changed at all. If it did, people would be getting jumbled, gibberish messages all the time. And if that had happened, I would have heard about it."

"And your fourth form of entropy?"

"That's associated with the power kernels. Any black hole has a temperature, an entropy, a mass, and maybe an electrical charge. If it's a kernel, a Kerr-Newman black hole, it also has rotational energy and a magnetic moment. And that's all it *can* have—no other physical variables are permitted. A kernel sends out random particles and radiation according to a process and a formula discovered a couple of centuries ago. What it emits only depends on the kernel's mass, charge, and spin. For a small black hole—billion-ton, say—the emitted energy is up in the gigawatt range. That's what the kernel shields are for, to stop that radiation. The entropy depends on the mass of the black hole, but I think we can rule out this one. If Wolf's Negentropic Man were dealing with kernels, he'd have to be a superman. Nobody could live for a second inside the shields. All you find in there are sensors, data links, and spin-up/spin-down equipment for energy storage and generation. Here." He had thrust a data cube into Manx's hand. "What I've been saying is all basic stuff. You'll find it explained here."

Leo had taken the cube. Sitting alone in an outer chamber of the habitation bubble, he had played it through twice. It was beginning to make some sense, considered as a set of abstract statements. But it had little to do with the capering man who had haunted Behrooz Wolf. Manx peered at the cube, closed his eyes for a moment or two, and was asleep before he knew he was near to it. All thoughts of entropy vanished. He dreamed that he was far from here, again on Earth, again roaming the old Chehel-sotun temple in Isfahan. But this time he was in free-fall, unhampered by that crushing gravity. He could not have chosen a more welcome dream.

Sylvia Fernald had the greatest need for total privacy. She was talking to Cinnabar Baker through a hyperbeam link. It was voice-only, hugely expensive to operate, and there was still an annoying thirty-second line delay before a reply could be received.

"You must return to the harvester," Baker was saying. "All of you, and at once. There are developments here that dwarf the space farm's problems. How soon can you leave?"

"I'll have to go and tell the others." Sylvia replied immediately, but she could imagine Baker at the other end, chafing at the transmission delay. "So far as Leo and I are concerned, we can leave at once. But Aybee and Wolf are reviewing the farm's data bases. That may take a while."

There was a pause that felt more like half an hour than half a minute. "You can't wait for that." It was the voice of command. "When you get back here, you'll understand why. Leave now, as soon as you can. I'll explain when you get here. One more thing. Have you been able to get closer to Wolf?"

"Not in the way you mean." But somehow I got turned on watching him eating, Sylvia recalled. Would you call that progress? Fortunately, it was a voice-only link. Sylvia was sure her face would have betrayed her—if her voice was not already doing that. "I'll see what happens on the way back," she said. "But I'm not optimistic. I'm sure he finds me as revolting to look at as I find him. And Leo told me Wolf is still infatuated with a woman he left on Earth."

There was a final annoying delay. "He didn't leave her on Earth," Cinnabar Baker said at last. "She left him, to run off with somebody from the Halo. Big difference. Keep trying. Link ends."

New problems on the harvester, Sylvia thought. What's

happening to the Solar System? It's one damned thing after another.

She hurried out of the room. She was heading for Bey's quarters in the higher-gravity region of the habitation bubble when the impact occurred.

CHAPTER 13

No recording instruments on the Sagdeyev space farm survived the impact. The whole encounter had to be deduced from other evidence.

The object hit the southern hemisphere of the habitation bubble, close to the pole. It was a jagged brown chunk of the primitive solar nebula, mostly ammonia and water ice, and it massed about eighty million tons. With a relative velocity of a kilometer a second, it smashed clear through the bubble and emerged from the side of the northern hemisphere. It also missed by thirty meters a collision with the shields of the power kernel and so failed to assure the immediate death of all humans on the farm.

The momentum that the impact transferred to the habitation bubble did three things. It broke the bubble loose from the farm's billion-kilometer collection layer. It left the bubble with a new velocity vector and a new orbit, sharply inclined to its old one. And it set the bubble spinning around the central power kernel as it caromed away into space.

Two thousand machines were left behind on the detached collection layer. After the first confusion they managed very well. The smarter ones herded the others into tight little groups, then settled down to wait for instructions or rescue. Whether that took place in one day or in one century made little difference. The smart machines knew enough to keep things under control for a long time. Not one of the two thousand was damaged.

The humans on the farm were less lucky. Four of the farmers were in chambers on the direct path of the intruding body. They died at once. Two others were left in airless rooms and could not reach suits. The rest of the farmers followed the standard emergency procedure and were into the lifeboats and clear of the bubble in less than a minute.

The visitors from the harvester were both more and less fortunate. Their chambers were not on the main line of the collision, and the impact was felt at first as no more than a short-lived and violent jerk of acceleration. Leo Manx, Sylvia Fernald, and Aybee Smith did not know the emergency routines specific to the farm, but they had been trained to react defensively. High acceleration of a habitation unit equaled disaster. They did not wait to see if the integrity of the bubble's outer hulls had been breached. As soon as they picked themselves up after the first shock of collision, they headed for the survival suits. They could live in them for at least twenty-four hours. Aybee had a mild concussion. Leo had five cracked ribs and a broken leg, but his deep-space training allowed him to override the pain until he was safe in his suit.

Bey Wolf was in much deeper trouble. His room was closest to the line of destruction. Worse than that, he lacked the right reflexes. He knew there had been a major accident, but he had to attempt by thought what the others did by instinct.

He had been thrown headfirst and hard against the communications terminal. Drops of blood from deep cuts on his cheek and forehead were already drifting across the room when he came to full consciousness. His head was ringing, and he was nauseated. He wiped at his face with his shirt and staggered to the door. It was closed. Beyond it he heard a hiss of air, and he could feel the draft at the door's edge.

The sliding partition was tight-fitting but not airtight. He had maybe a couple of minutes before the pressure dropped too low to be breathable. Just as bad, a faint plume of green gas was seeping *into* the room, and the slightest trace was enough to start him coughing. Wall refrigeration pipes must have ruptured. He might choke before he died of lack of air.

Suits. Where the devil were they kept? Bey hauled himself across to the storage units on the other side of the room. He jerked them open, one after another. Everything from chess boards to toothbrushes spilled out. No suit.

He caught another whiff of gas, coughed horribly, and mopped again at his bleeding face. What now? Where else might a suit be kept? Don't panic. *Think!*

He realized that if the data terminal were still working, it could tell him what he needed to know in a couple of seconds. He was moving across to it when the knock came on the door.

The sound was so unexpected that for a moment he did not react at all. Then he had a terrible thought. If someone out there in a suit were to try to come in . . .

"Don't touch the door!" he shouted, but already his voice sounded fainter in the thinning air. Asphyxiation, not poison gas, would get him. He was aware of pain in his ears and the cramping agony of trapped gas being forced out of his intestines.

"Bey?" The cry from outside was muffled. It was Sylvia. "Bey, can you hear me?"

"Yes. Don't open the door."

"I know. Do you have a suit?"

"Can't find it."

"By the data terminal. In the footlocker."

He did not waste air replying. The suit was there, but he had to fight his way into it. He was growing dizzy, panting uselessly. He got his legs and arms in and pulled the suit up around his shoulders. But the helmet was too much. He concentrated all his attention on the smooth head unit and managed to place it roughly in position. But he could not seal it. Anoxia was winning. The room was turning dark. At the edge of unconsciousness, Bey realized how much he wanted to live.

He was fighting the seals—and losing—when there was a crash behind him and a rush of escaping air. His lungs collapsed as the pressure dropped to zero. When Sylvia arrived at his side he was almost unconscious, still groping single-mindedly at the helmet. She slapped it into position and turned the valve. The rush of air inside the suit began.

She bent to look into the faceplate. Bey's face was a mottled nightmare of fresh red blood and cyanotic blue skin. As she watched, the oxygen-starved look faded. The chest of the suit gave a series of shuddering heaves. Alive. Sylvia grabbed Bey's suited arm and began to drag him. She had come at once, as soon as her suit was on, and she did not know the cause of the problem. Another crash or explosion might happen at any moment. Like any Cloudlander, she fled for the safety of open space.

The exit wound of the colliding chunk provided the widest and easiest way out. Sylvia and Bey accompanied a mass of flotsam, flying out into space with the last puff of internal air from the bubble.

Bey was unconscious. Sylvia, shaking with exhaustion, held him tightly and looked around them. The collection layer of the farm had been left far behind. The surviving farmers had moved their lifeboat close to the shattered bubble, and half a dozen of them were preparing to reenter through an air lock. They had a clear duty toward their missing fellows: rescue or space burial.

Sylvia could see the ship that she and Bey had arrived on. It floated a few kilometers clear of the bubble, apparently undamaged, its warning beacons a red glow against the stars. She was not sure that she had the strength to get there. She set out, dragging Bey along with her. When she was nearly there she saw a suited figure jetting across to help her. It was Aybee.

"Leo?" she asked.

"Inside. Banged up, but not too bad." Aybee took over and hauled Bey along behind him. "How's with the Wolfman here?"

"Hurt some." She was shivering. "He should be all right. Where's our other ship?"

Aybee waved his arm through a wide circle. "You tell me.

The beacon's not working. I don't know how we'll ever find it."

As he passed Bey through the lock, Sylvia took a last look around. There was no sign of the ship Aybee had arrived in. It was lost somewhere in the darkness, indistinguishable from a million other pieces of stellar flotsam.

She collapsed as she stepped out of the air lock. In the past twenty minutes she had forced her body all the way to its physical limits. Any more help for Bey Wolf would have to come from someone else.

Bey woke up three times.

Pain was the first stimulus. Someone was hurting his face, stabbing again and again at his cheek and forehead. "A bit crude," a voice said. "But it'll do. Couple more stitches, I'll be all done. You're a mess. You hearing me, Wolfman? No beauty prizes for you." The sharp pain came again, followed by a wash of icy fluid across his face. Bey grunted in protest and drifted back to unconsciousness.

The second time was more alarming. And more painful. He woke and tried to touch his throbbing left cheek. He could not do it. Something had him firmly held, unable to move. He began to struggle, to pull randomly against his restraints. He was too confused and dizzy to analyze what was happening or why, but he fought like an animal, straining as hard as he could. It was futile. He was working against straps designed to hold a human body secure under a ten-g acceleration. Exhausted after just a few seconds, he lapsed again into unquiet sleep.

Pain and consciousness came faster the third time, and with them—at last—vision. He was lying with his eyes open, staring at a woman's face. It was only inches away from him, pale and still. There was a tracery of blue veins on the temples and the violet-black smudge of deadly fatigue below the closed eyes. He studied it, puzzled by its familiarity. Who was she? That rounded brow was well known to him. He tried to lift his arm to touch the delicate skull and the fine red hair. He could not do it. They were strapped side by side, lying on a single narrow bunk and securely held in position.

As he placed his fingers on the release mechanism of his harness, awareness returned. And with it, fear. He remembered. Violent impact. The panicky hunt for a suit. The fight for air. Sylvia's appearance at his side just as that fight was lost.

He had a vague, surrealistic memory then of the nightmare ride through space, stars blurred points through a bloodstained visor.

"Sylvia!" She did not move.

Bey struggled free and sat up. He was again on the transit ship, and the McAndrew drive was on. They were moving with an indicated acceleration of a couple of hundred g's. He was lying in the same bunk with Sylvia Fernald. On the other bunk, strapped in and wrapped like a cocoon from neck to ankles, lay Leo Manx. As Bey straightened up, Leo's eyes rolled toward him.

"Where's Aybee?" Bey asked.

"I don't know. But the last time I saw him he was all right." Leo turned his head slowly and gingerly. "It is Sylvia I have been worrying about. I cannot move, and I cannot see her monitors. How is she?"

Bey scanned the condition sensors, supplementing that with his own touch to her cheek and forehead. "Out cold, but everything shows normal. What happened to her? And to you, too? And where's Aybee? And where are we heading?"

"Mr. Wolf, I am sure you can ask more questions than I can answer." Leo Manx's silky voice was gruff. He was either in much pain or terribly ill at ease. "I'll do my best. Sylvia Fernald made a supreme physical effort when she saved you, but it was too much for her. She collapsed as she reached the ship. At my suggestion and with the medical system's concurrence, Aybee extended her natural period of unconsciousness. She should sleep until we are close to the Marsden Harvester —our planned destination, where we should now find Cinnabar Baker. What was *not* my suggestion—" Leo Manx grimaced with displeasure and then with pain. "—was the idea that I would be bound here like an Egyptian mummy, unable to release myself. If you would be kind enough to free the harness . . ."

"What happened to you?"

"Broken ribs and broken legs. Aybee exceeded his duties and his authority when he anesthetized me and then did this."

Bey moved to examine the telesensors for Leo Manx, spent a few seconds with the displays, and shook his head. "Sorry. The monitors agree with Aybee. You stay like that until it tells me something different. You should not move."

"Mr. Wolf, I assure you that I am quite able to—"

"Don't take my word for it. Try a deep breath." Bey watched as Manx tentatively inhaled and gasped with pain. "Case closed. What about Aybee?"

Manx rolled his eyes toward the tiny console crowded against the cabin wall. Everything on the transit ships was a third the usual size. "It was my expectation that he would be with us on this ship. Clearly, he is not. But according to the signal there, a message is waiting for us. I have been looking at the indicator for some time, but unfortunately I cannot reach it."

Bey went across to turn on the unit. As he did so he saw his own reflection in the display screen. Whatever Aybee's talents, plastic surgery was not one of them. Bey's face and forehead were crisscrossed with crude, ugly stitches, and the skin on his left cheek had been pulled down so far that the red socket of his eye was exposed. There was no chance that such a mess would heal cleanly. He would have to use one of the Cloudland form-change tanks. He switched on the set.

Aybee's image showed no sign of either excitement or injury. He scowled out of the display like a bad-tempered baby. "I don't know which of you will be watching this, but hi. If it's you, Leo, I didn't lie to you. I intended to come along as well. But the ship was awful crowded once I had you in your bunks, and with those ribs I knew you wouldn't enjoy anybody cuddling up close to you, the way Sylv and the Wolfman were doing last time I saw 'em. So." He shrugged. "I had to change my mind. And I haven't found any trace of the other ship. I'll look again, but if I'm delayed getting back there, don't be surprised. Here's a few things for you to chew on. First, the female farmer we talked to. She's dead. We'll never get any more about that woman she saw walking on the collection layer. Second, the farm can be saved, but the data banks are shot. So you should drop the idea that we can correlate the form-change problems with events on the farm and the collection layer. I was doing that when the bubble was hit, and I'll tell you the only thing I'd noticed. The form-changes starting to go wrong coincided with a doubling of energy use on the farm. That fact's for Wolf—you there, Wolfman?—and I hope you can make more out of it than I can. Bet you can't, though. Here's my last thought, and it's for anybody who wants it. From all I can tell, the bubble was hit by a Cloud fragment, one that was traveling unusually fast and from an unusual direction. Bad luck, you say? Except that the farm had sky-scanning sensors, and the bubble had a standard response system. That fragment ought to have been given a little laser nudge when it was millions of kilometers away, and missed us by a nice margin."

He smiled from the screen, a humorless grin. "Now, I know what you're thinking, Leo. It's old paranoid Aybee, at it again. But try it on the Wolfman—he thinks more the way I do. And while he worries that, here's one more thing for you. The equipment that protected the farm from space junk is the same type as we use on all the harvesters. Foolproof, triple-tested, infallible. If the farm can get hit, so can anything else. Nice thought, eh? Sweet dreams, you three. Think entropy."

The screen blanked. As it did so, the system alert inside the ship's cabin sounded its warning beep. They were close to crossover, the place where the ship rotated through 180 degrees, and they changed from acceleration to deceleration. For that thirty-second period, they needed to be strapped in.

Bey headed for the bunk, lying down again alongside Sylvia. As he did so, Leo Manx gave a gasp of irritation. "Mr. Wolf! Don't let it do that."

A spray syringe was creeping out of its holder above Manx and quietly positioning itself close to his neck.

Bey paused from his strapping in and checked the monitors. "Don't worry. It's only an anesthetic. Apparently the robodoc thinks you're being too active."

"But I have no wish to go to sleep, Mr. Wolf. Stop it!"

"Sorry. Can't disobey doctor's orders." Bey lay back on the narrow bunk, squashed up next to Sylvia Fernald. He watched as the spray mist passed painlessly through Leo Manx's skin and the other man fell asleep in midprotest.

Bey liked Leo and enjoyed talking to him. But at the moment he needed time to chew on what Aybee had said. If he had been allowed one guess as to something that might correlate with the deaths in the form-change tanks, he would have picked sabotage—something in the software on the farm's central computer complex. That fit the idea that feedback information was being tampered with or supplied incorrectly. What he would never have picked in a hundred guesses was the farm's total energy load. In fact, he could see no way that it *could* be involved.

He felt fully awake. His aches and pains were unpleasant, and there was a disturbing buzzing in his ears. But he could stand that. He lay back in the bunk, ready for a long, intense session of thought. By the time he saw the anesthetic syringe at his neck it was too late.

"Hey! No. I don't need—" Like Leo Manx, Bey fell asleep in midprotest.

Bey had checked Sylvia's condition and Leo Manx's, but not his own. He believed he was doing fine. The transit ship's computer disagreed. It knew that Wolf should have been safely asleep and resting, but it also understood that he was unlikely to obey a computer command. The machine had waited for crossover, knowing that Wolf would then have to return to his bunk. Then, satisfied once more with the physical condition of all three passengers, the computer turned to other matters. At its direction the speeding ship passed through crossover point and raced on for the second half of its journey to the Marsden Harvester.

The computer was justly proud of its performance. It encountered hardware problems so seldom that the automatic error-correcting codes were called on only a couple of times a year. Error checking and correction were completely automatic. No human realized it, but the ship's rate of signal-error generation was less than a thousandth of that of the computers on the Marsden Harvester——and less than a millionth of the rate for the now-destroyed computer on the Sagdeyev space farm.

CHAPTER 14

"War is nothing more than the continuation of state policy by other means."

—Karl von Clausewitz

"A thermonuclear war cannot be considered a continuation of politics by other means. It would be a means to universal suicide."

—Andrei Sakharov

Conflict between the Inner and Outer Systems was a battle between a cat and a kestrel, between a lion and an eagle. Each could hurt the other—perhaps fatally. But neither could possess the other's territory, or rationally want to do so. Fifty million people might annihilate twenty billion, but they could never subjugate them. No sane Cloudlander desired to live crowded into the Sun and the inner planets. And despite their enormous superiority in numbers, twenty billion could never control the sparse and infinitely dispersed inhabitants of the Cloud, constantly drifting outward, always farther from the Sun. No member of the United Space Federation could stand the cold, open space of the Cloud.

War was senseless. And yet war came creeping steadily closer. Its presence could be seen and felt—in the angry faces of people on the harvesters, in the hoarding of food supplies and metals, in the false confidence and self-righteousness of the government speeches, and in the tense warning notes that flew between the Inner and Outer Systems.

Cinnabar Baker felt it better than anyone. She was officially responsible for the operation and maintenance of the harvesters, but that position carried an additional duty as head of system security. It made Baker, the Most junior of the three people who ruled the Cloud, also the most powerful.

A couple of thousand staff members on her payroll sent back official reports from locations in the Cloud. Twice that number, scattered through the Inner System and the Halo, provided Baker's unofficial information network. If someone sneezed on Ceres and that sneeze might mean bad news for the Cloud, Cinnabar Baker wanted to know about it.

Bey Wolf had watched the big woman in action and asked himself: What makes Cinnabar run? The easy answer was the official one. She worked enormously hard directing the harvesters, and that work gave her satisfaction. But the innermost depth of Cinnabar Baker, the invisible place where the ego is so delicate that a feather's touch will bruise it, lay elsewhere. She loved and cherished her secret security operation. The network was her eyes and ears. She would do anything to keep it in place. Yet even that was not her secret pride. When word drifted in through the grapevine of an impending disaster at the Sagdeyev space farm, she could not compromise her sources. There might be a chain of a dozen informants involved, each with his own unreliability quotient and each with his own cover. Everyone had to be protected. No details had been available, no statement of how or when an "accident" might be expected. Cinnabar Baker had a choice: she could ignore the rumblings of her own intelligence net, or she could recall Leo Manx and the others from important work.

She had chosen to send that urgent recall message, but the news of the farm's destruction had not yet reached her. The farmers were too reclusive a group to offer frequent messages. Silence was not significant. She had no way of knowing that they were struggling to devise a makeshift communications link from the remains of the old one.

Baker had the habit of returning to her office after the evening meal, clearing her desk, and starting in again to work as though it were the dawn of a new day. She had arrived at the Marsden Harvester only that morning, but now, at an hour when most humans were settling in for their three or four hours of sleep, she was beginning to sieve through the mass of printouts of the day's incoming messages.

She had three types of informant. There were the ones she had carefully planted over the years, reliable Cloudlanders who knew what she needed and who understood how to screen important information from rumors and rubbish. Baker took any inputs from them seriously.

The paid informants were another matter. Loyal to no one, they tended to send her any old garbage, hoping that it might somehow be worth money. Their input had to be looked at hard, and almost everything was discarded or given little weight.

Then there were the revolutionaries. Small groups within the Inner System were working for the overthrow of their own government, and they were willing to form alliances with the Outer System in order to do it. They provided information free, and would be outraged at any suggestion of payment. Cinnabar Baker worked with them and used their input. But she had no illusions about their value. Most of her informants on Earth or Mars preached the overthrow of the United Space Federation, but they would never live in the Cloud or the Halo. Worse than that, they saw every event through the distorting lens of their own paranoia.

Cinnabar Baker had inspected Bey Wolf very carefully during their first meeting. Wolf's reputation for intelligence and insight was extremely high. But Leo Manx had told of a self-destructive, hallucinating man, obsessed with a former lover. That fit the pattern of an Inner System paranoid, one who might someday be converted to form part of her recruited group of unpaid informants.

She had dropped that thought in the first fifteen minutes of their meeting. Wolf was too strong and too skeptical, too cold and analytical. He could not be manipulated in the usual ways.

But there were also unusual ways. At the end of that first meeting Cinnabar Baker had set a high-priority trace on the whereabouts of Mary Walton. So far, she had two things. The first was a recent poor-quality photograph of Mary Walton standing with her arm around the waist of a stern-faced man. Even in that faded image, his eyes were the commanding orbs of a fanatic, blazing out of the picture. Scribbled on the back of the photograph were the coordinates of a location in the Kernel Ring, accompanied by a question mark.

Those coordinate strings had been noted as a place for future investigation, but not as a high-priority item. Baker had no idea how she might use any information on Mary Walton, but patience and foresight were two of her main strengths. She would never admit she was willing to work with anyone and anything to achieve her goals, but she would have found it hard to name a group she would reject.

That night there were ninety messages for her review. Half of them had come from official news reports, the rest from her own network. With Turpin crooning on her shoulder, his black head bobbing or tucked away under one shabby wing, she set to work.

Outer System first—she was not naive enough to believe that informants were needed only for the Inner System and the Halo. Most messages were simple statements of production or equipment problems. She skimmed through them, doing no more than confirm that the pattern of the past year was still present. The Outer System was going to hell. Navigation systems were failing, cargo transit vessels from the Inner System did not arrive, power systems were unstable or running close to failure, harvesters failed their quality control tests, communications were suffering inexplicable glitches, and cargo packages that dropped Solward from the Cloud were disappearing on the way. Aybee had done an analysis for her and had confirmed what she knew instinctively. What they were seeing was far outside the limits of statistical reasonableness.

In the mind of most of the Cloud's population, that left only one possibility: sabotage. And as the only instigator, the Inner System. Cinnabar Baker did not agree at all. She had her own ideas as to what was going on and who was causing the trouble.

"But it's *how*, Turpin. How can Ransome affect all the control systems? That's the problem, and no one can help me with that."

The crow made a rattling noise like a set of bone dice being shaken and stared at the sheets of paper with its head to one side. "It's a bugger," it said solemnly.

"Indeed it is." Baker turned to the reports on the Inner System. The profile there had been slower to develop, lagging the pattern in the Cloud by a year or two. Now it was unmistakable to anyone who had watched events closely in both regions. It was the same story of inexplicable failure. Transit ships were disappearing, massive food shipments were failing to arrive on schedule, and power supplies had become unreliable.

And the Inner System was reacting in a predictable way. They were blaming the Outer System. There was anger, and talk of sabotage, and threats of reprisals.

Cinnabar Baker could identify three people in the whole system who knew that the Inner and Outer Systems were not sabotaging each other. She was one. Her counterpart in the Inner System, a man whom she respected enormously but whom she had never met, was another. The third was the person who was causing all the trouble.

More and more, the lines of evidence converged on the Kernel Ring and on the shadowy no-man's-land of Ransome's Hole. She was feeling her way toward its location, but her informants in the Ring had a habit of cutting off contact without warning. She had lost half a dozen in a few months. Her adversary seemed to know everything she did as soon as she made up her mind to do it. She had looked unsuccessfully for the leak in her operations. She continued her efforts, assembling fragments, pulsing her web of informants, but she was still a long way from a set of coordinates for Ransome's Hole.

And when she had them, what then? It was not clear that a direct attack would succeed or, if it did, that the sabotage would cease. Baker sighed and rubbed the poll of Turpin, who was still quietly watching her flip the pages.

"Come on, crow. We've earned a break." She set down the listings and wandered off toward the door, the bird still gripping her shoulder. It was the middle of the quiet period, and every rational person was asleep. Baker met no one as she padded barefoot along half a mile of silent corridor.

As she opened the crèche door, the sounds began. Forty babies were crying, fifty more gulping and grunting as they were fed by the machines. Three hundred others were sleeping peacefully. The solitary human attendant was lying down at the end of the room, eyes closed.

Cinnabar Baker did not wake him. She did not want conversation. When she arrived at any harvester, an unheralded visit to its crèches was a high priority. To her, it was the heart of the world. She had never found a habitat where things were going well in the crèche and badly elsewhere.

She watched and listened for twenty minutes, walking along the aisles and occasionally picking up and holding one of the babies. They ranged in age from two days to two months. One newborn had been placed in a form-change tank for remedial work on a deformed limb. Baker peered in through the transparent port and checked the progress of the change. It was normal. She made a mental note to return in three days to make sure the outcome was satisfactory.

She checked the instruction monitors above each crib, noting the frequency and duration of the parents' visits. Finally she was satisfied. She stole away, rejuvenated, ready for hours more of tedious work.

The government of the Inner System knew Cinnabar Baker as a powerful, formidable woman. They would have been little comforted to know that she happened to be sterile. She was still the biggest threat to their independence and way of life.

Perhaps they were right. But if so, it was only because she could sense full-scale war looming closer and closer. Cinnabar Baker saw herself as the secret mother of the whole system.

Her children could not be allowed to fight each other, to kill each other. She would prevent that—even if the whole system had to be under her control before she could stop them.

To an inhabitant of Earth, all the harvesters were the same. They were remote, identical food factories, run by soulless machines and populated by a thin sprinkling of people.

Bey was beginning to learn the truth. Each harvester was different, as different as the separate planets and asteroids of the Inner System.

It had begun the moment they left the first air lock. He had been swathed from head to foot in flowing hospital robes that left only his eyes showing, strapped to a stretcher, and maneuvered swiftly inward from the surface. The sounds began in the first interior corridor. The Opik Harvester had been eerily quiet, but this habitat was filled with music, lush instrumental pieces that had not been heard on Earth for centuries. Each concentric set of chambers blended harmoniously into the next, even though the same work was never played in both.

Bey looked for the source of the music. It was invisible, projectors hidden behind the luxuriant green plants that climbed restlessly over walls and ceiling. He recognized them. They were an adaptation, a variant on the free-space vacuum vines popular in the Asteroid Belt.

And then there were the people. The ones he had met on the other harvester had been furious—angry at the Inner System in general and at Bey in particular. They had resented his presence enough to want to fight him.

The Marsden Harvester's population did not show rage. They stank with fear. The people he saw as he was hurried through the corridors gave him not a second look. They were afraid, preoccupied with other matters, and most surprising of all, many of them were sick or deformed.

"I've never seen anything like it," Sylvia said after they had moved past a group of agitated people. "This is the oldest of the harvesters, and usually it's the most peaceful. They're all scared."

"They look terrible."

"They do." She turned to face him. "And so do you. Those cuts on your face are bleeding again. I'd take you right to the form-change tanks with Leo, but Cinnabar Baker wants to see you first."

"It's mutual." Bey had been brooding over one fact since he had woken in the transit ship. According to Sylvia, it was Cinnabar Baker's order for an emergency departure from the space farm that had given Sylvia enough lead time to save them. "I have a question for Baker."

They had left the clean, open corridors of the harvester's periphery and were plunging on toward the center of the main sphere. The region they were in had been built before mastery of construction without metals had been fully achieved. The vines were absent, and the chambers were shabby past hope of disguise. The walls sagged inward, the floor was wrinkled and blackened, and hairlike outgrowths of hydrocarbon filament blurred the clean outline of lighting units and ventilators. To Bey it was oddly comforting. It reminded him of Earth's familiar run-down cities.

Cinnabar Baker's apartment was the one point of constancy. It was identical to the bland chambers she had occupied before, with plain furniture and drab beige walls. Turpin was perched on the back of a chair, as dusty and disheveled-looking as ever. The crow greeted the newcomers with a sinister muttering.

"Don't mind Turpin. He's been in a bad mood since we got here." Baker took a hard look at Sylvia, then at Bey's mangled face. She gestured to the gray chairs. "Ten minutes, Mr. Wolf, that's all I need. Then we'll get you to a form-change tank for remedial treatment—if you still want to go there."

"More problems?"

"And worse ones. Did you meet any people as you came here?"

"Dozens of them."

"So you know how they look. Do you know what's wrong with them?"

Bey shrugged. "Obviously, they're not using the form-change tanks. And some of the people I saw appeared old. They need treatment—soon."

"You didn't see the worst cases. The population of this harvester has the highest average age of any group in the Outer System."

"Then you have an emergency. Some of the people I saw won't last more than a couple of weeks. Why won't they use the tanks?"

"They're afraid to." Baker passed a card across to Bey. "Those are the statistics for the performance of form-change equipment on this harvester. I headed here as soon as I saw the figures. We're facing a ten percent failure rate—many of them leading to death. Some of the units are going wrong three-quarters of the time, and the results are hideous. People won't go near a tank, and it's hard to blame them." She frowned at Bey. "Mr. Wolf, why are you smiling? There is nothing funny in this."

"Sorry." What Bey was feeling was not humor. It was relief. "If I was smiling, it's because I can finally do something to justify my presence."

"Do you know what's wrong?"

"Not yet. But I will in a few days."

Both women were staring at him in perplexity. He realized that a smile on his stitched and battered face must be a gruesome sight.

"What we faced before were intermittent faults," he went on. "One in a million faults. That kind are almost impossible to track down. You can set up test procedures and observe for years, but you may never run across anything wrong while you're actually watching. Now we're in a different situation. I can set up monitors on a few tanks and be sure I'll find something on at least one of them in a reasonable time. Give me a day or two."

"Can you correct the problem?" Baker's face showed her own relief. "I know it's early to ask that, but we need to tell people something."

"If I can find it, I can fix it. And I'm pretty sure I'll find it."

"How?" Sylvia looked at Baker. "I don't want to be the pessimist, but we have to know how he does it. Bey has to go into a form-change tank himself in a little while."

She was *worried* about him. Bey Wolf's surprise was genuine. He had lived with form-change equipment for so long, it had never occurred to him that someday he might die with it. In that one area he was completely confident. "I'll tell you just what I'm going to do. It's no big mystery, and once you understand it, you can do it, too. I'm sure the form-change problems are software, not hardware—we established that on the space farm. We'll use a diagnostic program that exits the form-change program after every major step and performs a status check. When we find a software inconsistency, we run a ferret routine to trace it back to the block of instructions that produced it."

"Is it easy?"

"It's routine. It's exactly what BEC does when they are testing a radically new form. I'll show you how it's done. But before we do *that*"—Sylvia was standing up—"I have a request."

Cinnabar Baker nodded politely. Bey knew that she would have preferred him to get right down to work on the form-change process.

"You sent Sylvia an urgent message telling us all to leave the farm," he said. "Why did you do that? If it was just to get me back here to look at form-change problems, why drag Aybee and Leo Manx back, too? They still had things to do on the farm."

"Mr. Wolf, if you ever tire of the Inner System, there is a position for you in the Cloud." Cinnabar Baker nodded slowly. "You are very astute. I had a warning—a tip-off—that something bad was going to happen to the farm. The farmers themselves would ignore any request to leave, but it would have been criminal to leave the four of you there without warning."

"You were told that we were all in danger?"

"No. I was warned on your behalf, specifically. It was my conclusion that you were all at risk."

"Who told you? I suppose that you have a network of your own—people who serve as your informants, pass on to you rumors and gossip."

Sylvia looked uneasy at his comment, but Baker nodded again, her manner relaxed. "I do. Naturally, it is not something that we advertise."

"Does it work both ways—to *spread* information and questions through the system as well as collecting answers?"

"Only too well." Baker paused for a moment, looking around. "It may be happening now. I am not the only one who uses informers. Secret information leaks from my office so quickly that others often seem to know it before my own staff."

"That's fine. I want something spread as widely as possible, and I want it spread as a rumor."

"It can be done. What is it, Mr. Wolf?"

"I want you to get out the word that I was killed in the accident on the Sagdeyev space farm."

"Easy enough to do. But why do you want it?"

"Protective paranoia. Someone was after me when I was on Earth, trying to drive me crazy. I think they were still after me on the farm—it's a self-indulgent idea that someone would arrange to destroy the whole farm just to get me. But I believe it, and I think you do. If they know I'm here and still working for you, they'll keep trying. The safest person is a dead man."

"Dead man," Turpin repeated in a sepulchral whisper. "Dead man." He walked along the back of the chair and peered at Wolf with bright, beady eyes.

"Very well." Baker nodded, but Bey could see the doubt on her face. Was she continuing his own train of thought? If it was improbable that someone was seeking to end Bey's life or destroy his sanity, that person's continued failure was even more improbable. He had been too lucky. And it opened again the question as to why he was worth killing—or worth saving.

In his dog days at the Office of Form Control, Bey had sometimes thought of the detection of illegal forms as a vast game of chess. In that game he was the master player, one who controlled the movement of people and equipment on a giant board that spanned the space from Mercury to Pluto. It was a game that he had never lost.

Now another game was being played, on a much bigger board and with higher stakes. It was a battle over a territory that ranged from the Sun to the edge of the Cloud, one that stretched a quarter of the way to the stars, a new game that was spreading panic and anger and the threat of total war through the whole system. And this time Bey himself was nothing more than a pawn.

CHAPTER 15

A Kerr-Newman black hole, or kernel, *charged and rotating, is a highly dynamic object. The rotational contribution to its mass-energy can be extracted (or added to) using the Penrose process, and the kernel's own electric charge can be used to hold it in position, or to control its movement from place to place. Thus, such black holes are "live"; they can provide energy to or remove energy from their surroundings, in a controllable way, and they can be placed at any desired location. They are* power kernels.

A Schwarzschild *black hole is a kernel that is neither charged nor rotating. It is a kernel in a debased and limiting form, a spherically symmetrical object that has lost all electric charge and rotational energy. It is "dead," in the sense that one cannot extract from it in a controllable way any of its mass-energy. Unless it is "spun up" (i.e., given rotational energy using the Penrose process) it is not useful for power production.*

The Schwarzschild black hole is not, however, totally inert. Like any other kernel, it gives off particles and radiation from its hidden interior according to the Hawking evaporative process, at a rate depending only on its mass (smaller black holes emit more strongly than larger ones). However, the pattern *of this emission is predictable only in overall statistical terms. All events and processes occurring within a certain region about the center of any black hole, whether of Schwarzschild or Kerr-Newman type, are*

*unknowable. The interior of the black hole within this
"event horizon" constitutes, in some sense, a separate universe from ours.*

> —from the 2011 centennial Festschrift volume,
> compiled in celebration of John Archibald
> Wheeler's one hundredth birthday

Aybee was in trouble. He was smart enough to know it and
smart enough to realize he was unlikely to get out in a hurry.

His decision to remain on the ruined farm had been perfectly reasonable. There was too little space for him on the
transit ship. Leo and the others were in the competent hands
of the ship's emergency medical system, and Aybee himself
was not urgently needed back on the harvesters. His offer to
help the farmers had been politely—and predictably—refused. While they were maneuvering the habitation bubble
back into contact with the collection layer, Aybee had
switched to a long-duration suit and gone hunting.

He had two items he particularly wanted to find among the
thousands of bits of debris created in the collision. One was
the ship he had arrived in. It would almost certainly need
repairs, but it might be his quickest way home when he was
ready to leave.

With the help of the suit's microwave sensors he found it in
the first twelve hours. It was floating a couple of thousand
kilometers from the collection layer, with a small relative velocity. Aybee tagged it with a tracking beacon and went on to
the harder part of his search.

The central computer of the farm had been in the direct line
of impact. Not even a trace of it was left. But there must have
been backup storage for its records. It was in a region of the
bubble that had been smashed open by the impact but not
totally destroyed. Somewhere in the mess around the farm
Aybee hoped to find the secondary storage cube. It would be
small, no bigger than his fist, and he had no illusions about
how hard it would be to find it.

With so much debris of all shapes and sizes, the only hope of identification was through the data cube's reflectance spectrum. He selected the spectral signature for a data cube, set up a spatial survey for it, and settled down to wait. While the scan was being performed, he finally had time to look around.

And to gasp.

If he had been less busy, he might have noticed it hours earlier. A dark oblong stretched across a quarter of the sky, hiding the bright starfield. He cut in his low-light sensors and saw it at once as a massive cargo craft, drifting closer with unlit ports and with its drive off. It was the type used to carry food shipments from the Cloud to the Inner System, a low-acceleration ellipsoidal hull over a kilometer long and six hundred meters across. It felt close enough to touch.

Aybee did not consider for one moment that it might be a rescue vessel. The approaching shape was too dark and lifeless. He floated himself across to a tangle of ruined cabin furniture and set himself in the middle of it.

The hulk approached within two hundred meters of the battered habitation bubble. A dark port opened, and a file of suited figures emerged. Their suits were bulky, ending in a characteristic flared and massive lower section. That solid base contained low- and high-thrust jets; power supply; food, air, and water recycling systems; medical facilities; exercise units; and communications equipment. At the wearer's command, the flared bottom would open out to a thin-walled twenty-meter sphere, or couple with one or more other suits to form a common living volume.

Only one group used suits like that. Podders!

But these were Podders many billions of kilometers away from their usual haunts in the Halo. They were entering the dimly lit habitation bubble, passing to the interior through the gaping hole near the south pole. The bubble was on emergency power, but it was still far brighter than the dark cargo ship.

What was it doing here? It was inconceivable to Aybee that anything valuable was left on the farm, even including the machines and metals on the collection layer. And the Podders were showing no interest in those.

While he watched, another port in the cargo vessel began to dilate. It was huge, an opening nearly forty meters across in the end of the ship nearest the bubble. He stared at it, waiting for something to emerge.

It was completely free of the ship before he knew it was there, and then he did not see it. All he saw was a circling array of electromagnets. At their center sat a moving sphere of blackness, drifting slowly under their control toward the habitation bubble.

It was a kernel, totally shielded by electromagnetic baffles. At the center of that dark sphere sat a tiny, billion-ton Kerr-Newman black hole, its fierce sleet of radiation and particles balked and turned back on itself by the triple shields. The kernel had been halted. It hovered, stationary with respect to the bubble, and waited. The bubble's own main port was opening. Finally a second sphere of aching black emerged from the gaping port, its position controlled by surrounding electromagnets.

Aybee watched in amazement as the two drifting spheres changed places. The shielded kernel from the farm finally vanished into the cargo hull, and after a few minutes the new kernel was jockeyed into place by the bubble's port. It was nudged on down into the interior.

Aybee was bursting with curiosity. He nestled down into the tangle of space junk surrounding him and inched the whole assembly gently forward until he could see into the bubble's open port. He peered out through the mess of shattered furniture.

The kernel was replacing the one that had been removed. Aybee had noted the status of the farm's power kernel when he and Leo Manx had arrived. It had abundant rotational energy and was nowhere near depletion. There was no sense in replacing it—unless the Podders needed power and were swapping the kernel from the bubble for a dead one from their cargo ship.

It was a simple matter to test that idea. One look at the new kernel's optical scalars would tell Aybee what was happening, and that was a one-minute job if carried out next to its outer shield.

The port was closing, and one by one the Podders were leaving. As the final suited figure disappeared silently into the cargo hulk, Aybee headed for the bubble.

That was the exact point where Bey Wolf would have put his hand on Aybee's shoulder, told him to wait a moment, and asked a basic question. Where were the farmers? But Bey was billions of kilometers away. Aybee left his shelter of ram-shackle cabin furniture and headed into the bubble along the gaping exit wound of the earlier impact.

The farmers and their servant machines had accomplished wonders. Already the bubble's interior had been cleared of broken fittings. Makeshift bulkheads had stabilized the atmosphere of the interior and set up a new system of corridors that provided access to the habitable part of the bubble.

Aybee drifted down toward the bubble's center, where he found that the new kernel had been established in place of the original one. It had plenty of available energy—according to Aybee's recollection, almost exactly as much as the old one. The mystery was greater than ever. Why swap two identical kernels for each other?

He headed up a narrow stairway that would take him away from the kernel and toward the bubble's outer surface. At that moment he learned that the Podders had not left permanently. Three of them waited in a tight group by an exit duct, while a fourth was leading a group of three farmers out of the bubble at gunpoint.

Aybee ducked back into the shelter of the stairway and reviewed his options. He could wait, hoping that the Podders were finally done and were all leaving. Or he could take more positive action, heading out through the entrance wound cre-ated by the impact of the ice fragment.

The disadvantages of both ideas were easy to catalog. His hiding place was completely exposed to anyone who wan-dered by, and the way down to the kernel was a dead end. If the Podders wanted to be sure they had all the farmers, they would not overlook the surface of the kernel shields. On the other hand, he had no idea what might be waiting in the other direction. The Podders had first entered the bubble there, and some of them could be there again.

Bey Wolf would have waited. He was a great believer in putting off decisions, which he dignified as "keeping open all his options."

Aybee could not do that; he had too nervous a nature. After at most a minute he was hugging the side of the tunnel and creeping away toward the surface of the bubble. He was careful to look at the way ahead and turn every few seconds to make sure that he was safely out of sight of the four Podders behind him. He was doing that at the exact moment when a fifth Podder, also looking the other way, emerged from a narrow gap in the wall and ran right into him.

The suited figure did not bother to speak. He waved the gun he was holding at Aybee and gestured him forward.

Aybee could take a hint. He nodded and moved off along the tunnel toward the outer surface. The radio silence he had been observing earlier seemed pointless. Aybee scanned for the frequency the Podders were using and turned his suit to transmission.

"What are you going to do with me?"

The figure behind him grunted with surprise. Aybee realized it was a woman. "I thought you people didn't talk to anybody," she said. "None of your buddies said a word."

She thinks I'm a farmer, thought Aybee. But if I play that part too well, she won't tell me anything.

He grunted. "We don't talk much. But this is an emergency."

"Don't talk much and don't listen much, either." The Podder sounded disgusted. "I'm not going through all that spiel again. Do as you're told, and don't give us any trouble, and you'll be well treated. If you start cutting up, you'll find you're six to a cell."

The ultimate threat for a farmer. Aybee did not like the sound of it too much himself—he still had memories of the cramped trip to the Sagdeyev space farm with Leo Manx.

"Where are you taking me?"

"Are you deaf? Wait a minute." She moved around in front of Aybee and peered in through his faceplate. "I haven't seen you before. We didn't get you the first time through. Where were you?"

"Outside."

"And you came back in?" The Podder gestured him forward again. "Well, now I've seen everything. You were safe out in space, and you came back in. How dumb can you get?"

Aybee had three good reasons not to answer. First, he assumed it was a rhetorical question. Second, he had to agree in this case with the Podder's implied comment on his brains. He had been safe outside, where all he needed to do was wait for the Podders' ship to go away. Then he could have spent the next month inside the bubble, if that was what he felt like doing.

And third, he did not need to fish for more information about the Podders' immediate plans for him. He could guess them. They were close to the great hulk of the cargo ship, and a hatch was gaping open. With the woman close behind, Aybee drifted into the gloomy interior. He wondered how long it would be before anyone on the harvesters even noticed he was missing.

CHAPTER 16

"She did corrupt frail nature with some bribe,
    To shrink mine arm up like a withered shrub,
    To make an envious mountain on my back
    Where sits deformity to mock my body;
    To shape my limbs of an unequal size,
    To disproportion me in every part . . ."
        —William Shakespeare; *Henry VI, Part 3*

Every emergence was different.

Bey came out of this one dry-mouthed, wobble-legged, and furious. He knew the form-change process better than anyone. He could tell when parameters had been changed from their original settings, even when he was the subject, and this time he knew he had been through a lot more than simple tissue restoration.

The door of the tank sprang open, and he looked out. Sylvia Fernald was sitting by the control board, staring at him.

He roared with rage, a horrible squeal of unfamiliar vocal cords. "What the hell have you been doing to me?" The ionic balance of his body was still adjusting, and the chemical rush of anger was strong enough to propel him forward out of the

125

tank in one movement. "Don't try to lie. You've been meddling and you know it."

"You call it meddling when somebody tries to help you?" She stood her ground. "I've just saved you. You'd have been cut to bits as soon as people in the harvester knew you were here. No one from Earth is safe now."

"I can look after myself." Bey tried to gesture in anger, but his fist would not close. His body felt terrible, a bad size, a distorted shape. "A form-change like that—you could have killed me."

"I studied the change very carefully. It's a standard type of form for the Outer System."

"I didn't need a change."

"Wrong! You need a change. More than a change—you need a damned *keeper.* I've had it with you, and I don't care what Baker wants." Sylvia stood up. "You're an idiot, Bey Wolf, you know that? You come out here, an Earther, and you think you're God's gift to the Cloud." She gripped him hard by the arm and pulled him along the room. He stumbled after her, still too weak to put up more than token resistance. She halted by the door at the end of the room. "Take a look there. What do you see?"

Bey found himself in front of a full-length mirror. He was facing a nightmare, naked and thin as a skeleton, tall and stooped as a praying mantis. All the muscles had gone from his arms and legs, leaving ugly tendons and sticks of bone that ended in taloned hands and feet. His rib cage jutted like a dry wooden frame under tautly stretched parchment. The hair was gone from his head and body, and his browless eyes glared demented out of hollow sockets. His hairless genitals looked vulnerable and ridiculous. He stood frozen, his skull-head mouth gaping open.

"What do you see?" She had gone on shouting at him, but he had not even heard her. "What do you see?"

"You did this to me!" He shook his arm loose. "You're insane. You've turned me into a monster. I've got to get back in the tank, make this right again."

"No!" She stood in front of him, blocking his movement,

and he realized how tall he had become. They were suddenly eye to eye. "It's time you learned something, Behrooz Wolf— if you're still able to learn anything at all. I don't know what you see, but I'll tell you what I see, and it's the way everyone thinks in the Outer System."

She stepped back and swept him from head to toe with a searing glare. As his anger had calmed, hers had grown. "I see a passable-looking man for the first time since I met you. A man I would be pleased to know, a man whose company I might even enjoy. Not a damned monkey. Not a squat, hairy toad. Not a hirsute, jowly, Sun-sucking *midget* that no normal woman would be seen dead with. And *yes*, I did it to you. And *no*, I'm not sorry I did it. I sat by that damned tank for a hundred straight hours to make sure nothing was going wrong with the change I keyed in. And *yes*, I knew what I was doing. And *no*, I don't expect you to appreciate it. You're too graceless, too selfish, too self-obsessed, too wrapped up in your self-superior idea that anything from the Inner System has to be good and right." She was screaming at him. "So damn you, Bey Wolf. If you want to get back into that tank, go ahead. I won't stop you. And I won't interfere when the people on the harvester grab you and spill your guts."

Bey's body chemistry change was complete, and his condition was stabilizing. He was beginning to feel almost normal, but he also knew that the mood swings might be far from over. He stared fascinated at his image in the mirror and shook his head. "I look like a form-change *failure*. Those legs—you actually *programmed* for those legs?"

"They're great legs."

"They're revolting. Look at them! Too short, too white, too bowed." He turned to face her. "You're serious, aren't you? You think I should thank you for this."

"You should go down on your knees and kiss my hand. My God, I was doing you a favor." She had stopped shouting at him. "You're supposed to have brains. Use them. You asked Cinnabar Baker to announce that you had been killed on the space farm so you could explore the problem without people knowing who you were. How well would that have held up when people saw you? You *had* to change. I suppose you thought that you'd blend right in with the rest of us, with your ridiculous Earth body."

"All right. But why didn't you warn me?"

"Would you have agreed to this body if I had?"

"Never." Now that he was not angry, Bey was feeling a bit guilty. She had sat by the tank for days, looking after him, and he could see how pale and tired she was. "But do you blame me for feeling that way? Would you have let me change *you* so you look like an Earthwoman?"

"Don't be disgusting."

"Well, then. But I'll admit it, you're right about one thing, and I want to apologize for shouting at you. It's an odd thought, but in this stick-insect body I *will* be less noticeable here." Bey took another look at his reflection and grabbed for a robe by the door. It was suitably long and full—when he had it on he could see nothing but his hands and head. "That's better. I'd rather not see myself. But I still wish in some ways I could get back in the tank. I don't seem to be *done*."

"Are you feeling sick?"

"Not exactly. But I'm certainly feeling a bit Plantagenetish."

"A bit *what*?"

"You know. Or if you don't, you should." Bey held the robe tight around him, stood up as straight as he was able, and declaimed: " 'Deformed, unfinished, sent before my time, into this breathing world scarce half made up, and that so lamely and unfashionable, that dogs bark at me as I halt by them.' Richard the Third. One of my all-time heroes."

She stared at him. Finally she laughed. "My God, Leo was right. You *are* insane. You're worse than Aybee. Totally crazy."

Bey considered her statement. He was a bit light-headed, definitely that, but it was not his strongest feeling. "More like totally starving. Whatever you did to me, it left me hollow. Can I get some food?"

"We can try. And you'll have your big test. We'll see if you can pass—as a Cloudlander. Here, wait a minute." Bey was all ready to head out of the door. "You'll never pass in that outfit."

"You all seem to dress the same. There must be a uniform near."

"Wrong again." Sylvia gestured at her own gray suit. "I'm still just the way we came off the ship, but I wouldn't dream of mixing with other people here like this—or in the old uniform. You seem to think all the harvesters are the same. They're not alike, any two of them, in either their layout or their people. This harvester is super fashion-conscious. Nobody here would be seen dead in those yellow suits we wore on the Opik Harvester. If we want to be inconspicuous, we have to follow local ways. Come with me. It's right next door."

The room she led him to had rack after rack of clothing, all gaudy, varied, and extreme. Bey hesitated, then shrugged. "I've no idea. You know how to make me blend in. Pick something."

Within two minutes she had selected a pair of skintight peacock-blue suits with matching footwear and tall egg-shaped hats. They seemed designed to make Bey look even taller and thinner and were, in his opinion, the most ridiculous outfits he had ever seen.

He stared in disbelief at his reflection. "We can't go out in public like this. Everyone in the harvester will laugh at us."

"They won't even notice. Not in this harvester."

"But the people we saw as we came in from the ship didn't look like this."

"They were maintenance and operations crews. In uniform. You wouldn't know them if you saw them off duty."

Bey started for the door, then paused for a last look in the mirror. "Are you *sure*?"

"Trust me. You look quite handsome." Sylvia tucked her arm in his and led the way. "Remember, until you get the hang of that body in low g, you let me set the pace. Pretend we're a couple. Don't talk much at first, and if you don't know how to move, just let me drag you along."

They set off along a mysterious zigzag of corridors and

stairways. Bey knew he was lost within one minute; in ten minutes, he knew why the Cloudlanders had picked their preferred forms. He was shaped just right for a low-g environment. He could pivot his top-heavy body around its center of mass and use his long arms to control the direction of his movement, unhindered by excess muscle or fat. Even the air somehow smelled better, but whether that was his new physiology or his imagination he could not tell.

The hall they came to was crowded for a room on a harvester. Bey's initial worry—that it was too public a first appearance for his new body—vanished when he saw the general behavior. A peculiar sense of panic and excitement filled the air. No one took any notice of Bey and Sylvia. A couple of hundred noisy people were milling around a dais at one end, and as Bey looked at them he felt reassured. He was one of the most conservatively dressed. Pink sequined pantaloons and curved-toe slippers competed and clashed with scarlet tunics and glittering black hose. Earth taste was nonexistent.

At a gesture from Sylvia, Bey slipped into an eating cubicle at the back of the room. Sylvia in the next cubicle was out of sight unless she stood up to look over the partition, and one-way glass in the front wall allowed both of them to see the rest of the hall. Most of the crowd was clustered around a scarecrow of a man with a blue skullcap, a long white robe, and a mask that covered the lower half of his face.

"You have a choice!" He had a muffled, booming voice, echoing from the room's bare white walls. "I can *give* you a choice. If you do not like the idea of form-change, if you do not care to face the terror of the tanks, *there are other ways*. Ancient secrets, the mysteries of Earth's antiquity, means of treating illness that do not depend on the use of form-change tanks."

"Nothing good comes from Earth!" The shout came from somewhere in the throng of people.

"From today's Earth, you are right." The man on the platform turned to that part of the crowd. "I think we ought to destroy Earth and all the Inner System." There was a roar of approval from the crowd. "But that does not mean that the knowledge of Old Earth is useless. All our ancestors once lived there! I have learned Earth's old secrets."

Bey spoke to Sylvia, busy ordering food in her cubicle from the table server. "What's he talking about?"

"I was going to ask you the same thing. He said something about knowledge coming from ancient Earth."

"The distilled wisdom of long-dead ages," the booming voice was continuing. "Three hundred years ago, the knowledge that I possess was tightly held by a small group of people. When form-change came in, the need for their skills disappeared. They lost their power. Their special learning vanished. But not forever! By intense research, I and my assistants have repossessed those lost skills. We are the New Aesculapians." He held up two clear bottles, one filled with a cloudy green liquid and the other filled with small white spheres. "Whatever your ailment, we can help you! One of these will be the answer."

"Oh, my God." Bey had been chewing on a bland yellow wedge of material that Sylvia had ordered. He almost choked, then spoke with his mouth full. "I never thought I'd see this."

"What is he offering?"

"Pills and potions. Panaceas. He's saying he's a doctor!"

"You mean a—a *physician*?" Sylvia groped for the old word. "There are no such people in the Cloud."

"Nor on Earth, anymore—there hasn't been for two hundred years. I didn't think there ever would be again, anywhere." Bey was ecstatic. "Before purposive form-change was developed, there were thousands of them. They were enormously powerful, just like a priesthood. Those clothes and masks he's wearing were their robes. I wonder he isn't spouting the Hippocratic oath and writing prescriptions."

"Writing *what*?"

"Purchase approval for chemicals. They used to treat diseases with chemicals, you know—and with surgery, too."

"Surgery. Isn't that *cutting*—"

"Right. Cutting people open. Before it was outlawed, they were allowed to do that. I hope he's not proposing it here."

The white-coated man was being mobbed by people shouting out their problems. He had been joined by half a dozen acolytes, who were beginning to hand out vials and packages. Sylvia opened the door of her cubicle and stepped out. "I have to tell Cinnabar Baker about this. We can't allow it."

"No." Bey came out quickly to grab her sleeve and restrain her. "First we get samples, have them analyzed. I'll bet they're totally harmless. Come on."

They had not finished eating, but the food and drink had been enough to produce another mood change. Bey was getting a little sleepy and extremely cheerful. He began to make his way toward the center of the crowd. Sylvia caught up with him and pushed in front. "Not you. I'll do it. I can move easier than you. You stay right there."

She eeled into the mass of people and returned a couple of minutes later with a bottle in one hand and a packet in the other. She held them up triumphantly, but just before she reached Bey, she halted and her expression changed. She was looking right past him.

"Here comes your real test." She leaned close and spoke rapidly. "If you pass this one, you're home free."

Bey slowly turned. Heading toward them across the room was a smiling woman dressed in a cloudy dress of flaming pink. "Sylvia! I had no idea you were here."

"I just arrived." Sylvia squeezed the woman's hands in both of hers, then stepped back. "Andromeda, this is Behrooz. He's also visiting the harvester. Bey, this is an old friend of mine, Andromeda Diconis. We studied optimal control theory together, many years ago."

"Too many. But Sylvia was always better at it than I was. That's why I'm here, in my boring little job, while Sylvia roves the system." The woman had taken Bey by the hand and was giving him a head-to-toe stare. Her glittering blue eyes and full mouth held an odd and unreadable expression. "Very nice clothes you have—you *both* have. Perfectly matched. What are you doing here?"

"Behrooz works on communications equipment," Sylvia said before Bey could speak. "He's an expert on it."

"We can certainly use some of those here. Where are you from, Behrooz?"

"The Opik Harvester."

"Ah. Such a dull place—I would never want to live there. And you are a communications *expert*? How impressive." Andromeda Diconis was still holding Bey's hand, but it was Sylvia she spoke to next. "I'm sure he is an expert on many things. But my dear Sylvia, whatever happened to your other friend? What was his name, Paul?"

"Paul Chu. I suppose you didn't hear. He disappeared on a mission to the Halo."

"Oh, yes, now you mention it, I did hear that. But I thought he came back. Someone here said they'd seen him just a week or two ago. Anyway, we don't want to talk about *him*, do we?" Andromeda finally released Bey's hand and reached up to straighten his collar. Her fingers ran over the hollow of his throat. "Not when you've been able to make new friends, Sylvia. And very attractive friends, too. I'll tell you what, I'm going to stay here and have something to eat. Would you and Behrooz"—Bey earned a dazzling smile—"like to wait for me, and then we can all go to the concert along the corridor?"

Sylvia placed her hand firmly on Bey's arm. "Not today. We've just eaten, and Bey has had a very hard day. He needs to rest now."

"I'm sure he does. I'm sure you *both* do. But it's wonderful to see you again, Sylvia, and I'll call you tomorrow." She reached forward and stroked Bey's forearm. "And I really look forward to seeing you again, Behrooz. Once you're properly *rested*."

Bey tried to smile and nod, but Sylvia was already towing him off toward the exit. He waved to Andromeda Diconis and received a blown kiss in return.

"What's the hurry?" he asked as soon as they were out of earshot. "Was I making her suspicious?"

"Not in the slightest." Sylvia's manner was a mixture of pleasure and irritation. "You passed perfectly. Couldn't you tell? She'd never have acted that way if she thought for one moment that you were from the Inner System. She's the perfect Cloudlander, looks down on everything inside the Kernel Ring. But Andromeda was all ready to eat you for breakfast."

"If I was passing perfectly, why drag me away?" Bey rather liked the idea of being eaten for breakfast by Andromeda.

"Because Andromeda has to think that I'm jealous—the way she would be. She thinks she understands our relationship exactly, and that's the best thing that could have happened. Andromeda's a total bitch, but she took you at face value, as a Cloudlander. And she's the universe's greatest gossip. Give her a day or two, and everyone will know that I have a new companion, a man from the Opik Harvester."

"Isn't that dangerous? They may want to meet me."

"She'll tell people that I'm jealous of you and want to keep you all to myself. It's a perfect reason to let us stay private while you work. But that's something we'll worry about tomorrow."

"Uh uh." He yawned. "Tomorrow, and tomorrow, and tomorrow. Great word. Great speech. Hmmm."

Sylvia had noticed the change in Bey since leaving Andromeda Diconis. Another common aftereffect of a long session in the tanks was hitting him. He was on a high but was fast running out of adrenaline and energy. The surprise of waking in a strangely different form and the stimulus of the new surroundings had been enough to give him a lift for the past few hours, but that was fading.

"Come on. Before you fall asleep in the corridors." His exhaustion had been a convenient excuse to leave Andromeda, but it was true enough. Bey Wolf would need a good rest before he was fit to work on the Marsden Harvester's form-change problems.

She led him away toward his assigned quarters. Bey did not speak, and by the time they arrived his eyes were closing. Sylvia steered him to a bunk. He was asleep before she could add another word. After a few moments she gently removed the bright blue clothes and the extravagant hat and secured him in the bunk with loose straps. He would become used to low-g sleeping soon enough, but he might be disoriented when he first woke.

He lay flat on his back. Sylvia looked over the sleeping body with approval. "Pretty good job I did with you, Behrooz Wolf, if I say it myself. Andromeda was fascinated, and she's a connoisseur. 'Very attractive friends,' eh? We'll have to fight to keep her away from you."

Sylvia frowned, remembering another of Andromeda's comments. Someone on the harvester had seen Paul Chu recently. Even if it were no more than a bit of gossip, Sylvia needed to follow up on it. Cinnabar Baker had pointed out the problem. When one talked of war and sabotage, all roads seemed to lead to the Kernel Ring; but no roads led to Black Ransome, or to Ransome's Hole—unless she could track the lead to Paul, and he could provide the pathway.

She started for the door, then paused. She must not go back to the hall too soon. Andromeda had her own ideas about what Sylvia and Bey were doing at the moment, and Sylvia wanted to keep that idea intact.

She forced herself to wait for almost two hours, thinking hard and watching the steady rise and fall of Bey's bony chest. At last she headed for the concert hall.

The lights had dimmed automatically. Bey lay in darkness, listened to the faint hissing of the air ventilators, and wondered what had wakened him. He was almost in free-fall, floating with only the imperceptible tether of a pair of retaining straps. And he was not ready to wake. He felt groggy with sleep, so tired that it was an impossible effort to open his eyes.

"Bey!" The voice came again. It was no more than a whisper, but it jerked him at once to thrilling wakefulness. It was a sound to rouse Bey from the dead.

He opened his eyes. The projection system in the corner had switched itself on and revealed the interior of a dark room. In the center of that open space, her face illuminated by the faint gleam of a single red spotlight, sat Mary Walton.

"Bey!" The soft call came again.

"Mary. Where are you?"

"Don't try to answer me, Bey. This message was prere-corded, so I can't hear what you're saying. It is triggered when you respond to your name and open your eyes."

She was as hauntingly attractive and as crazy-looking as ever. Bey even recognized her outfit. It was the one she had worn when she played Titania, a long russet gown that should have been dowdy but glowed with fairy tints of warm light. He had last seen it locked in a closet of his Earth apartment. Her voice was even more familiar, as wonderful as ever, with smoky, husky tones that made Bey hear sexual overtones even in her comic speeches.

"I don't want you hurt, Bey," she went on. "I've already saved you many times, back on Earth and on the space farm, but I don't know how many more times I can do it. You have to stop what you're doing, leave the harvesters, get back to Earth."

"How did you know where I am?" Bey responded automat-ically, forgetting that she could not hear him.

"You are being used, you know, by the Outer System." She had not paused. "It's not your problem, but they'll try and make it yours. The Outer System is going to break down more and more, and if you try to stop it, it will kill you. Say no to Cinnabar Baker, whatever she suggests. When Sylvia Fernald tries to sleep with you—she will, if she hasn't already—re-member that she's doing it as part of her job. You are nothing to those people." Mary raised her hand. On her middle finger glowed a huge kernel ruby, the rarest gemstone in the system. "It may be over between us, Bey, but don't ever forget that I'm fond of you. I saved you when the messages were making all the others die or go mad. Give me credit for that. Good-bye now, and please take care. Sleep well."

She waved. The projection unit's image slowly faded, until after twenty seconds Bey could see nothing but the ghostly glimmer of the kernel ruby. Finally that, too, was gone. The sleeping chamber was again in perfect darkness.

Bey was sweating hard, and his heart was pounding. He was filled with a mixture of excitement and amazement.

Mary's final words had been a grim joke—he would not sleep now, not for hours. He loosened the straps that had held him snugly in position and made his way across to the projection unit. It should hold a recorded copy of that whole message.

The recording storage was completely blank. Naturally. Bey was not even surprised anymore. After the Negentropic Man, after the projected images that were filling the Outer System, and Mary's ability to leave a message for him wherever she apparently chose, no other anomaly of the communications system could be ruled out. It was all impossible.

But one impossibility throbbed in his head harder and harder the longer he thought about it. If Mary knew where he was, then perhaps she could find a way to send a message. But *how*, in a total region of space so large that the whole Inner System was no more than a dot at its center, had she *known* where he was?

She had known of his trip to the Sagdeyev space farm. She had learned of his return. She had tracked him to these quarters within a few hours of his arrival there. How? How did she know?

He would *never* get to sleep. *Never, never, never, never, never*. With that single word resounding in his head, he went drifting irresistibly toward the slumber of total exhaustion.

And it was in those final moments, swimming down toward new unconsciousness, that Bey had a first inkling as to how Mary knew what was happening so quickly. He tried to catch the thought, to study it; but it was too late.

He was asleep.

CHAPTER 17

Aybee had a problem. He wanted his captors to think he was from the space farm and not a representative of the Cloud's central government. On the other hand, he could not afford to meet any other farmers. They would know at once that he was not one of them, and they would have no reason to hide that fact from the Podders. For the moment, at least, he seemed safe. There were plenty of Podders, easily recognized from their suits, visible near the lock of the cargo vessel, but he could see no sign of farmers.

Steered along by the woman behind him, Aybee went drifting on into the interior. From the outside, the ship had been an inert, lifeless hulk, a derelict abandoned in the early days of Cloud colonization. Within, the airless enclosure was filled with activity.

Aybee looked around with a professional eye. They had entered through one of the ship's forward ports. The outer hull arched away from them, a great curved span of carbon fiber sheet with strengthening beams of hardened polymers. From the inside it seemed much more than six hundred meters wide. There was enough interior space for whole cities, complete with everything from food and power production to swimming pools and game fields. But there were signs that the ship was more than a simple colony.

The first giveaway was the bracing struts and massive electric cables. They ran through the whole interior, and there was no reason to have them unless the ship had to withstand acceleration. Aybee did a quick mental calculation and decided that the mechanical and electromagnetic stiffening was consistent with about a two-g thrust.

That at once told him something else. At two g's, the ship was over a year's run away from the Podders' natural home in the Halo. There had to be some way of moving people and materials faster than that. Aybee looked again around the cluttered and dimly lit cargo shell and saw the expected equipment far away near the outer wall. A high-acceleration ship hung there, its McAndrew drive off. Its design suggested that it would allow up to three hundred g's before the gravitational and inertial accelerations were in balance. Aybee studied that ship very closely. With it, the Marsden Harvester was only twenty-four hours away.

The second oddity was the presence of transparent internal partitions and numerous internal air locks. Cargo hulls were rarely pressurized, and the Podders had no interest in living within an atmosphere. Their suits were all the air supply they cared to have. So who wanted parts of the ship to be air-filled, and where were they?

Finally, there were the kernels. Aybee could see a dozen places where the local spherical structure implied housings for shielded kernels. That suggested a monstrous power demand. One kernel would be sufficient for normal operations of a volume this size, even if it were a full-scale colony ship. The alternative explanation, that the kernels were being used for some other purpose, made no sense without more data.

Aybee turned back to the woman behind him. Inside the ship, she had put her gun away. "What are you going to do to me?"

"Just keep going. You'll find out in a few minutes." She relented. "Don't worry. We don't kill people without a good reason."

But we do kill people *with* a good reason? Aybee wondered what a good reason was. Trying to escape? Lying about one's identity? Being a spy for the Outer System government?

They were entering a new section of the ship, passing through an interior lock into an enclosure with opaque walls. Aybee heard the hiss of air and looked questioningly at the woman.

She nodded. "Transition point. Here's where I leave you. Get out of your suit and go through the inner lock." She switched to some other transmission frequency, had a conversation that Aybee could not follow as he was removing his suit, and gestured him forward. "Move it unless you like to breathe vacuum. I'll be exhausting this lock again in thirty seconds."

Aybee had been worried when he took off his suit, because underneath it he was not dressed like any of the farmers he had seen. But apparently the Podders were no experts on space farm attire; certainly the woman did not give his clothes a second glance. He went on through.

A man and a woman were waiting for him on the other side of the lock, facing him across a curved table.

More mystery. Neither of them had the stunted form and compact build preferred by Podders or the elongated shape of a Cloudlander. Aybee was in about a twentieth of a g field, which suggested that the room had to be close to a kernel. Both the people in front of him appeared comfortable with that, which meant they were not likely to be from the Inner System.

The woman gestured him to a seat opposite her. She had black hair, black skin, and a wary look in her eye. "Leila tells us that you talk," she said. "Good. That's a nice change from your buddies."

Aybee sat down, hunching low in the chair. "All right, so I know how to talk. What happens to me now?"

"That depends on you. I don't suppose you know any physics?"

"I know a bit." It was no time to act insulted.

The other two people looked at each other. By this time Aybee had decided what they were. They had the build of Inner System inhabitants but not the Sunhugger look. Both of them hailed from farther out, yet both of them were used to gravity. That meant the Kernel Ring, living in close proximity to shielded kernels.

"We'll test that in a little while," the man said. Aybee noticed that he was wearing a kernel ruby in his shoulder epaulet. "D' you know math, too?"

"Some." There was a fine line to be walked. Too much knowledge might be as dangerous as too little.

"Then if you know an adequate amount, you'll have a choice. Either you can go to a Halo development project, a long way from here, and work with no one but a few of the other farmers and a lot of machines. That's what all your friends will be doing, helping to build a new farm—the Halo is short of metals, too. Or if you're really willing to work with people, we have a more interesting prospect to offer you."

"I don't like the sound of no farm. I've had it with farms. Tell me about the other thing."

"Not yet." The woman was looking at him suspiciously. "First, we want to hear *you* talk, and make sure you can say more than a few phrases. You can start by telling us why you're different from the rest of the farmers. They haven't said ten words between them."

That was a nasty question. If he seemed too different from the other farmers, these people would wonder why. If he were too similar, he would be sent out to the edge of nowhere and spend the rest of his life building a collector to sieve stray atoms from nothing.

If you have to lie, make the lies little ones. "I was the interface," he said at last. "With people from the harvesters. When engineers came to the farm, *somebody* had to work with them. We all had a psych profile run. I looked like the best choice. So I got special training. I sorta liked it, wanted to do it more. Mebbe even get a job away from the farm."

The man nodded, but the woman leaned forward and stared Aybee in the eye. Her own eyes, glowing brown with a yellow center to the iris, gave her a feral appearance. She had the dedicated face of a fanatic. "Did you interface with the group that came to the space farm from the Opik Harvester just a couple of days ago?"

"Yeah." Aybee did not even blink. "They insisted on a face-to-face with us. I met 'em, four of 'em. My special training came in real useful."

"How long were you with them?"

"Not long. Ten minutes, mebbe. I been wondering what happened to 'em since the impact. Were they all killed?"

"Why do you care?"

"Dunno. Guess I wondered if they were here, too. They're like me, don't mind working with other people. *Are* they here?"

"No. They went back where they came from. We saw their ship leaving."

Aybee hid his relief. But the woman was suspicious again. "Why do you care about them? Never mind, I'll accept that you talk. It seems to me maybe you talk a little too well. I don't know how you could stand it on the space farm."

"Let's give him the test," the man said. "If he's lying about what he knows, we don't have to waste more time talking."

The woman shrugged and slid two sheets of paper across the table to Aybee. "Write your answers right there if you want to," she said. "Or say them out loud to us. We don't care."

"I'd rather write. If you have something I can write with." Aybee had seen the first page of questions and had a new worry. If the tests were all like this one, he needed time to think. He was being asked things so elementary that he was not sure how much ignorance he should feign. For what those people had in mind, ought he to know Newton's laws of motion and Maxwell's equations and the classical definitions of entropy? Almost certainly. But how about Price's theorem and spinors and Killing vectors? They were on the list, too, along with Newman-Penrose constants and Petrov classification. He had written papers on each of those, but he did not want anyone to suspect that. The questions themselves were also a tantalizing hint as to the work he might be expected to do. He would certainly be working with kernels.

He took the pen they gave him and carefully wrote out his answers. Two wrong out of each ten. That ought to be about right.

Aybee could see the irony of it. For half his life he had been trying to do well on stupid tests; now he had to do just well enough to be accepted but badly enough to be plausible.

He handed back the sheets and for the first time in his life sweated while he waited for test results. The man was reading his answers, and his expression was guarded.

At last the man looked up. "Did you work with the kernel on the space farm?"

"Some. Part of my job—to check power use and rotational state. Learned how to measure the optical scalars. That was all."

"You're not afraid to go near a kernel?"

"Not if the shields are in good working order."

"I'll second that." The man flipped the pages casually onto the table. He turned to the woman. "What do you think, Gudrun? It's your decision."

She nodded. "Do you work hard?"

At last, a question that Aybee could answer comfortably. "You bet. Harder than anyone I know. Try me."

"I guess we will. You have to know one more thing before you say yes or no. If you join us, you'll have a chance to become a full part of our group. We have big plans, but we're few in numbers. That means wonderful opportunities. But many people do not understand the importance of our goals. Once you join us, you'll be considered a rebel by the Outer System. Now let me ask you directly. Do you want the assignment?"

"I think so." Aybee nodded his head slowly. He had to appear interested, but cautious. "The Outer System never did nothing for me. I never asked to be out on the farm. Guess I'd like to know more about your deal, though, before I'm sure."

"Fair enough." For the first time the woman smiled and held out her hand. "You're on for a trial run. I'm Gudrun. This is Jason. What's your name?"

Spacehooks. What's my name? Better pick somebody real.

Aybee groped for the name of his first instructor in calculus. "Karl Lyman."

"Welcome to the program, Karl. Are you tired?"

"Nothing special."

"Then let's go and eat." She saw his expression and laughed. "I don't mean *with* me. Don't worry, we know what people are like in the Outer System. You can have your own cubicle; you won't have to look at anybody taking meals. But I want to find out a bit more about you and tell you what you'll be doing." She gave him another look, one of a shared secret. "I liked your answers to that test, and I think maybe you were wasting your time on the farm. You may be able to go a lot farther with us than you realize."

As they stood up, she moved to his side and looked up at him. "One thing, though. You're too tall for this place. We don't even have a bed to fit you. When you've started work, Karl, we'll give you a spell in a form-change tank and cut you down to size."

Aybee put on a worried frown. "D' yer think it's safe? I mean, we've had bad trouble with form-change equipment on the farm. Bad stuff coming out of it. Suppose yours don't work right, either?"

Gudrun and Jason exchanged a quick look. "Don't worry your head about that," the man said. "That's something we can guarantee—absolutely. You'll have no trouble with our form-change equipment."

They led the way on into the interior of the ship. Aybee, following close behind, pondered that final remark. Gudrun and Jason, whoever they were working for, had plenty of confidence and conviction. They acted as though they had a direct pipeline to the secrets of the universe. Could they deliver a safe form-change operation, though, where the whole Outer System was failing?

Aybee wondered if he had become an instant convert to their fanaticism. Somehow, he was sure they could deliver what they promised.

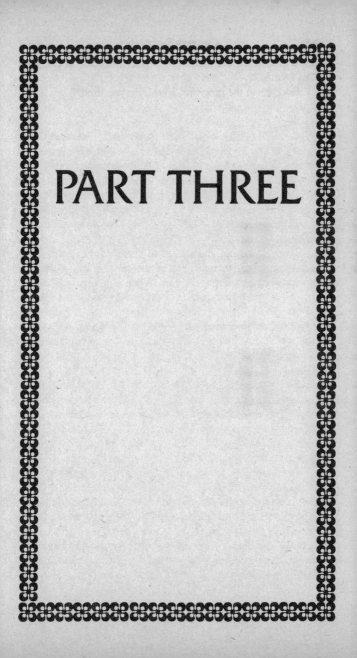

PART THREE

CHAPTER 18

"So when this world's compounded union breaks,
Time ends, and to old Chaos all things turn."
—Christopher Marlowe

Bey Wolf had inherited a good stubborn streak from his German father and a subtle and suspicious mind from his Persian mother. Both parts of the combination were needed now. He was stuck in the middle of a rank impossibility.

He had analyzed defective form-change runs. They ranged from minor flaws too subtle to be detected in outward appearance to grotesque end forms that could never have survived in any environment known to Bey. Every one was different, but in one way all were alike. The ferret routines he had introduced into the purposive form-change programs confirmed that there had been systematic modifications to whole sections of code; they pointed always to the same impossible blind alley. The changes were no accident. They were so complicated that they had to have been generated by a computer— but in a place where no computer capability existed on the harvester.

He swore and grumbled and grunted to himself. His work had gone on obsessively for several days, broken only by hurried meals and occasional naps. He had not washed or changed his clothes. He was surrounded by empty disposable plates and cups, listings, diagnostic trace routines, system flow diagrams, and his own scribbled notes and questions. Paper was everywhere, sprawling across the floor and over every available surface.

Bey was totally frustrated and oddly content. No one on the harvester could help him, and he did not want help. He wanted to solve it *himself*. He did not admit it, but intense concentration was also a form of therapy. He wanted to keep the disturbing thought of Mary Walton's visitation out of his head.

Sylvia Fernald had stopped by a couple of times in the first day of work. She had watched his efforts sympathetically, spoken to him, and left when it was clear that his mind was elsewhere. On the third day Leo Manx had also appeared. He came to the door of the room several times, stared in disgust at the mess, and hobbled away. The wounds he had received on the space farm were not yet fully healed, but he was in no apparent discomfort.

When Leo came by for the fourth time, he stayed, standing silent in the doorway and puzzling over a blue folder he had brought with him. Bey Wolf ignored him until a final and irrefutable statistical analysis came back on the display screen. At that point he swore at length, switched off the unit, and turned to the other man.

"That does it. I know exactly *what* happened—and I've no idea how."

Manx looked up from his own musings. "If you've discovered anything useful, you're making more progress than I am. What have you found? Cinnabar Baker will want to know."

Wolf waved his arm at the sea of listings covering the floor around them. "I have output trace listings of everything. Do you know how the harvester computer system works?"

Manx frowned at the question. "Well, I feel sure it's a straightforward distributed system. There's computing capacity and major storage in a couple of hundred nodes located at different points in the harvester, and local storage with limited compute power at a few hundred more. Everything is tied together through a fiber communications system. It's exactly like the integrated computer system on the other harvesters—or in your own Office of Form Control, back on Earth."

"My ex-office. So there's nothing unusual about the arrangement?"

"Of course not." Manx had stepped gingerly into the middle of the paper jungle and was carefully collecting the listings into neat piles. "Bey, you must have known all this days ago—you couldn't generate these message traces without knowing."

"I thought I did." Wolf grabbed an elaborate schematic. "The general structure is shown here. I took this, and I began to search for places in the system where spurious coding sequences could be introduced to modify the form-change programs. Watch now."

He switched on the wall-size display screen. "I've color-coded this. You need to know what they mean. The blue network is the overall connection plan for the distributed computer system. The red nodes show where we have data storage; green ones show computer elements. Purple dots are sensors—data collection points for the computer system. Orange dots are form-change tanks. They have some of their own storage and computer power, but they rely on the master system for some data and computation. Understood?"

"Perfectly. I hope there's a point to all this."

"There is. Just watch. I spent days working it out. You're going to see my ferret routines, chasing down all the places where false code might have come into the system. We'll do just one case now, for a form-change anomaly they had in the resource control office of this harvester. Watch the moving yellow tracer." Bey entered the command and leaned back in his chair.

For a moment or two the display was static. Then a fine yellow line appeared at one of the orange dots and crawled across the screen. It reached a green node and divided there, then two yellow daughter traces continued on their way to a red element of the schematic.

"Picking up data from two different banks," Bey said. "That happens a lot."

The yellow lines crept onward, reaching new computer nodes, sometimes branching, sometimes terminating there. After thirty seconds a complete tree structure had been established, starting at a single form-change tank and spreading across half the screen.

"That's one complete form-change operation," Bey said.

"It's too complicated. I can't follow all that structure."

"Nor could I, without help. The central controller used whatever computer power happened to be available—that's why you see so many green nodes in use. It's a horrible mess. Now, I'm going to add the other hundred and fifty-six cases, all at once. You'd expect the picture to become even worse, impossibly complicated."

"It's impossibly complicated already."

"I agree. But it simplifies. Watch." Bey entered a new command. The whole screen lit up with a tracery of moving yellow lines. They each began at a form-change tank and branched and zigzagged across the display. Thirty seconds later the screen steadied. Leo Manx shook his head. Lines were everywhere, a tangled mass of knotted interconnections, convoluted and horribly interwoven.

"I hope you don't expect me to read anything useful out of that."

"With a little help you will." Bey was busy again at the terminal. "I agree it still looks like a gigantic mess. So I wrote another program to help sort it out. I asked for a statistical analysis of the places where each branching set *ended*. That would tell me how often the form changes were using a particular data storage bank, or a particular computer. If one storage area or computer was receiving unusually heavy use, that would be a good place to do some troubleshooting. Take a look at what I found. The program flags every terminating node that occurs more than two sigma away from the mean for all nodes."

A couple of dozen points on the screen began to blink. Leo

Manx stared at them blankly. "Very interesting," he said after a few seconds.

"You're wrong. It *is* interesting—once you look at those nodes more closely." Bey stood up and went to the wall display. "Some end at computer elements; some end at data banks. Very reasonable. But what about this one?" He was pointing at a flashing purple point on the screen.

"What about it?"

"Leo, remember the color code. Purple. That means it's a *sensor*—a place that collects data for the computer system."

"That's not surprising. There are sensors on each form-change tank."

"True. Not surprising—*if* this were a sensor associated with a form-change tank. It would be collecting physical readings from the tank and using them in the programs. But this sensor should have nothing to do with a form-change process. And *every* form-change anomaly has a branch that ends there. That sensor was involved *every single time* we had a form-change problem."

Manx had stood up and was craning to see the blinking point next to Bey's finger. "I don't know which sensor that is. Are you sure it's not a form-change monitor?"

"I checked it a dozen times. It's not. So I decided that it had to be a signal coming from *outside* the harvester, maybe something we were picking up on beamed data from an external antenna. It's not that, either."

"Don't keep telling me what it *isn't*." Leo Manx was losing his usual courtly politeness. "We have to check this directly. Which sensor is it?"

"I'll tell you, but you're not going to like the answer." Bey tapped the display. "That sensor is inside the harvester, but it's in the hardest place of all to check. It monitors the radiation level from the harvester's kernel, and that means it's sitting where we can't get at it. *Inside* the kernel shields."

Leo was shaking his head. "You're suggesting that somebody put a computer and a data storage unit in there? It couldn't happen. Nothing but hardened sensors can operate inside the shields—even the remote-handling machines that manipulate the kernels don't have programs."

"I know. But I'm convinced there's *something* there, inside the shield. Some information source, some chaos generator for the form-change process. It's the 'negentropic' influence again—spurious information that's the source of disruption for the whole system."

"But the other problems we've had were nothing to do with form-change!"

"We've gone past form-change now, Leo. Form-change just happens to be highly sensitive to signal control sequences. Problems show up there first. But what I've found takes us into kernel control theory, and that's a different game. I don't know enough about Kerr-Newman black holes to decide what's going on. That's why I've been waiting for Aybee to get back from the Sagdeyev space farm."

"Then you might have to wait a long time. He's not there."

"But he's on the way back, isn't he?"

"I'm afraid not." Leo Manx retreated to a cleared area of the floor and sat down cross-legged. "Before I came here I was with Cinnabar Baker. She'd just had a report from a repair and maintenance crew who had reached the farm. Apparently it's totally deserted. No farmers, no Aybee."

"More mechanical trouble?"

"No signs of that. The bubble was halfway repaired, reasonably habitable. But deserted. It was just as though everyone had decided to down tools at the same time and leave. We have no idea why they went or where they went. Or even *how* they went. Baker says that no transit vessel was missing. All they took with them were their suits. There was no sign of new violence."

"So it could be worse. Aybee's probably safe. And he's a survival type." Bey left the screen and flopped down untidily on a pile of output listings. He was almost at home in his new body, but the odd center of mass offered occasional surprises. "But it's very bad for me. I don't know who else to ask."

"We have other experts on the kernels."

"Not like Aybee. I need somebody who thinks around

corners." Suddenly Wolf's labors were catching up with him.
He was exhausted.

"And so do I." For the first time, Leo Manx held up his
own blue folder. "That's why I came to you. You've got your
problems, I've got mine. Aybee got me started on this before
we left the farm. I need him as much as you do. But he told
me to talk to you if he wasn't there—I don't know if you
cherish the notion, but Aybee suggests that you and he think
about things the same way."

"He's wrong." Bey made no attempt to take the proffered
folder. He was still staring moodily at the display screen.
"Aybee's smarter than I am, but he makes me feel a thousand
years old. I don't have his childlike faith. If I can't solve my
own problems, I'm sure I can't solve anybody else's."

It was a dismissive comment; at that point Leo Manx was
supposed to stand up and leave. Instead he inched forward
along the floor and placed the folder open on Bey's knees.

"The Negentropic Man," he said. Bey looked down at him,
then shook his head.

"Where he came from," Manx went on. "What he means.
Aybee listed four ways of thinking about entropy: thermodynamic entropy, statistical mechanics entropy, information
theory entropy, and kernel entropy. But he couldn't suggest
which meaning was appropriate."

"Nor can I."

"That's all right. I don't want to ask you about that." Manx
lifted one sheet from the folder. "Aybee suggested that if we
want to make progress we ought to examine the exact time
when your hallucinations occurred. I've made a list of everything that you told me when we were in transit from the Inner
System. Now I'd like to make sure it's complete."

Bey stared gloomily at the list. He knew what Leo was
doing: exactly what he would have done himself with a reluctant partner. Bait him with something he was interested in,
reel him in slowly, and hope that after a few minutes he could
be dragged far enough to be useful.

Well, what the hell. It was a game two could play, and Bey
had gone as far as he could in the form-change tracking with-

out allowing time for his ideas to sort themselves out.

"You only want to hear about my seeing the Negentropic Man? You know that Sylvia is sure he's Black Ransome?"

"I know. We have only her word for it. Isn't the Negentropic Man the only person you saw in your hallucinations?"

"He was, until a few days ago." Wolf did not look up. He was not sure he wanted to tell anyone at all about Mary's strange visit. It felt remote and improbable. Even the day after it happened, he had become half-convinced that he had dreamed the whole episode. "I saw Mary Walton," he said at last. "After I came out of the change tank."

"You mean—saw her in person?"

"No. A recorded message, left in my sleeping quarters."

"And you didn't tell Sylvia or Cinnabar Baker?"

"No." Bey hesitated for a moment, evaluating the risk. He decided that he had to trust *somebody*—they could not all be spies. "Leo, I had a reason why I didn't talk about this. We have an information leak here. We arrived from the space farm just a few weeks ago. No one knew we were coming; no one even knew we had survived the 'accident' there. No messages were sent out from here *after* we arrived, saying we were here. I know, because I checked the message center myself. And yet, as soon as I went to my sleeping quarters, a planted recorded message from Mary Walton was waiting for me. Leo, until I was taken to those quarters, I didn't know *myself* where I would be sleeping."

"So that's why you didn't talk about it to me, or Sylvia Fernald, or Cinnabar Baker?" Manx was full of unfocused energy that made his arms and legs jerk like a puppet's. "Bey, I know you're not used to Outer System ways, and I know where you're heading. But it's crazy. Those are terribly serious charges that you're making, and it's just as well you told this only to me. I can absolutely assure you that Sylvia and Cinnabar are not providing information leaks."

"Not *intentional* ones, maybe. But think back, Leo. Somebody seemed to know we were going to the farm almost before we set out. Somebody knew we were here the moment we arrived."

"Then it must be somebody on the harvester staff."

"On two different harvesters? We left the Opik Harvester; we came back here to the Marsden Harvester. Are you suggesting that there are *two* leaks, both close to Cinnabar Baker, one on each harvester?"

"Then who? I hope you don't think that *I*—"

"There's an old Earth saying: 'Everyone's suspect but me and thee; and I'm none too sure of thee.' I thought about you. But I don't see how it could be. When we arrived here you were in pretty bad shape, and you went straight to the tank for remedial form-change work. You weren't conscious until after this happened."

"Your faith in me is touching. I wonder why you're telling me now."

The bait was taken. Time to reel in the line. Slowly. "Because I need your help, Leo. And I want your word that you won't pass this on to anyone, unless we've discussed it first. And I mean *anyone*."

"Not Sylvia? Not even Baker?"

"*Especially* not Baker. Can't you see that if we're logical, her office is the only place where the leaks can start? Don't tell her anything, unless it's at a meeting that I've arranged, in a place I arrange. I think we should talk to Sylvia and see how she responds to the idea of a spy in our group. Will you come with me, right now, and do it?"

"Under one condition." Manx took back his blue folder and looked at it in a puzzled way. Somehow the whole conversation had headed off in an unintended direction.

"Anything reasonable."

"Then you take a shower first. I don't want Sylvia or anyone else we meet to think that smell is coming from me."

"Is this the Leo Manx who dragged me out of Old City? All right. If you insist. Let's go."

Later, Bey would describe the shower as a wasted effort. As soon as he was scrubbed clean and dressed in clean clothing to Leo Manx's satisfaction, they headed for Sylvia's quarters.

But she was not there. No one knew where she was or

when she would be back. Twelve hours earlier, Sylvia Fernald had requisitioned a high-g transit ship. She had headed inward, toward the edge of the Halo, traveling fast and traveling alone. She had told no one her mission, and no one on the harvester seemed to know her destination.

CHAPTER 19

"Stone walls do not a prison make,
 Nor iron bars a cage."
              —Richard Lovelace

"But empty space does a pretty good job
of it."
       —Apollo Belvedere "Aybee" Smith

The training schedule was rigorous but reasonable. Four hours of theory in the morning, a food break at which all the trainees were expected to eat together and discuss what they had learned, four hours of practical work in the afternoon, and then the evening free, but with enough reading, interactive education sessions, and quizzes to fill at least another six hours before sleeping.

The program was scheduled to continue for seven weeks. Aybee kept his head down for the first couple of days, watched what the others were doing, and tried to fall nicely in the middle of the group when it came to tests and answering questions. That was not so easy. The rest of the trainees were a miserable, mismatched set who had apparently been dragged in from random sources. In Aybee's not so humble opinion, none of them had the least idea of any kind of science, and a couple of them acted positively half-witted. They offered bizarre answers to the simplest mathematical questions—Aybee could not figure out how they came up with such odd replies.

On the third day he made his first request. He was not used to eating food with other people; it would be a lot less of a strain if he were allowed to take the midday break alone. Could he get permission?

Gudrun looked doubtful, but she agreed. There were twenty-four trainees, and Aybee's absence would not make much difference to the discussions. "Remember, Karl," she added. "If you hurt your progress because you can't talk to others while what you've learned is fresh in your mind, you'll have no one but yourself to blame. If the reason you're doing this is that you find the work difficult and you're embarrassed to talk with the others, come and see me. I'll arrange personal coaching for you."

Aybee/Karl nodded politely. He had gained an hour. The morning classes so far had covered routine general relativity material three centuries old, and he did not need to discuss that with anyone. More than that, he did not want to. The big danger was that he would reveal how much he knew about the subject.

The evening work was a joke. He did not need to do the reading, and he could handle all the rest of the assignments in the middle of the day. His next request to Gudrun was a little more risky. He handed in a perfect test, which he was usually careful to avoid doing, and went to see Gudrun that afternoon.

She beamed as he came in the door. "Well! Smart Karl. You don't seem to be harmed by missing the midday sessions."

"Hope not." Aybee had the horrible feeling that he was her favorite trainee. She always looked at him in a special way. "But I'm not used to high gravity. Not like the farm. I sleep bad here. Wake up a lot in the middle of the night. If I'm all done with my work an' that happens, could I look around the ship?"

He saw the danger signs. Her smile vanished, and she was

staring at him suspiciously. "Look at *what* in the ship, Karl?"

"Dunno. Whatever." He waved his arm vaguely around them. "Power supplies, maintenance shops. Anything."

"Oh, that shouldn't be a problem. But only if you still do well enough in your training. Let's see how you perform in the next few days."

She was not worried about security—she was worried that he would take too much time wandering around and flunk! Aybee made fewer deliberate mistakes on the tests, and three days later he had his permission. He was fascinated to see what was off-limits: armories, main drives, and the areas where the suits and transit ships were kept. It made good sense for them to keep him out of there until they were absolutely sure about his loyalties. It was also no big loss. So long as they were steaming along to nowhere, Aybee did not like the idea of leaving the ship until he knew exactly where he was.

There was one big unexpected freedom. He would be allowed to go to the kernels and do what he liked there. Gudrun must have decided that he was not interested in suicide by fiddling with a power kernel and blowing up the whole ship. It also tended to confirm what she had said at their first meeting. When the training course was over, he would be working with the kernels.

The first night he had permission to wander, he could not use it. A formal evening meeting was scheduled for all the trainees. After a special dinner that Aybee did not eat, they were subjected to a four-hour session of live and recorded speeches, slogans, and arm waving.

Gudrun stood up and offered her version of system history. Between the millstones of the Inner and Outer Systems, the inhabitants of the Halo had been crushed for over a century. The Kernel Ring was a borderland, a dangerous region of scattered high-density bodies. As a result, all the travelers from Sunhugger territory bypassed it on their journeys outward. They were quite willing to exploit its energy supplies, but none of the wealth generated from the Kernel Ring's resources was ever returned to it. That was unjust and intolerable. Finally, it was going to change. The balance of power had shifted. The Halo had a born leader, and the revolution had begun.

Jason came next, and he was worse: The Outer System is composed of oppressive tyrants! The Inner System is decadent! It supports an idle and growing population by the efforts of our people! Both federations deserve to fall! You are all part of a great reform that will achieve those ends—and soon!

Aybee hid his yawns, but he noticed that the other trainees were lapping it up. Gudrun, Jason, and the handful of other permanent crew of the ship knew how to whip up enthusiasm. They had enough for everybody. Gudrun stood up again for another statement. A special announcement would be made on the ship in a few days, reporting an event that was truly extraordinary. All training would be interrupted when it happened, and everyone would have two days free. The group cheered.

Aybee cheered as loudly as anyone and wondered if propaganda had a cumulative effect. If so, he would have to find a way to escape before his own brain was softened.

Escape seemed harder and harder. All the access points to suits, transit ships, and weapons were guarded not by humans, which would have been bad, but by machines, Roguards that did not sleep, could not be distracted, and could not be persuaded.

Aybee decided that he needed a radically new approach. The next night, he set out to prowl the ship.

He had no illusions about the size of the task that faced him. The ship was small compared with the central sphere of a harvester, but it was still huge. With a length of two kilometers and a diameter of six hundred meters, the ship he was on had enough internal volume to house a couple of million Earth people—or one or two space farmers. Podders and the rebels of the Kernel Ring sat somewhere between those two extremes, but Aybee could not guess at the ship's internal structure from the limited regions he had seen in training.

Fortunately, he did not need to. Overall ship schematics were held in a central data bank, and he had been studying them in the evenings for over a week. There were half a dozen blank spots in the plans, which he assumed corresponded to regions of special privacy, but all the rest of the ship was there.

As an experiment, he headed outward toward the surface. The ship had been built to carry cargo, and so all the internal bulkheads and corridors were a later addition. The whole habitat interior had an unfinished and neglected look. Mildewed partitions were warped and grimy, and at central communications nodes, masses of cables and fiber lines festooned the walls and ceilings.

Aybee wandered on, committing everything he saw to memory. If the need ever arose, he wanted to be able to run through the ship blindfolded.

No one questioned him; no one stopped him. In a few minutes he was at an observation port, peering through the outer shell of the hull to the stars beyond. He could tell from the positions of the constellations that the ship was heading Sunward, but that was all he was able to deduce. He watched quietly for ten minutes. There were no signs of other man-made vessels out there or of natural bodies of the Outer System.

When he finally moved on, easing his way along the hull toward the nearest air lock, a Roguard appeared at his side before he had gone fifty meters. It seemed to ignore him, but it moved as he did and did not respond to his questions and commands. Twenty meters before he reached the lock, it passed silently in front of him and extended a broad polymer net to block his path.

Aybee did not try to talk to it. The machine was too stupid for logic. Instead, he turned to head away from the surface. When he was forty meters from the ship's hull, the machine dropped behind. He turned to look and saw it disappearing through a service aperture. Aybee did not go back. If he did, he was sure that it or its sister Roguard would be there again to balk his progress toward the air locks. Instead he headed down the gravity gradient for the nearest kernel, two hundred meters away.

In the corridors he encountered a couple of dozen maintenance machines and three humans. The machines offered him friendly greetings. The humans, each two feet shorter than Aybee, said not a word. They hardly looked at him, and they seemed preoccupied with their own worries.

Was it his trainee's uniform, which made him so much lower in status than anyone else on the ship that they would not even talk to him? If so, that was fine with Aybee. He traveled on along a dirty passageway coated with the grime of a decade's neglect. Somehow the controller of the cleaning machines seemed to have lost the narrow alley from its memory.

He passed down a narrow final stair just wide enough for his skinny body, and he was there. The shielded kernel was not the one that had been removed from the space farm. It was a monster. Even at the outer shield's thirty-meter radius, Aybee judged that he was standing in a field of over a twentieth of a g. That put the kernel mass at nearly eight billion tons. It must have been found near the middle of the *Zirkelloch*, the circular singularity that formed the center of the Kernel Ring.

That did not mean it was particularly useful as a controllable power source. If it were a slowly rotating kernel, approximately a Schwarzschild black hole, it was useless for anything except raw heat.

Was this one rotating?

Aybee fixed his eyes on one point on the ceiling and crouched low. No doubt about it, the kernel was both massive and rotating extremely rapidly. He could feel the inertial dragging as the kernel's spin rotated the reference frame along with it, tilting the local vertical.

He turned his attention to the controls. Most of them were already familiar to him. There were a dozen superconducting electromagnets holding the charged kernel firmly at the center of its spherical shields. They appeared standard, no different from systems Aybee had seen in dozens of other energy-generation facilities.

There was the energy-extraction mechanism itself, clearly

identifiable by its plasma injection units. The system was unusually finely calibrated, allowing far smaller changes to the kernel's rotational energy than any that Aybee had seen before, but that was an easy technological refinement, within the power of any kernel user. It was not clear why anyone would *want* to do it.

The first sign of real oddity came in the sensor leads. They were ten times as big as Aybee had expected, suggesting a high signal-carrying capacity, and they ran to a substantial computer sitting right on the outer shield.

A computer to do what?

Inside the shield, the spinning black hole of the kernel was sending out a seething stream of radiation and particles. That random energy emission was a nuisance, and the shields were a necessity to reflect it back on itself. At the same time, the sensors monitoring the outward flood within the shields allowed the mass, charge, and angular momentum of the kernel to be measured to one part in a trillion.

Aybee crouched on the dull black surface of the outer shield, staring at the computer and its connecting cables for a long time. He would have loved to follow those optic bundles a meter or so farther, beyond the shields. It was impossible. There were hatches for robot access, but he would not have survived a moment inside the shields.

He stood up, puzzled, and stared thoughtfully at the sensor leads for a few minutes. When he finally wandered through the corridors back to his own quarters, his head was whirling with ideas and conjectures. He had theories but no way to test them. What he needed was a long spell of quiet thought.

What he found when he arrived at his room was Gudrun. She was sitting on his bed. She had abandoned her silver-blue uniform and badged cap for a brief black exercise suit and purple skin makeup. Gudrun nodded at him and patted the bed next to her.

Aybee eyed her uneasily and remained standing. "I was just taking a look around."

"I know. Sit down, Karl."

He placed himself at the far end of the bed. "I'm doing all

right, aren't I?" He cleared his throat. "I mean, no problem with my work."

"Just the opposite." She inched along closer to him. "Karl, you've been doing well, but I'm convinced you could do a lot better. Some of your answers on the tests are so concise and clear, they're better than anything in the training manuals. I'm using them as reference material. Where do you get them from?"

Aybee swore internally and shrugged. "Dunno. I just write what I think of."

"If you can think that way consistently, there's more in your future than a job as a maintenance engineer. I want to do something special with you."

"What do you mean?" Aybee did not like the look in her eye.

"I want to take you to meet the big boss—the head of the whole revolution and movement. We have his orders to sift for unusual potential and report it to headquarters." She misread his concern. "Don't worry, I wouldn't send you there alone. We'd go together, just you and me, on one of the special high-acceleration transit ships. I'd be your sponsor."

"When?" The training course had five more weeks to run.

"In a couple of days. Jason and the other assistants can handle the training course easily enough. It's five days travel from here to headquarters in the new ship, but we wouldn't waste the time. You have a lot to learn. I'd give you personal coaching and special training." Gudrun had moved Aybee all the way to the end of the bed, and he could not retreat farther. Her golden-brown eyes were gleaming. She took his hands in hers and stared at him possessively. "And we still haven't done that form-change, have we? The one that we talked about when you signed on. You're still too tall for comfort. We'll work on that. There might be some spare time for a form-change on the journey, too. I want to make you look more like one of us—less like a Cloudlander." She squeezed his hands. "What do you say, Karl? It's a one-time opportunity."

Five days confined to a high-g transit cabin with Gudrun.

Five days of "personal coaching" and "special training." What did that include? He had horrible suspicions. Aybee avoided her gaze, but she was very close. Everywhere he looked he saw nothing but bare flesh, plump thighs, arms and shoulders and breasts.

"Well, Karl, what do you say?" She was whispering, close to his cheek.

Aybee closed his eyes in horror. Do I have a choice?

He took a deep breath. Look at it this way, Apollo Belvedere Smith: You go to headquarters and the chances of finding out if your ideas are right are a hell of a lot better there than they are here. Whatever happens on the journey, you can handle it. So say yes quick, before you decide you can't stand the idea.

He nodded, eyes still closed. "It sounds . . . wonderful."

He felt Gudrun's hand on his thigh. "I'll make sure that it is," she said. "We'll leave tomorrow. I'll put a form-change tank and size-reduction programs on the ship, too. You can use them as much as you want to. But you'd better get some rest now, Karl. You need your rest."

"Yeah." Aybee swallowed. "I think I do."

She was moving slowly away from him. He could breathe again. He looked at her red lips and half-open mouth. She seemed ready to eat him.

Just make sure the form-change tank and size-reduction program is there, Gudrun, he thought. I'll use 'em, all right. In fact, if this trip is anything like I imagine, I'll use 'em over and over. I'm going to arrive at headquarters as a two-foot midget.

CHAPTER 20

"I disapprove of every conspiracy of which I am not a part."

—Cinnabar Baker

Sylvia Fernald had agonized over the decision for a long time. Who should be told what she was planning to do, and how much should they be told?

On the one hand, her attempt to contact Paul Chu was in no sense an official mission. She had not been ordered to do it or even asked to think about it. On the other hand, Bey Wolf and Aybee Smith believed that the rebels were behind the technical malfunctions in the Inner and Outer Systems, and they agreed with Cinnabar Baker that the rebels' end objective might be to instigate an all-out war between the other two parties. If that were the case, and if Paul were part of the rebel group, a dialog with him was supremely important. Sylvia knew of no one else who might be able to open that dialog. Paul had always been secretive and mistrustful, but he would talk to Sylvia.

Wouldn't he? They had been very close, but in the final months she had never known what Paul was thinking or even what he was doing. But surely he would at least *talk* to her— they had been partners for more than three years. On the other hand, if he had become a rebel himself, she ought not to be talking to him, and if she did meet with him, she should not tell anyone she was doing it.

Sylvia wondered and worried and at last settled for a compromise. Since she would be using a Cloudland ship in her travels, someone in government had to know and approve it. But the fewer people who knew, the less the danger that her mission would be leaked to others.

Sylvia looked at her options. Leo Manx was a good man but pedantic in approach and—much more dangerous—apt to gossip. Bey Wolf would not talk, but he would probably try to stop her. Aybee, her first choice, was off who knew where, and all her other close friends in the harvesters would be overwhelmed by the implied responsibility. They would feel a compulsion to tell their superiors—who might then tell anyone.

In the end, Sylvia called Cinnabar Baker directly and asked for a private meeting. If the information were likely to end with Baker, it might as well begin there.

The other woman asked her—typically—to come to her quarters that same day, but at one o'clock in the morning. Sylvia spent the next twelve hours making final preparations for her departure and rehearsing what she was going to say to Baker. But when she finally entered the bare-walled apartment, she forgot about her prepared speech.

Cinnabar Baker looked terrible. She had lost fifty or sixty pounds, and her gray-toned skin was lined and pouchy. From time to time she rubbed at her eyes, wheezed deep in her chest, and produced a rumbling cough. Turpin sat blinking on her shoulder. Each time she coughed, the bedraggled crow provided an impressive imitation of the sound. He must have had plenty of time to practice.

"I know." Baker saw Sylvia's dismay. "Don't tell me I look like hell, and don't worry. It's not permanent. I've been overworking, and everyone here is scared to let me near the formchange machines for a remedial session. The machines are so messed up, people are afraid I'll turn into a pumpkin. What can I do for you? We have ten minutes."

Sylvia jumped into her description of how she had found a trail that should lead to Paul Chu. Half her explanation proved unnecessary—Cinnabar Baker knew more about the relationship with Chu than Sylvia had dreamed. Baker waved her on past that, then listened in a silence broken only by her coughs and hoarse breathing.

At the end of it Baker sniffed and pinched the end of her nose between her fingers. "I've heard your reports, and the ones from Leo Manx. Do you agree with him that the rebels are behind Bey Wolf's problems with the 'Negentropic Man'?"

"I think so."

"You've saved Wolf's life at least once, probably twice. Do you know what the ancient Chinese, back on Earth, used to say if you saved a man from drowning?"

Sylvia shook her head in confusion. Cinnabar Baker had lost her.

"They would say you are then responsible for the welfare of that man for the whole rest of his life. Let me ask you, how much of what you're proposing to do is for the sake of the Outer System? And how much are you doing to help with Wolf's personal problems?"

The suggestion floored Sylvia.

She had acted to save Bey on the transit ship and on the space farm without thinking for a moment about her own motives. She would have done as much for anyone. And as for sitting beside the form-change tank while Bey Wolf was in it . . .

"Don't bother to answer that." Cinnabar Baker was moving on. The allotted ten minutes had passed. "Tell me this instead. You're proposing to leave at once. What's the hurry? Why not wait a few more days?"

"More days?" Turpin repeated.

Sylvia shook her head. "I daren't. Paul Chu is at that location to perform a facility conversion, adding a low-g drive— probably to a cometary fragment. That means he'll be working alone except for machines. We'll be able to talk freely. But that will last only another couple of weeks, then he'll be leaving. I don't know where he'll be going next."

"Does he know anything about this?"

"Not a thing. I didn't suggest to *anyone* that I might try to visit him. You're the only person who knows I'm even thinking of it." She saw the slow nod of Cinnabar Baker's head. "You will approve it, then?"

Baker grunted. "Fernald, I never did like Paul Chu. I remember him, and I don't believe he'll do one thing to help you." She held up her hand. "But before you begin to argue, let me tell you I'm going to approve your request. You ought to have this job for a day. You'd approve *anything* that might give you a toehold on our problems. The Cloud's technology is all going to hell, people daren't go near the form-change machines, we've been receiving communications from some of the other harvesters that suggest the populations there have all gone crazy, and I just had a report from the other side of the Cloud about a bad accident on another of the space farms. To top that off, one of our inbound cargo ships was destroyed yesterday, and the Sunhuggers are blaming *us* for it—saying we blew up one of our own vessels!"

She sighed. "All right. You've heard enough of that. Of course I'll approve it. Go do it, and use my authority if you need it to get your ship. But one other thing," she added as Sylvia stood up. "This has to be a two-way street. You won't tell anyone where you're going. And I won't tell anyone, not even the Inner Council, what you are trying to do. If you get into hot water, I'll have to disown you. I'll even deny that you had my permission for a transit ship. We have a firm policy, you see: We don't deal with the rebels in any circumstances. Understood?"

Sylvia bit her lip, then nodded. "All right."

Cinnabar Baker reached out and took her hand in an unexpected gesture. "We never had a meeting tonight, Fernald, and you leave by the other exit. I have another group of people waiting outside. Good luck, and good hunting. You'll be a long way from home."

"From home," Turpin echoed hoarsely. The crow wagged his head. "Way from home."

That had been eight days earlier. Eight days of silence and solitude. Sylvia had maintained strict communications blackout all through the journey, even when the ship's drive was inactive and it was easy to send or receive signals.

But as she slowed to approach her final destination, the rendezvous only a few minutes away, her nervousness increased. The urge to send some kind of message back to Cinnabar Baker grew stronger. Sylvia had been provided with an ephemeris for a body in an orbit skirting the outer part of the Kernel Ring; she was told that Paul Chu should be there. But the positional data had come with an admonition to strict secrecy—and nothing else. She had not been told the nature of the object to which she was traveling, or whether it was large or small, man-made or natural, a colony or a military base. She had *assumed* a cometary fragment—why else would he be installing an add-on drive unit—but suppose that was wrong?

Well, she would know soon enough. At last the body was visible. From a distance of five kilometers it was like an irregular, granular egg, shining by internal lights. Sylvia turned the high-magnification sensors onto it. She was confused, and her nervousness had increased. The object was about three hundred meters long, too small to be a harvester, a colony, or a cargo ship, and the wrong shape for a transit vessel. That fit with the idea of a small comet nucleus, still rich in volatiles. Yet the pattern of ports and lights implied an inhabited body, and two docking ports and air locks were clearly visible on the surface.

If it were a natural body, then it was one that had already seen some internal tunneling and modifications. The newly installed drive unit was easily recognized, gleaming at the thicker end of the lumpy body.

Delay would not help, and she had not come so far for nothing. Sylvia was already in her suit. She allowed the transit ship to dock itself gently against the bigger port, opened the cabin, and went straight to the lock.

It was open, contrary to standard safety regulations. And the *inner* lock was open, too, which meant that the interior of the body was airless. If Paul Chu were inside, he was wearing a suit or he was a corpse. Sylvia noticed how loud her own breathing sounded in the helmet. She set her suit receiver to perform a frequency sweep and passed on through the inner air lock.

The first chamber had been carved from the water ice and carbon dioxide ice of the cometary interior, and it was clearly intended as a workshop and equipment-maintenance facility. There were plenty of signs that it had been recently inhabited, with cutting torches still attached to their fuel bottles in a tool shop chamber and an electrical generator in standby mode. Three or four construction machines were waiting patiently against one of the walls. Sylvia regarded them with irritation. They were obsolete models by Cloud standards. If they had been made just a little bit smarter, she could have asked them what was going on. As it was, they had been designed with a specialized vocabulary and understood nothing but mechanical construction tasks. If no one came along to give instructions, they would wait contentedly for a million years.

She passed on through a sliding partition, deeper into the interior. The scan on received signals had produced nothing, so she switched to an all-frequency broadcast. "Paul Chu. This is Sylvia." Her suit repeated the message automatically, over and over, and listened for any reply.

She had reached the temporary living quarters built by the machines near the center of the body. He was not there, but she saw many signs of his recent occupancy. That was definitely his computer link, the one he had used for ten years. No Cloudlander, no matter how long he was away from the Outer System, would ever leave metal objects strewn so casually around unless he knew he would be coming back soon or had been forced to leave in a great hurry.

Or dead, her mind said insistently.

She pushed away the thought. Perhaps Paul was somewhere on the other side of the body, or perhaps he had been temporarily called away.

But called away to what? And to where? She had seen no sign of other bodies in her approach, and her suit radio had an effective range of many thousands of kilometers.

Then suppose that he did not *want* to meet her and was hiding away to avoid an encounter? That thought rejected itself. How could he be hiding when he had no idea that she was even coming? He thought she was back in the Outer System.

Almost against her will, Sylvia set out to explore the desolate interior. Sometime, far in the past, it had been a human home for a long period. There were kitchens, bedrooms, even chambers set up for entertainment and exercise. Those rooms held harnesses, stretch bars, and workout machines, each with dials to measure effort level and progress. But over all the equipment and instruments lay a thin layer of sublimed ice. No one had touched anything there for years, maybe for decades.

In less than half an hour she was convinced that there was no one anywhere on the hollowed-out comet. She was alone. And only a few moments later she felt a strange vibration beneath her feet and sensed a slight pressure on the front of her suit. She knew at once what was happening. The air locks had been closed on the body's surface, and the interior was filling with air.

She set off, hurriedly retracing her steps toward the lock through which she had first entered. When she was halfway there a flicker of movement appeared at the end of a corridor.

"Paul?" She paused, her hand on the wall of the corridor. "Paul Chu? Is that you, Paul? Who is there?"

The corridor supported a full atmosphere, and her voice went echoing along the narrow passageway. There was no reply, but suddenly a little machine came scuttling into view and moved toward her. Ten feet away it paused. Sylvia was thrilled to see it. Unlike the others she had seen, this one she recognized as a very advanced model, one that was scarcely out of the development labs. It was a GA machine, a general assistance model that would perform hundreds of tasks with vocal direction and little human supervision. If it had to, it could fly her home in her own transit ship.

"What's been happening here?" She advanced on it confidently. No machine would harm her—no machine *could* harm her, except by accident. "Where are the people? Is Paul Chu here?"

It said nothing. The arrays of detectors on the front of the machine had tilted her way, and there was no doubt that it was aware of her presence. But when she was within a couple of paces, it began to back away. A second machine of the same design had appeared at the end of the corridor and advanced to stand next to the first.

"Come on." Sylvia was becoming impatient. "I want answers. Don't pretend you can't understand me, I know you're a lot too smart for that. What's been going on in this place?"

From a circular aperture at its base, the second machine suddenly extruded a pair of long, rubbery arms. Before Sylvia could retreat, they had moved forward to circle her ankles.

"Hey! Let go of me!"

It took no notice, and then arms from the first machine came forward to wrap around her forearms and waist. She was gently lifted off her feet and held in midair. Both machines moved in unison along the corridor, holding Sylvia as delicately but firmly as an armed bomb.

"There is no problem." The first machine finally spoke in a voice that Sylvia recognized at once. It sounded just like Paul Chu. "We will be going on a journey. You will be quite safe. One moment."

While Sylvia struggled as hard as she could, yet another pair of arms appeared to check the closure of her suit helmet.

"What do you mean, a journey? Damn you, let go of me. Take me to see Paul Chu. *I order you to release me.*"

That *had* to work. No machine could hold a human against her will, unless it was to save a life.

"We cannot do that." The voice was suitably regretful and apologetic. "We cannot set you free; not yet. But we can take you to Paul Chu's present location. Maybe you will see him there."

"When?" They were already in the lock, and there was a hiss of escaping air.

"When we reach our destination. Ten days journey from here."

They were outside, drifting along in a glimmer of starlight. The second machine had stayed behind at the lock, so she was held only by her arms and waist. Sylvia saw a new shape in front of her, a small ellipsoidal object only twenty meters long. It was like no ship she had ever seen. "We can't fly in that." She spoke into her suit radio, offering what should have been for a machine the ultimate threat. "If you make me fly in that, it will *kill* me."

"Not so." The machine sounded shocked, but it did not even pause. "Otherwise, of course, we would never permit it. Ten days will quickly pass. Perhaps when we are on the way you would like to play chess with me? We will be alone."

"I hate chess!"

As Sylvia was carried into the ship, she had a final unhappy thought. She had given Cinnabar Baker the coordinates of this destination and had felt pleased with her foresight. But how much use would that information be wherever she would be in another ten days?

CHAPTER 21

"Any sufficiently advanced technology is indistinguishable
from magic."

—Arthur C. Clarke

Aybee had seen many transit ships during his wanderings
through the Outer System. The design was standard. It dif-
fered only in detail, depending on whether the fabrication was
done at the Vulcan Nexus, whispering its way across the surface of the Sun, or out in the Dry Tortugas, wandering the
remote and ill-defined perimeter of the Oort Cloud.

Each transit ship had a thick disk of dense matter on the
front end. Each one also had a passenger cabin that could slide
backward or forward along the two-hundred-meter central
spike jutting out behind the mass plate. The McAndrew vacuum energy drive sat at the plate's outer edge. The whole
assembly looked like an axle with only one wheel attached.

It was a shock to be taken by Gudrun to the front of the
ship and be shown a smooth, spikeless ellipsoid just twenty
meters long.

Aybee stared at it as if he were in the audience at a magic
show, waiting for the missing bluebird to appear. "Where's the
rest of it?"

"There is no more." Gudrun laughed. She was bubbling

175

with excitement. "I told you, Karl, the surprises are just beginning. This is the ship for our journey. It arrived from headquarters two days ago."

Aybee made a complete circuit of the outside. The ovoid had a smooth glassy hull, polished and unmarked. He could see his own distorted reflection in the convex surface. That alone was sufficient to make it out of place in the dingy and grimy environment of the old cargo ship. It was as new as its surroundings were old. Odder yet, it showed no sign of a drive mechanism. There was nowhere to attach the massive disk that balanced gravity and acceleration, and the clear ports suggested that at least half the internal space was passenger quarters.

As a supposed trainee, Aybee could not tell Gudrun what he was thinking. Either this supposed ship was a total hoax and would go nowhere—or there were whole realms of physics unknown to the best minds in the Inner and Outer Systems.

Instead he asked, "Who built it?"

"Headquarters. It's very new and very fast. The old ships took weeks to get to headquarters—it's over six hundred billion kilometers away. We'll be there in five days!"

"What's the acceleration?"

"That's not relevant. This works on a new principle. They are making more of them, but today there are only a handful of others like this ship."

But there ought to be *none* like it, Aybee reflected. He did the instant mental conversion: five days for six hundred billion kilometers meant about five hundred g's. Then he at once ignored his own answer. The range calculation made sense only if the ship performed like a transit ship, with an acceleration phase, a crossover, and a deceleration. There was no reason for that assumption. If the ship were as new as it seemed, headquarters could be on the other side of the galaxy. Aybee had no idea how it could function. At the moment he did not even know what questions to ask.

"How is it powered?" he said at last. "With a kernel?"

That was fishing. The transit ships used the McAndrew vacuum drive, not kernels.

"No. But apparently it has a low-mass kernel at the center."

Curiouser and curiouser. Even a small kernel weighed a few hundred million tons. Why accelerate that mass if one did not need it?

They went aboard, and Aybee's confusion performed a quantum jump to a higher-level state. The internal living space on the ship was ten times what he had expected. There was too little space for any reasonable power supply, engines, or drive mechanism.

In the back of his mind Aybee had already decided that a new and first-rate intellect must have arisen in the rebel communities of the Kernel Ring. That was the only way to explain something as radically different as the new ship. But once inside and looking around, he was forced to drop even that idea. Too many things were new and unfamiliar. Out of a dozen different internal systems, he could identify and explain maybe half of them. And those few hinted at something that Aybee had been groping his way toward for the past four years, a new landscape just beyond the horizon.

Aybee had a clear image of current science, of its peaks and valleys and gray clouded areas where theory failed. Technology advanced constantly, but it depended on models of the physical world that were often centuries old. It advanced by ignoring the foggy regions, those places where deep understanding had not been achieved and where the subtle paradoxes lurked. Aybee had charted those anomalies. It was shocking to find the misty curtain suddenly blown aside and a new world stepping forth in full-blown glory.

Gudrun had no such worries. She sat down confidently at the control board and began to follow the simple sequence of instructions provided by the panel's prompting. The new ship did not seem to amaze her, but Aybee recalled the description of the Outer System Navy: a system designed by a genius to be run by idiots. And when he thought of the level of genius needed to come up with a whole system so different from anything he had ever seen, his skin crawled with excitement.

Five days. That was how long he would have to explore

everything and find out how it all worked. Aybee had been dreading so long a trip with Gudrun, but now he wished that the travel duration were double. His usable time would almost certainly be much less than five days. Gudrun would insist on talking—or worse—for part of it, and she also wanted him in a form-change tank, wasting more precious hours.

Even while she was finishing the command sequence to move them out of the cargo hulk and on their way, Aybee was thinking hard. What he needed was a complete reversal of roles: Gudrun absent and Aybee free to explore the ship. How could he manage it?

Cinnabar Baker would have solved that problem in a moment. With stakes so high, Gudrun had to be out of action for the duration of the journey. One blow would do it; then the disposal of a corpse or the confinement of an injured body to the medical unit.

Aybee had plenty of brainpower. The idea that Gudrun could be killed or injured occurred to him at once. She had finished the control sequence and had moved to the communications unit. As she crouched before the panel with the headset shielding any of his actions, he picked up a heavy data storage case and moved to stand directly behind her. It would take only a moment, a single strike to the unprotected skull.

Now!

Aybee stared the possibility full in the face—and blinked. For the first time in his life he was forced to face one of his own limitations: He was not particularly fond of Gudrun, but regardless of logic and motivation he could not harm her physically.

He put down the case and stared at her in total frustration. At the same moment, she swiveled around in her chair to look up into his face. Her expression was curious, somewhere between cold and startled. Aybee could visualize a five-dimensional knotted manifold and manipulate its topology in his head, but he could not read that human countenance. If he had, he would have recognized a look of fear.

"I've been in touch with headquarters," Gudrun said after a few moments. "I said we'll be on our way any moment now."

Aybee nodded. It hardly seemed like a universe-shattering revelation.

"And I'm afraid we can't do the things we'd planned," she hurried on. "There have been changes. I have urgent work to do on the journey, so you'll have to occupy yourself as best you can. Don't come in here."

Without another word she went through to the aft part of the cabin and slid the door closed. Any child could see that something had happened to upset her very much.

But if Aybee was a child, he was the little boy who had suddenly been given the run of the candy store. He stared after Gudrun for all of ten seconds, until he heard a high-pitched whirring from somewhere beneath his feet. A new mechanism had come into operation.

Aybee felt no acceleration, but he suspected he might be hearing the drive. It was easy enough to test the idea. The McAndrew propulsion system produced a faint sparkle of eldritch light as high-speed particles collided with the occasional hydrogen atoms of free space. He went across to the port and peered out.

And gasped. There was no pinpoint twinkle of drive interactions. Instead, the whole starfield had been replaced by a tangled rainbow of color, rippling across his field of view.

From that moment, Aybee forgot all about Gudrun for many hours.

CHAPTER 22

"I often wonder what the vintners buy
One half so precious as the goods they sell."
—Omar Khayyam

Behrooz Wolf claimed to have no conscience. He denied having brains. What he had in place of both, he said, was a little voice that whispered in his ear, urging him to take actions that his natural indolence discouraged.

That voice was interfering with his work. What he *wanted* to do was solve the mystery of the demon of form-change, that impossible chimera that could live in the radiative inferno inside a kernel shield and send a stream of misdirection through the computer system to the rest of the harvester. And if it could do it to form-change, he realized, it could do it to everything else. It was the key to wholesale delusions and impossible sensor messages. Even the Negentropic Man himself, and Mary's visitation, and failed mass detection systems. *Something* had allowed that cometary fragment to crash undetected into the Sagdeyev space farm.

That was what he *wanted* to do: to work on technical problems. So why was he wandering the interior of the Marsden Harvester seeking a woman whose last name he had not at first remembered?

It could only be the dreams; persistent, chaotic images that came in the middle of deep sleep. He saw flashes of Mary in indescribable danger and of vague menace creeping toward her. He heard cries of fear and pleas for help.

Or was it *Sylvia* that he saw? The visions blurred and faded, one face flowing to another, as he watched. And were they dreams, or were they messages, like the first one he had received from Mary? When he woke he was never sure what he had experienced. All that remained was the feeling of urgency.

Bey wandered on. He was looking for Andromeda, but Andromeda who? Leo Manx had never heard of her. Bey went to the central data bank and asked for a complete listing of all the Andromedas—Diconis, that was the name he had been groping for, but the computer offered only a general location within the harvester. She was a woman with no permanent partner and no particular job. Bey started with the dining area where they had met and widened his sphere of search from there.

His new form had a stamina level inferior to that of his Earth body. After seven hours of roaming the harvester's corridors, asking for a woman everyone seemed to know and no one was able to locate, he was wilting. He needed food. He gave up his search, headed for the nearest dining area—and found Andromeda Diconis.

He dropped the idea of food and filled a jug with purpled red wine when he saw her. He did not expect to enjoy the meeting—So why am I doing it? he asked himself. She was alone, dressed in a cleverly cut garment that suggested body curves where there were none. He had to hurry, since she was carrying a tray of food and about to enter a dining cubicle. He grabbed his jug and a cup, hurried that way, and crowded in after her.

She gave him a first amazed stare, then a gasp of pleased recognition. "Why—Behrooz. What a nice surprise."

"I have to talk to you."

"But I'm about to eat." She gestured to the tray in front of her. "You'll have to wait until I've finished. Unless—" Her face turned pink, but her eyes were gleaming before they looked away from his. "Unless you were thinking of staying here while I do it."

"Sure. Here, we'll share this." Bey placed the wine on the table between them and heard her gasp. He might be getting into more than he realized.

Andromeda was looking around, checking that no one else had seen Bey enter the cubicle. "Wait a minute." Her voice was breathless, and she quickly set the table controls to make all the walls opaque. "There—if you are sure you really want to?"

"I do. I'm sure." Bey picked up the flagon and poured wine. He did not think Andromeda was a woman who did favors for nothing. Who was it who had said that Paris was worth a mass? One of the Henrys. Well, Sylvia was worth more than that. According to his estimates, she had saved his life at least twice. And she had sat for days by the tank when he had gone into form-change to make sure nothing bad happened there. Sylvia was worth it, whatever it took. Bey followed his instincts, picked up his cup of wine, and drained it.

Andromeda had taken a spoonful of a clear soup, but she was hesitating with it poised in front of her mouth, watching him drink. Bey stared right at her, not letting her off the hook. After a moment she gave a little shiver, pursed her lips, and sipped in a determined way. She swallowed, blushed, and said, "I hope you don't think I'm like this all the time. I mean, I'm really a very respectable woman."

"I know. Sylvia says you're the tops." Bey gulped more wine and watched Andromeda lean forward and lick her lips. Her nipples were pushing against the indigo fabric of her dress. He was even getting excited himself. Maybe the Cloudlanders knew something that Earth people had never learned about the serious business of eating. Bey struggled to keep his mind on the job at hand. "She says the two of you go way back together. You were big buddies until she set up with Paul Chu."

"We were." Andromeda swallowed another lascivious spoonful of soup. "I was very disappointed when that happened. I mean, he was *nothing*. Little, and fat, and full of strange ideas."

Lady, that was me two weeks ago. Bey leaned across, poured a full glass for Andromeda, drank deeply from his own glass, and nodded agreeably. He had not eaten for a long time, and the alcohol was pumping straight through to his bloodstream. Andromeda was beginning to look much more attractive. "I don't know why she started to hang out with him." He leaned forward. "Wasn't he part of some sort of religious group?"

"Not *religion*. Revolution." She gave Bey another knowing look, waited to be sure he was watching, and took a deliberate swallow of wine. Her face was flushed, and her lower lip swollen. "He was into revolution, and borderland politics, and all that rubbish. I don't know how much she told you about the two of them, but they were an item for a long time. I think she still has the hots for him. I don't know what she told you, but in my opinion she hasn't got him out of her system."

"Was she asking about him?" The question was overly direct, but Andromeda was too preoccupied to notice. She was sitting with a forkful of food poised in front of her. Not until Bey fixed his eyes on her again did she slowly place it in her mouth, pull the food free with her white teeth, and chew steadily while he watched. The pulse in the hollow of her throat was throbbing.

"She was asking." Andromeda finally swallowed and put down her fork. "She was asking about him, and I told her how I thought she could get in touch with him."

"You *know* that?"

"I'm fairly sure I do. He was here secretly, but he wanted certain people to be able to reach him. I know who they are."

"And you could tell me?"

"Well, not immediately." Andromeda licked her lips again. "It would take time to find them. But we could look together."

Bey knew what was coming. "'There's a divinity that shapes our ends, Andromeda, rough-hew them how we will.'"

"I'm sorry?"

"Shapes our ends." Lord. He had had far too much to drink—but too much for what?

Andromeda laughed. "You're such a *strange* person—not at all the way you look. If you want to search, I can tell you where we should start." She moved closer to Bey. Andromeda had lost all interest in eating. "I have their names and locations—but not with me. Back in my private quarters. We'd have to go there. If you want to."

She paused and looked at him inquiringly.

With a wild surmise. Silent, upon a peak in Darien. Lord, he *was* drunk.

"Well, Bey." She had stopped smiling. "Do you want to?"

"'Being your slave, what should I do but tend upon the hours and times of your desire?'"

"What?"

"I mean, let's go. Now. To your place. I want to."

"Mm. Are you *sure*?" She was playing hard to get. "I mean, what about Sylvia?"

"'I have been faithful to thee Cynara, in my fashion.'" I mean Sylvia. I mean *Mary*, for God's sake.

"What?"

"I mean, I'm quite sure. Can't wait. Let's go." Bey lurched to his feet, clutching the half-full flagon of wine. She was out there somewhere, in the featureless gulf of the Outer System. He was going to find her. If he had to lay his body down to do it, that was part of the game. *Whatever* it took, he was going to find her. But not quite yet.

Leo Manx stared at him in disbelief. "Let me get this straight. You're leaving tomorrow for these coordinates." He tapped the sheet he was holding. "In the wilderness. And you don't want me to come with you. I'll second that. You don't want to tell the harvester controllers where you're going. All right, if you say so. But what are you hoping to accomplish?"

Leo Manx was a good listener. Bey outlined his ideas. At the wilder moments, Leo muttered to himself but did not interrupt. "How are you proposing to prove all this?" he asked at last.

"I'm going to bring one back. A live one." Bey was white-faced, exhausted, and somewhere between stoned and hung over. Four days of wine, drugs, and Andromeda Diconis was not an experience for the fainthearted. They had wandered the harvester together from one end to the other. Andromeda believed in stimulation rather than sleep. If he survived, Bey wanted to see her again. He had to know where she got her energy. "But if I don't make it back," he went on, "there has to be at least one person who knows exactly where I'm heading and what I think is going on. That's you."

"But how am I ever going to persuade Cinnabar Baker that what you're doing makes sense?"

"You don't start with Cinnabar. You *end* with her, and only if I don't come back and there's absolutely no other alternative. I told you the danger. Did you do what I asked you to?"

"As much as I could. Have you ever tried to brief your boss without telling her what's going on?"

"A hundred times. It's the first rule of self-preservation. Do you have them in a safe place?"

"The coordinates? Sure I do. But you realize those coordinates are almost certainly *not* the location of Ransome's Hole? They're too far out of the Kernel Ring."

"I know. But they're the only starting point I have, and I feel sure Sylvia went there. I'm leaving now. If everything goes to hell, you know what to do. Give me thirty days, then if you don't hear from me, assume I'm dead and gone."

He was ready to go, but Leo Manx stopped him. "Bey, you tell me you need thirty days before I panic, and you're not frantic now about Aybee. So why don't you give as much breathing room to Sylvia? Maybe she's working her own agenda. You could ruin it for her."

Leo deserved an answer, but Bey did not have one. All he had was that small voice again, whispering in his ear. It said that Aybee might be fine, and Bey might be fine, but Sylvia was in trouble. Or was it telling him that he owed more to her than he did to Aybee, and so he had to worry more about her?

Bey could not turn off that voice, but he could sometimes see through its strategies. He was in a hurry to leave, but not perhaps for the obvious reason. If he found Sylvia, she might lead him to Paul Chu. And Paul Chu might lead to Black Ransome. And Black Ransome was the Negentropic Man, that grinning, dancing figure who had driven Bey near insanity and forced him to leave Earth. *That* was who Bey was after. Wasn't it?

Maybe. The inner voice insisted on the last word. You want to get even with Black Ransome, I can believe that. And you want to solve the mystery of the kernels, which begins and ends with Black Ransome. But aren't we conveniently forgetting one other little thing? If you find Black Ransome at the end of the trail, who else may you find with him? And what will gallant Bey Wolf do then?

CHAPTER 23

"Time to worry, time to fear,
The Negentropic Man is here."
—crèche song of the Halley Harvester

Aybee Smith was a helpless prisoner, boxed up in a ship with a woman who would not talk to him, racing toward an unknown destination, heading for a meeting with people who were sworn enemies of everything that Aybee's civilization stood for.

Any logical person would have been worried sick about his future. And logic ruled Aybee's whole life. He loved logic; he lived by logic. And yet he did not give any of those worries a single thought. He was busy with something far more important.

The ship was a treasure box of mysteries. Beginning with the puzzle of the drive mechanism—no high-density balancing plate and no acceleration forces—he had listed twenty-seven devices that required some new technology or, beyond mere technology, some new physical principle!

With a mental clock ticking always in his mind—five days! too little time!—Aybee had forgone the luxury of sleep or rest. No matter what they did to him at his destination, he could sleep when he arrived there; at the moment the exploration of the ship was his only goal.

Gudrun appeared from her locked quarters only for a few minutes twice a day, when she found it necessary to use the ship's single galley. Aybee was eating randomly, snatching food when he could bear the interruption to his work. He and Gudrun met in the galley only once. She avoided his eyes and did not speak. He did not even notice. A new insight had occurred to him, a possible basis for the ship's garbage disposal unit, which somehow removed the mass from the ship but did not eject it to open space.

While she prepared her meal and fled, he sat motionless and gaped at the blank wall. Aybee worked in his head. He transcribed results only when everything was complete. So far he had written nothing.

He had performed a taxonomy of those twenty-seven anomalies, placing them neatly into four major categories. Thus:

(1) Inertial versus gravitational mass: Half a dozen devices on the ship, including all its positional and navigation systems, could be explained very well in one simple theory—*if* Aybee were willing to abandon the principle of equivalence. He was not. He would give up his virginity first.

(2) Heat into motion: Another set of devices on the ship made sense only if heat could be converted *perfectly* to other forms of mechanical energy; in other words, if Aybee were willing to give up the Second Law of Thermodynamics.

The Negentropic Man again! In a closed system—and what was more closed than the ship?—Aybee was asked to admit an entity that would decrease entropy. He remembered Maxwell's Demon, that tiny imp who was supposed to sit in a container sorting molecules. The fast-moving ones would be allowed to pass in one direction, the slow-moving molecules in the opposite one. Maxwell's Demon had been introduced in 1874, but Szilard had banished it completely in 1928. Hadn't he?

Aybee was not sure anymore. But he certainly did not want

to give up the Second Law of Thermodynamics. Eddington's words were graven in his memory:

"The law that entropy always increases—the second law of thermodynamics—holds, I think, the supreme position among the laws of nature. If someone points out to you that your pet theory of the universe is in disagreement with Maxwell's equations, then so much the worse for Maxwell's equations. If it is found to be contradicted by observation, well, these experimentalists do bungle things sometimes. But if your theory is found to be against the second law of thermodynamics I can give you no hope; there is nothing for it but to collapse in deepest humiliation."

Aybee agreed with that. Wholeheartedly.

(3) Force-field aberrations: By the end of the third day Aybee had devised an alternative theory that explained how the drive might work, but it involved the introduction of a new type of force similar to the ancient and long-discredited concept of "hypercharge." Aybee shrank from such *ad hoc* leaps into darkness. "*Hypotheses non fingo*"—"I don't make new assumptions." If that had been good enough for Isaac Newton, it was good enough for Aybee.

(4) Information from nothing. All the rest of the ship would work fine—if only it were possible to create information from random noise! Chaos to signal, that was all Aybee needed. The ship's communication system seemed to *depend* on that impossible capability. Could he accept it? Aybee knew exactly where it would lead him, and he did not like it. He would again need a way in which entropy could be decreased. It was the Negentropic Man popping up again in a different but equally unappetizing form. Aybee hated the whole idea.

Five days flew by. The approach to their destination was an irritating distraction but finally a necessary one. Aybee would not stop thinking about the physical problems—he *could* not stop thinking—but at least he would have an obligatory break from it.

One hour before arrival, Gudrun appeared grim-faced from her cabin and moved at once to the communications terminal. She was wearing a spacesuit, and it was clear that she was very nervous. But her feelings were not obvious enough to break through Aybee's shield of obsessions. He went on working until the very moment when the ship docked and the lock began to open. Then it was not Gudrun's voice that brought him out of his reverie; it was the clatter of metal from within the lock itself.

"There he is!" Gudrun had run to the opening and squeezed through it. She turned to point back inside. "That's Karl Lyman. Be careful—he's dangerous!"

The air lock on the ship, like its passenger quarters, was far bigger than on an ordinary transit vessel. Aybee stared into it and saw to his amazement that it was crammed with armed men, all in full space attire and squeezed tightly together. There were eight or nine of them; to a Cloudlander, that many people in one place was a major gathering. Gudrun had pushed into their midst. As he watched, all the weapons lifted to point straight at him.

"Into your suit," an uncompromising voice said. "If you have an explanation, you can give it later."

It was not a time to argue. One shot from any of those weapons would pierce the average hull. Aybee had a suit on and was ready to go in less than thirty seconds. He nodded as he closed the final seal. The outer lock opened, and air hissed out into vacuum. One of the guns lifted and gestured. "Outside."

One step behind Gudrun, Aybee moved on through the lock. It had been three days since he last looked out of an observation port, and he stared around with keen interest. The strange rainbow aurora had vanished, presumably disappearing when the drive went off, and the familiar starfield was all around. The Sun was visible off to his right, noticeably more brilliant than it had been when the journey had begun. Aybee made a quick assessment of its apparent magnitude and decided that they were somewhere on the outer edge of the Kernel Ring.

The ship had docked on the perimeter of a structure that was no more than a minor way station, a long skeletal framework of struts with clamps to hold ships in position and massive tanks for fusion fuels. The group moved to a little pinnace propelled by a high-thrust mirror-matter engine. Their real destination was a few kilometers Sunward, a dull darkness whose size and shape could be assessed only from stray glints of sunlight splintering off external ports and antennas.

The body was roughly spherical, perhaps five kilometers across. Aybee stared at it with the greatest interest. If he were unworried, it was not because he was confident of his own fate. He was simply unable to drag his mind away from the new physical universe suggested by the ship he had arrived in. And if he had any emotion, it was anticipation; whatever he had seen in transit, there would be greater marvels here, where the transit ship had been built.

Aybee did a quick analysis. The sphere ahead might be a source of ships, but it was not itself a ship. It was also the size and shape of a cargo hulk, but it was not being used for cargo. There were no signs of a drive mechanism, and there could be none, since the delicate spikes and silvery filaments of exterior antennae were incompatible with accelerated motion. No stronger than tinsel, they would be crushed and deformed by the slightest of body forces.

It could be a colony, like the Outer System's free drifters, or it might be a converted factory, originally dedicated to the production of a particular line of goods.

Aybee abandoned speculation. They were moving to a huge airlock built into the hull's convex surface, and already several of the party had their hands ready to break suit seals. Aybee waited. If anyone attempted to breathe vacuum, he would not be the first. He was amused to note that Gudrun had positioned herself as far away from him as possible, at the opposite side of the lock. The escort had apparently formed their own conclusions about Aybee's threat to them. No one held a gun at the ready, and half of them did not even bother to look at him.

The inner lock opened. The group moved quietly forward into a large, bare chamber with a flat floor and a local gravity field that varied irregularly from one point to the next. To Aybee, that suggested the resultant vector from many kernels scattered through the interior of the body, each adding its own field component.

The man in front halted and turned around. At his gesture, Aybee removed his own suit with the rest. For the first time he could assess their physical appearance. Most of them had the short, stocky build that he associated with the Inner System and the Kernel Ring, but two were long and lean, as much Cloudlanders as anyone Aybee had ever seen. They were probably not recent arrivals, either, since they were not dressed in Outer System style; their arms and legs stuck wildly out of clothes far too small for them.

Gudrun was staring at him in fear and horror. Aybee felt tempted to go across, wiggle his fingers in his ears, and see if she screamed. What was she expecting? Someone to appear in a puff of smoke and carry her off to hell?

Instead he nodded amiably to the others in the group. "Well." They all stared at him. "You got me. What happens now?"

"That depends on you." The speaker was a black-haired man with dark skin and a thickset build. Aybee recognized the voice as the one that had been ordering him around. "I was told to get you here, that's all. If Gudrun is right"—the man spoke as someone who already knew her well—"then you're in trouble. We don't like spies here. If you're innocent, you'll have to prove it."

"Guilty until proved innocent. Nice. Where's here?"

Several of the men stirred uneasily at Aybee's question. "Got a bit of nerve, haven't you?" the stocky man commented. "What did you tell him, Gudrun?"

"Nothing." She was defensive. "At least, not very much. I thought until we were on the ship that he was just a new trainee that we captured on the Sagdeyev space farm. How was I supposed to know he's a Cloudland spy?"

That produced another reaction from the rest of them, and a couple of guns were again pointed at Aybee.

"I don't think you want to believe this," he said. "But I'm not a spy, and I've never been one."

"He's lying!" Gudrun's face was flushed with anger. "He even gave me a false name. He says he's Karl Lyman, but his real name is Smith—Apollo Belvedere Smith."

That shocked Aybee more than he wanted to admit. He could see how he might have revealed by his actions that he was not from the space farm or that another farmer might have said he was not part of that group. But how could anyone know his real name? Unless he had taken to talking in his sleep, he had never mentioned his name since the accident back on the farm.

"*Is* that your name?" one of the tall, thin escorts asked. "Because if it is, then, man, you're in deep trouble." He turned to the rest of them without waiting to hear Aybee's answer. "There's an Apollo Belvedere Smith who works for Outer System headquarters. High up, staff position. So if this is him, he's definitely a spy, and we have to—"

"I tell you, I'm not a spy." Aybee cut him off before the other man could finish. "I'm a *scientist*—"

"He's lying!" Gudrun shouted. "He's no scientist. He lied to me."

"He did," said a quiet new voice from behind the group. "And yet, oddly enough, he is not lying now. He is telling the exact truth."

Everyone spun around. A small, lightly built man had stepped into the chamber through its open inner door. He was dressed in a tight-fitting suit of rusty black, and on his head he wore a peaked cap of the same sable tone. His face was fine-boned and pale, with an odd little smile on the thin lips, but that expression was belied and dominated by the eyes. There was no smile there, only a dark and piercing look that demanded and held attention.

Aybee found his attention drawn to those eyes. It took an amazing effort to look away. He heard Gudrun gasp. She, at least, had not been expecting the new arrival. But she had to be less surprised than Aybee himself. For although the dress was quite different and the teeth no longer incongruously blackened, Aybee recognized the man standing in front of them. It was the Negentropic Man, just as he had danced and capered through Bey Wolf's tormented memories.

The newcomer stepped forward, and the others moved aside to make a corridor. Right in front of Aybee, the man stopped and looked up. Aybee was a head and a half taller. The thin grin widened.

"As you said, Apollo Belvedere Smith, there was no lie. You are a scientist, and Cinnabar Baker thinks you are the best in the system." He held out his hand. "Let me welcome you here, and let me introduce myself."

"That's not necessary." Aybee took the outstretched hand and decided it was time to do more than just deny everything. He had to establish independence. "I know where I am. This is Ransome's Hole. And you are Black Ransome."

If Aybee had expected a shocked response, he was disappointed. The other man frowned just a little and gave Aybee's hand a dry, firm shake. "I'm Ransome, true enough. Some call me Black Ransome, although that is not my name. And some call this Ransome's Hole, too, though I would never do so." The smile returned, warm and embracing. "I'm going to welcome you here, whether you want it or not. You've come a long way, and we must talk. You may be very valuable to us. Come on."

Aybee had apparently been switched in status from prisoner and spy to welcome guest. Gudrun gasped, but there was no murmur of dissent from anyone. The force of Ransome's personality was too strong to brook argument. Instead, the group of people moved to leave a clear path to the door. He turned and left, confident that Aybee would follow.

That annoyed Aybee. So Ransome was to lead, and he was supposed to trot along behind like some pet animal? No way.

He left the chamber just behind Ransome and tagged along until they were out of sight of the other group. But then he paused and looked around. Ransome went on, almost out of sight in the curving corridor, heading deeper into the sphere along a spiral path whose field in less than fifty meters fluctuated from almost zero g to a thirtieth of Earth gravity. The floor turned in the same space through 180 degrees. In any other structure, Aybee would have known just how to interpret that. The path must wind its way past two shielded kernels, one below the "floor," the other, forty meters farther on, above the "ceiling"—which had become the floor.

That was the only logical explanation, but Aybee's new experiences on the transit ship had taught him to mistrust preconceived ideas. He slowed his pace and hunted backward and forward, seeking a point of maximum field in the corridor floor. If he were now close to a kernel, he would feel an inertial dragging.

He went down on his hands and knees and put his head close to the floor, moving it slowly about. While he was in that position he saw a pair of black-clad legs standing a few feet in front of him.

"If you're going to travel all the way like that," Ransome's calm voice said, "it will take you a long time and I won't wait. I'll send one of the machines back here to show you the way. It *is* a kernel down there, you know. What else did you think it might be?"

Aybee stood up. He was still young enough to hate looking like a fool more than anything in the world. For the rest of the journey through the interior of Ransome's Hole he trudged grumpily along right behind Ransome.

In a few minutes they came to the end of the corridor and passed through into a great hemispherical chamber, furnished to a level of luxury that Aybee had never seen. Glittering silver sculptures of human and animal figures were everywhere. The domed ceiling housed a huge sprinkler system, able to deliver anything from a fine mist of rain to a total deluge. Fruit trees and flowering vines, trained in elaborate espaliers along walls and trellises, grew beneath in disciplined variety. At the center of the chamber stood its most spectacular feature. A forty-meter globe of greenish

water was held in position by the gravitational field of the
kernel at its center, and brilliantly colored fish were swimming within it. Fronds of weed and branched coral grew
down on the kernel's outer shield, and an external lighting
system created ever-varying patterns of light and dark within
the clouded interior.

Aybee goggled. No one had anything like that in the
Outer System, not even the three general coordinators.

Ransome had caught his expression. The shorter man
shrugged. "Not for me, Aybee Smith. That isn't my taste at
all." He sounded amused and tolerant, far from the fanatical
rebel promised by his reputation. The ogre of the Kernel
Ring was easy company, lulling one to relax and listen to
him.

"But sometimes you have to do these things, don't you?"
Ransome went on. "For the sake of the less scientific. Stick
around here for a while, and you'll see worse. Maybe you
should think of this as my version of the Hanging Gardens of
Babylon."

The what of what? Aybee decided to look it up when he
had a chance. Meanwhile, he could not help changing his
mind about Black Ransome. The man was treating him like an
equal rather than a prisoner, and given Ransome's reputation
and authority, that had to be flattering.

"Now, this *is* my own taste," Ransome said. "A person
can really work here." He led the way through a gleaming
door of white metal, on into a sparsely furnished room
about eight meters by six. A long desk, half-covered with
random piles of data cubes, stood against one wall. Half a
dozen displays were mounted above it on plain beige walls
that carried unobtrusive light fixtures, the biggest holograph
projectors Aybee had ever seen, and no decorations of any
kind. Elaborate computer consoles were built into the surface of the desk itself.

Ransome sat down on one of three easy chairs and gestured
to another one. Now that they had arrived, he seemed in no
mood to speak. There was a long, uncomfortable pause, with

Aybee standing waiting and Ransome staring blank-eyed at the wall.

At last Aybee tucked himself into a chair. They had been made for Ransome's convenience, not for a tall Cloudlander, and his knees came up near his chin. "So I blew it," he said. The personal failure had been troubling him since they had first reached Ransome's Hole. "Mind telling me how?"

Ransome raised dark eyebrows questioningly, but still he did not speak.

"I mean, my *name*," Aybee added. "Gudrun knew it, and you knew it. But I told her I was Karl Lyman when she found me on the space farm, and nobody did a chromosomal ID check on me. You shouldn't have had any idea I was lying. So I must have done something dumb. I'd just like to know what it was."

Ransome shook his head. "You demean yourself, Aybee Smith. It was not your failure. Watch." He nodded to one of the displays and played briefly with the miniature console set into the arm of his chair.

The screen glowed. Aybee had half expected to see the result of some unsuspected test conducted on the space farm or perhaps on the dark cargo hulk. Instead, a color image appeared. It was Sylvia Fernald, seen full face. After the flicker of a fast audio search, her image steadied and began to speak.

"We thought Aybee would have been here long ago," she was saying. "Now it looks as though he was captured along with the others. Do you have any idea where they were taken?"

"Not yet." The voice was Cinnabar Baker's, and as the field of view on the display scrolled across and down, Aybee realized that he had to be viewing the scene through her eyes.

"I hope he has the sense to lie low until we can trace him," Sylvia said from outside the field of view.

"If we ever can," Baker said. "We have no clues so far. If he's still alive—we're not sure of that—he could have been taken anywhere in the system." The screen showed the main display in Baker's own office. It held a listing of the names and physical descriptions of all personnel of the space farm, plus Aybee's own personal data.

"You know Aybee," Sylvia said. She appeared again in the picture. "If he is alive, he'll be looking for a chance to get away—"

"As I'm sure you were," Ransome said. He cut off the display, and Sylvia vanished. "But once we knew you had not left the Sagdeyev farm with the others, we could identify you from your description and take special precautions."

Aybee was still staring at the blank screen. "That was in Baker's private apartment. It was seen through her own eyes!"

"Indeed." Ransome leaned back comfortably in his chair. "Aybee Smith, you are surprised. You should not be. My resources for the collection of information through the whole system—even within the coordinator's private apartment—are unmatched. Cinnabar Baker keeps no secrets from me. I know every word that is said, in every one of her meetings. If you want more proof of that, I can easily provide it. I have been aware of your own existence and of your potential for more than three years. Had I realized that you were with Behrooz Wolf on the space farm, I would have prevented the accident there."

"Could you have stopped it?"

"With ease. I controlled the whole destiny of the Sagdeyev farm, from form-change units to matter detection systems. But before we come to something so specific, let us be general. You are a young man, and you are fascinated by science. Let me ask you, do you have equal interest in politics?"

The tone in Ransome's voice was still casual and detached, but Aybee detected a heightened level of interest. He shook his head. "Politics isn't for me. I leave that sort of stuff to people like Baker."

"Ah. To be young. You will change as you grow older. If you do not know politics, do you know the theory of dissipative systems far from equilibrium?"

"I know all the classical work, Onsager and Prigogine and Helmut. And I've followed what Borsten has been doing on iterated function spaces in the past few years." The abrupt turn in the conversation was baffling, but Aybee was on familiar ground. Maybe they were going to talk about science at last.

"In that case you will readily follow what I am about to tell you, even if you at first have trouble accepting it." Ransome's eyes were like magnets, drawing Aybee's attention against his will. "I can demonstrate to you that the whole civilization of the Solar System is on the brink of massive change—total and irreversible change. I know this, and soon everyone will know it. In the language of dissipative systems, we now stand at a bifurcation point, at a singular moment on the time line. As you know, this bifurcation implies an instability. In such situations, the future of a large system can be controlled by small forces. I have such a force at my disposal—the same force that guarantees we occupy a singular point in time. But before the new system can emerge, the old order must crumble and fade. The process has begun; you have seen the signs, in the general breakdown of the Outer System. From its ruins, we will create the new order. Today's divisions into Inner System, Halo, and Outer System will disappear. There will be a central government, a single point of power and control. It will be here, under my control. My office will become the center of the Solar System." He leaned forward toward Aybee, eyes dark and hypnotic. "The program to accomplish this is well advanced. But in certain scientific areas I need help. You are well equipped to provide it, and I can guarantee that you will find the work totally fascinating. And think of the prospect. You will help to define the future! You will help to *create* the future. What could compare with that?"

He paused and looked at Aybee expectantly. His voice had never risen a decibel, always completely thoughtful and reasonable. But in terms of its persuasive power, it was like a triumphant shout.

Aybee struggled to resist the feeling of enthusiasm and well-being that was flooding through him. He had always been a loner, never one to join any movement, and some small corner of his brain was fighting back. But it *was* a small corner—most of him was in there cheering for Ransome.

He forced himself to think again about his journey to Ransome's Hole. He wanted to hear about the new scientific advances that had made the little ovoid ship possible. If Ransome were the genius behind those developments, Aybee had to hear the theory—all the theory. Instead he was listening to a man talk about politics. Was it conceivable that the scientific genius and the would-be emperor were the same person? Aybee knew very well the sacrifices and the demands on time and energy called for by great scientific advances. He was prepared to meet those demands, but could anyone combine such a life with an attempt to take over the Solar System? Surely not.

Aybee felt the flood of enthusiasm giving way to rational thought. He knew it was no time to argue with Ransome. Instead he nodded slowly. "What you are telling me is fascinating. I'd like to hear more."

He was not surprised when Ransome accepted his apparent conversion. The other man projected so powerfully, he was probably amazed by anyone who did not become his follower on first exposure.

Ransome stood up, so warm and friendly and convincing that Aybee began to have second thoughts about his motives. "You have much to learn, Aybee Smith. To the few thousand people already devoted to my cause—yes, we are still spread that thin—I am their only scientific expert. They see me as their prophet, and as the source of all the new technology. But there is a limit to what one man can do, and I have no more than scratched the surface of the possible. That has been enough to allow us to begin the reorganization of the system. You will help me to take our work much farther. When you are ready, we will go to the laboratories. You can begin work there as soon as you like. The facilities are the finest that we can provide."

He paused and frowned. "Of course," he added mildly, "there are certain precautions taken for such sensitive work. As you will appreciate, it would be intolerable if word of our plans and discoveries were to leak prematurely to the Inner or the Outer System." He smiled. "The monitor systems are automatic, and beyond my control. Attempted escape would unfortunately and inevitably lead to your capture, perhaps to your death. Now. Shall we proceed?"

CHAPTER 24

"Mary, Mary, quite contrary
 How does your garden grow?
 With spinor fields, and kernel shields,
 And pretty men all in a row."
 —crèche song of the Opik Harvester

The self-reproducing machines that alone made possible the rapid development of the Oort Cloud had never been so important in the Inner System. Fifteen billion humans were quite self-reproducing enough. Bey Wolf, accustomed all his life to human limits on work habits and energy levels, had not yet made his adjustment. He knew in the abstract what a group of machines could do, but their actual performance still amazed him. And they never seemed to stop work, even when Bey could see nothing useful to be done.

The odd logic of that had been explained by Leo Manx on their original trip out to the Cloud. "It's actually more economical of resources to keep them working," he said. "You see, if they're *not* working, they're programmed to make more copies of themselves. And that takes more materials."

"But why not just switch them off?" Bey asked.

Manx shook his head. "They're designed for continuous

use. If you don't want them to decline in performance, you have to keep them busy."

Typical Outer System design philosophy, but Bey was looking at a good example of what Manx had meant. Sylvia Fernald had approached the same destination and found the darkness and silence of a mausoleum. To Bey, near to rendezvous just seven days later, it seemed inevitable that the body had looked then much as it did now, gaudy, bustling with activity, ablaze with internal lights. Half a dozen ships lay in the docks, and the irregular egglike outline of the surface was blurred and softened by a tangle of free-space vines, tilting their silver and black webs to drink in the miser's dole of radiation from distant Sol. The idea that the whole body had been dark and deserted as recently as two days earlier never occurred to Bey.

Its small size was a surprise. In the Inner System, a few hundred sets of orbital elements covered everything significant. The vast majority of planetoids were uninhabited and likely to remain so, except for mining operators. Travel to any of the interesting destinations took one to a body at least tens of kilometers across, with an associated population center. There would be thousands of people there at minimum, if not the billions of Earth, the hundreds of millions of Mars, or the tens of millions of Europa and Ceres.

That Sylvia would come so far to arrive at a body with a handful of people was perplexing to Bey. However, it might also make his own task easier. He was seeking Sylvia, but beyond that he had another motive. He sought the trail that would lead him onward to the right location in the Kernel Ring and the Negentropic Man himself. Whatever lay there, it was an improbable end point for Sylvia's travels.

There was little point in trying for an inconspicuous arrival. Space radar systems would have marked his progress and projected his arrival time when he was millions of kilometers away. Bey ignored the manual controls and allowed the docking to proceed automatically. He did not put on a suit. He was not being overconfident, nor was he a fatalist. Any dangers would derive from humanity rather than nature, and they would call for intelligence, not speed or strength.

The lock opened. He drifted through and found himself in the middle of a fairy tale. The interior of the body had been converted to a single chamber hundreds of meters across. Its vaulted walls were painted in red and white and gold, and vast murals reached up to the domed ceiling. Unencumbered by gravity, needle spires and slender minarets rose bright from the outer surface next to Bey, and lacy filaments arched between them.

He looked instinctively for signs of a kernel and headed for it right across the central chamber. No matter that he had spent much of the past week brooding on the impossible possibility of a demon inside a kernel shield, some indestructible, pachydermous, and unimaginable end product of infinite formchange that would bask and bathe in the radiation sleet within the shields. Never mind that thought. There would be a local gravity field near a kernel, and he yearned for it, even if it were a weak one—Earth habits died hard.

As he approached the outer kernel shield he was struck by a shocking thought. In his fascination at the sights within the lock, he had missed a central mystery. He could see almost the whole of the body's interior, and although a dozen machines were visible, there was no sign of another human being. Had he come all that way on a wild chase that would end on a deserted pleasure sphere? He knew such things existed, created as the hideaways of wealthy and reclusive individuals of the Outer System. They were maintained by their service machines, patiently awaiting the arrival of their owners, and for ninety-nine days out of a hundred they were uninhabited. If no one at all was there, his journey would have been a complete waste of time and effort.

Down on the kernel's shield Bey saw another oddity. Amid a riot of free-growing plants, a little bower had been created using a woven thicket of plaited vegetation to form a living roof and walls. The sight gave him an irrational shiver of premonition along his spine.

"Sylvia?" His voice was unsteady. Logically, he had no

idea what came next, but the dark recesses of his hindbrain knew it already. He floated on down toward the kernel's shield. "Sylvia," he repeated. "Are you there?"

A sudden giggle came from the inside of the bower, and a curly-haired head peeked out past the tangled leaves. "Bey? Oh, my word. What have you done to yourself?" The laugh came again, this time full-throated. "'Bottom, thou art translated.' You're so long and thin—and no hair! I knew it; you let them put you in one of your horrible form-change machines." It was Mary, moving out to meet him and filling his arms. "Oh, Bey, you're here at last. It's so good to see you again."

The questions had tumbled through Bey's head one after another. How had Mary known he was coming? How had *anyone* known he was coming? That information was supposed to be a close secret. Why was Mary here? Where was Sylvia? Mary had recognized him instantly, despite his changed form, but how had she been able to do that?

He thought everything and at first asked nothing. Mary was a drug that had lost none of its strength. She still ran through his veins. He felt light-headed with unreality.

"Right here," she was saying. Bey found himself led by the hand into the little bower and seated on a rustic bench fabricated to resemble aged and knotted wood.

It was typical of Mary that she felt no need to explain anything, and just as typical that she wore a costume equally alien to both the Inner and Outer Systems. Her print dress of faded dark purple flowers on a pale gray background belonged to another century. It fit perfectly with the bower and with the woven basket hanging over the end of the bench. She was wearing a hint of flowery perfume, light and fresh.

Mary was playing a part—but which one?

"How did you know I was coming here?" Bey forced himself to ask that question, and at the same moment had a suspicion of the answer. He had told Leo Manx to tell no one—but did Leo have that much self-control? All it might have taken was one short conversation with Cinnabar Baker, and for Leo telling Baker was still second nature.

Mary was smiling at him as sunnily and possessively as if they had never parted. He thought for a moment that she had ignored his question, but then she said, "It's just as well for you that I learned you were heading this way, and better yet that no one else saw the message before I could take care of it. Otherwise you'd have found an armed guard waiting instead of me." She snuggled against him and laughed when she found that her head touched not his shoulder but halfway down his chest. "Oh, Bey, I've been taking good care of you. I changed all the messages that were going to you. If it weren't for me, you'd have been dead or crazy long since."

Bey had learned long ago that Mary did not lie. If her answers failed to match the real world, that was only because her perceptions of reality were so often awry. She had been protecting him, or at least she believed she had.

"What happened to Sylvia Fernald? She was supposed to be here." He was rewarded with a frown of disapproval.

"I know all about her. The two of you have really nothing in common."

"That's not true." Bey half agreed with Mary, but he felt the perverse need to defend Sylvia. "We have lots in common. She's educated. She saved my life—twice. We get on well together, and she's a—a nice, kind woman," he ended lamely.

"'Be she meeker, kinder than, Turtle-dove or pelican, If she be not so to me, What care I how kind she be?' They used to be *your* lines, Bey. Have you changed that much?"

"I came here to find her, Mary."

"I know. And I came here to stop you searching anymore. I know where she is, and she's safe enough. But you don't want to go looking for her. It might put you in danger."

"From whom?"

Mary shook her head. Bey knew exactly what she meant. She would not lie, but she would refuse to speak. They had slipped into the old relationship, just as though Mary had left Earth—and Wolf—no more than an hour before.

"I won't stop looking," he went on. "There's more at stake

here than me or Sylvia. The whole system is coming unglued. That has to be stopped."

She turned her head and looked up into his face. "The same old Bey. Saving the world. You ought to know better. You worked half your life for that stupid Office of Form Control, and what reward did you get at the end? They threw you out, with never even a thank you."

"They had a good reason."

"You haven't changed at all, have you? Still honor and glory and once-more-unto-the-breach, dear friends." She rubbed her hand across his chest. "Bey, if only you could stop living in the past and the future, and live in the present for a little bit, you'd have so much more fun."

If anyone in the universe lived in the present, it was Mary. The signal was clear and tempting. Bey heard all his internal voices shouting at once to justify the action: 'A few hours delay can't make any difference' . . . 'Mary will become your ally, and she can take you straight to Sylvia' . . . 'Mary scorned now would be your bitterest enemy'. . . . 'You've been away from each other far too long'. . . . 'All the time you thought she had forgotten you, she was *protecting* you' . . . 'Live in the present . . .'

Bey turned and leaned down toward Mary's waiting face. Her eyes had closed.

'But where has Mary been all this time? And what has she been doing?' Amid all the clamor of emotions, that single questioning whisper in Bey's mind was drowned out completely. It did not stand a chance.

A few hours had stretched into a day, and then into two and three. It was a long time before Bey saw a possible approach to the problem.

Mary was immune to all forms of logic. He had known that for years. It was maddening, but it was also part of her charm, and it meant that she would be unmoved by any rational reason for taking Bey back with her to the Kernel Ring and, ultimately, to Black Ransome. Kernel demons and form-change anomalies and Systemwide hallucinations meant nothing to her. Another motive was needed, something that went deeper than logic; Bey had lain awake for hours trying to think of one and had returned again and again to a single question. Why had Mary come to meet him, secretly? She was apparently not trying to capture him, and she had made it clear that she did not intend him to stay with her permanently.

He thought he had the answer. Mary had come for personal reassurance. She knew he had traveled a vast distance in pursuit of Sylvia Fernald. Mary hated to give up any man. The idea that she had been superseded by Sylvia, so that she could no longer move Bey at her whim, was intolerable. She wanted to show that she still owned him and could still control him.

Bey looked at the sleeping form stretched out next to him. So far the demonstration must have been to her satisfaction. Now he had to make use of the same fact.

The most difficult thing was to be casual and convincing enough. Mary did not lie, but she had a sixth sense that told her when others were doing it to her. The best way was to make her feel that any decision was her idea.

Bey dropped the first word while Mary was showing him around the elaborate new gardens that the machines had built under her direction in a single day. It was in answer to Mary's complaint that he was too bony to lie next to in comfort, and it took the form of a vague comment on his part that the standards of beauty for women were very different in the Inner and Outer Systems.

"For the Cloudlanders, curves are out," he added. "And yet that doesn't mean that a Cloudlander will be unattractive to somebody from the Inner System—or that a Sunhugger disgusts somebody from the Cloud."

Mary had not reacted to the comment, but Bey knew she had registered it. He waited. It was hard to keep his own mental processes under control. Emotion and real affection for Mary were competing with his long-term logical plan, and Bey knew from experience that logic could lose.

Later in the day Mary was studying a recording of one of her own old performances, as Polly Peachum in *The Beggar's Opera*. She remarked how good she had looked as a redhead.

Bey agreed enthusiastically. "My favorite hair color. As a matter of fact, naturally red hair—" He paused and went silent. Mary also said nothing. Sylvia had red hair.

They watched the performance together. When Macheath was looking at Polly and Lucy Lockit and singing, "How happy could I be with either, were t'other dear charmer away," Bey knew that Mary was watching him from the corner of her eye.

She was preoccupied for the rest of the day. Late in the evening she suddenly asked him if he and Sylvia Fernald had been lovers.

"Of course not!" Bey sat up. "You've seen her, you know how tall and gawky and strange she is. And she has a longtime partner of her own, back in the Cloud, so she wouldn't look at anyone else. And did you know when I arrived at the Opik Harvester, she said that I looked like a hairy little monkey? To her, I'm totally hideous . . ."

Bey went on with his protests just a little too long. He did not need to point out to Mary that his own appearance had changed considerably since the arrival at the harvester, to a form much more pleasing to Sylvia Fernald's tastes. On matters like this, Mary's instincts reached a conclusion ten times as fast as any logic.

The next morning Mary was very quiet. At midday she casually announced that she would be returning to the Kernel Ring. If Bey wanted to take the risk, he could accompany her. Did he want to go? If he did, he ought to get ready.

Bey, equally casual, accepted. However, he did not feel satisfied with the way the conversation had gone. He had achieved his objective, but his little inside voice would not keep quiet. Too easy, it said, much too easy. When a difficult goal is achieved with no effort, it's time to be suspicious. You want to get to the Kernel Ring? Sure—and maybe someone else wants you there, too.

CHAPTER 25

"In Ransome's Hole you'll lose your soul
   (We won't come to find you).
With Ransome's breath you'll meet your death
   (The Dancing Man's behind you).
Ransome takes one,
   Ransome breaks one,
      Out—goes—you."
      —crèche song of the Marsden Harvester

Bey had been wrong. He might be the only person who would ever know it, but still he hated the idea.

Back on the Sagdeyev space farm he and Aybee Smith had agreed to differ. Aybee felt that a life without surprises was no fun. Bey agreed, but he pointed out that ninety-nine of any hundred conceivable surprises were unpleasant ones. That was why he tried to analyze *all* outcomes of a situation rather than just the one he liked best. Aybee agreed—in principle—but he pointed out in turn that complete prediction was impossible in anything but abstract theory; the cussedness of the real world promised that the actual outcome would be unanticipated. Bey agreed, but he suggested that *any* chance of successful prediction was better than no chance. Aybee nodded. Honor was satisfied, and they moved on to other subjects.

Bey truly believed what he had told Aybee. When he had set out to follow Sylvia Fernald into the depths of the Halo, he had foreseen and analyzed four scenarios. One, the search might reach a dead end, and he would return to the harvester. Two, he might find Sylvia, but she would have discovered nothing useful and would already be at her own point of frustration, so they would *both* go back. Three, Bey might be captured and detained before he found Sylvia or reached Ransome's Hole. Fourth, he might be captured after he reached the Kernel Ring.

The idea that he would find *Mary* rather than Sylvia at that first location was so preposterous that it had not been in his thoughts at all.

So Aybee had been right. Bey allowed himself the luxury of a moment's irritation, then he inspected the ship that Mary had arrived in.

His reaction to it was not so strong as Aybee's. He had done little space travel, and although he knew that the ship was radically different in appearance from the ones he was used to, he did not realize how much new science had to be in it. He also had many other things on his mind. With Mary at her sunniest, most affectionate, and most demanding, he had little time to worry about spacecraft. She was in a holiday mood. If she thought for a moment that she was taking Bey toward danger, it did not show in her manner.

She complained only at the end, when the ship neared its destination in the central annulus of the Kernel Ring. "We're *crawling*. Why do we always have to go so *slow* when we're nearly there?"

"Safety requirement," replied the hollow voice of the ship's main computer. "Proceed with caution. Danger zone."

The computer was treating the region with great respect. They were picking their way through the maze of debris, unshielded kernels, and high-density fragments that littered the central part of the Kernel Ring. Those shards were the relics of a catastrophe four billion years earlier, when a toroidal region of space-time had suffered gravitational collapse and spewed high-mass elements toward the Sun. Life on Earth owed its existence to the event, but that was of no interest to the computer. Like Mary, it too lived in the present. Currently this location housed the freaks of the Solar System: collapsed objects invisible to deep radar and massive enough to destroy a ship, side by side with corotating kernel pairs whose signals played havoc with navigation systems.

Bey had never been here before, but he knew the place's reputation. The Kernel Ring had been left undeveloped for a good reason. A thousand ships had been lost in the early days, before transit vessels to the Outer System learned to fly high above the ecliptic.

Danger, the small voice in his ear said. *Danger*. Ninety-nine of any hundred conceivable surprises are unpleasant ones. But the shiver in Bey's spine was not fear. It was excitement. Ransome's Hole was visible; or, rather, it was invisible, a dark occulting disk against the continuous starfield. And it was *big*, big enough to contain anything: armies, weapons, factories, cities, monsters and treasures and mysteries unguessed at. Bey stared at nothing and was stirred by emotions he had not felt for years. He was in the past again, pursuing illegal serpent forms into the black depths of Old City. He was eager to begin, wondering if and how he would survive. The same ineffable force was quickening his pulse, drawing him on and tugging him down into danger.

While he was watching, brief flashes of blue-white fire sparked on the black disk. He recognized them. Short-range drive units. Five small vessels were heading out toward them.

Bey glanced at Mary. She frowned and shook her head. "Not my doing." But she did not seem too surprised.

Within a couple of minutes the five had been joined by others. Surrounded by an escort of a dozen pinnaces, the ship drifted to a docking and attached to a lock. The hatch swung wide, and Bey followed Mary out.

A dozen armed soldiers were waiting, their weapons raised and ready. Two paces to their rear stood a short, black-clad man with folded arms. His face was thin, with prominent bones, a sharp nose, and a trace of a self-confident smile. Bey stared at those piercing eyes, and after a few seconds the unmoving features before him seemed to shift and flow, reassembling themselves like an optical illusion to a different and familiar pattern.

The Dancing Man—the *Negentropic* Man, without the clownlike scarlet suit and black filed teeth but unmistakably the same in face, body, and movement. Bey shivered. The face and burning eyes brought frightening memories from the edge of death and madness.

"Full house," the Negentropic Man said. He stepped forward, still flanked by his guards, and nodded approvingly at Wolf. "I am Ransome. I have been curious to meet you for a long time, Mr. Wolf. When a man or woman refuses to commit suicide or to become insane, no matter what the external pressure, that person is of interest to me. And here you are, in my home." He turned, and his wave took in the whole habitat. "You see how obliging the universe can be. If I had originally set out to lure you here, I might well have failed. But by allowing you to sail freely with the winds of space, you arrive even before I am ready for you."

Ransome placed his arm possessively around Mary's waist. She did not resist, but she gave Bey a strange, uncertain look.

"So you have me. What happens now?" said Bey. He had seen eyes like that three times before in a human head, but none of their owners was living.

"For the moment, nothing." Ransome was disconcertingly at ease. "I have unfinished business with two of your friends, and then a couple of other things to take care of. You will have to bear with your own company for a little while. Later you and I must talk. I feel sure that we are going to be working together." Ransome gave Bey a dismissive, self-confident little nod and turned to go. Mary followed without a word.

"Mary!" Bey called after her as the guards moved to separate him from them. He received a brief glance in return from lowered brows, then he was being hustled away. The guards escorted him deep into the habitat's interior and finally stopped at an oval door. They ushered him through without comment and left at once, but as they went a bulky machine took up guard position at the entrance.

How long was the "little while" that he would be on his own? Ransome's joking tone had suggested that it might be quite some time. Bey turned in the doorway and stepped close to the Roguard. It stood solidly blocking his path.

"Allow me to pass. That is an order."

"The order cannot be obeyed." The voice was soft-toned and polite. "Egress is prohibited. You lack authorization."

"Who has authorization?"

"You do not have authorization to receive information on authorizations."

Bey retreated. He had not expected a useful answer, so he was not much disappointed. He went to sit at the table in the little dining area and pondered his situation.

Against the initial odds—and suspiciously easily—he had found his way to Ransome's Hole. He was in the middle of the enemy stronghold, unarmed and surrounded by guards, held prisoner by a probable megalomaniac with the power to destroy the Solar System; he had to decide what to do next.

What *could* he do?

After a few minutes he stood up and made a leisurely and thorough survey of the living quarters. They were perfectly adequate for a stay of weeks, months, or even years. The walls, floor, and ceiling were white, seamless, and solid. There was a comfortable-looking bed, a large and well-equipped washroom, a full food-production facility, a small computer with its own recreational and educational data bases, and even a small exercise unit that included simple form-conditioning. Notably absent was any type of communications equipment, audio or video.

Bey went to the little form-conditioning unit, turned it on, and reviewed its capabilities. It was the simplest and cheapest of the commercially packaged form-change systems. The options it offered were minimal. They included monitoring and feedback for standard muscle tone improvements, routines for minor physical repair such as sprains and bruises, and a couple of low-g/high-g conversions modules; that seemed to be all.

Bey opened the cover and checked the telemetry inputs and

internal storage. It was a BEC unit, completely self-contained, and the hardware was standard and quite powerful. That meant the weaknesses were in the software. The programs that came with the unit lacked all the more substantial form-change functions—it did not even permit eye adjustments, which Bey had needed for nearsightedness since he was a teenager.

What was he supposed to do when everything began to look fuzzy? Squint, or make himself eyeglasses? He closed the cover of the unit in disgust. On Earth no one had used anything so primitive for over a hundred years.

Bey went once more to the open door and tried to walk directly through it. The waiting Roguard again blocked him. He put his hand onto the machine's exterior, estimating its strength and sensitivity. It did not move.

"How long will I remain here?"

"That information is unavailable." There was a pause, then the machine added, "It will be no longer than two years, since the food supply has been set for such a period."

"Two years! That's terrific news."

"Thank you."

Bey closed the door in the Roguard's face, went to the bed, and stretched out on it. He should have known better than to waste his time talking. No machine of that type could recognize sarcasm.

He closed his eyes, but he had no thought of sleeping. There was a job to do, and it was a big one. The first step was a rough time estimate. How long would it need for development and testing, and then how long for the process itself to be completed? If the answers came out too high, he might as well relax and forget the whole idea.

Within ten minutes Bey had a first estimate. Five weeks, total, if he worked day and night. That was far too long. He had to cut it somehow by a factor of at least three. It was time for something rough and ready and less than perfection. The logic flow and accompanying condensed code for an alternative approach began to take shape in his head.

The next estimate came out at two weeks. Still too long, and he had taken all the legitimate speed-up steps. It was time for desperate measures. He had to begin accepting higher physical risks.

Bey lay on the bed for another four hours. At last he sat up, ready to start. As he made his last-minute preparations, it occurred to him that he had one unexpected asset. Ironically, the wild card in his favor was the Negentropic Man himself.

In his lectures to the beginning class at the Office of Form Control, Bey Wolf used an analogy:

"Purposive form-change is a *process*, a tight interaction of life-support machinery and real-time computer code." The display on the wall behind him provided a flow diagram, bewildering in its complexity. "There's a typical sample up on the screen—a straightforward one, as a matter of fact. By the time you get out of here, that will seem simple and familiar. But knowing how to read one of those schematics won't be enough to protect you. To be useful in this office, you have to see *beyond* the detail, to grasp a whole form-change picture in one swoop."

The wall display changed to show an old-fashioned map, bright with colors and dotted with fanciful illustrations. "Each form-change is a journey from a defined starting point to a defined end point. But those journeys all cross a part of the great ocean of form-change. Some areas of that ocean have been explored completely, and all commercial form-change programs navigate within that charted region. But beyond the safe waters lies a wilderness, unmapped and unknown. And *dangerous*. Never forget that.

"Everyone who tries a radically new form-change experiment is embarking on a trip through the unknown. And when you work in this office, you often have to follow the route of the pioneers, across those perilous waters.

"Now, we can't provide an infallible pilot across that unknown sea. No one can. But what we *can* do is teach you what to look for. You'll learn to recognize—and avoid—the shoals and reefs of form-change, the whirlpools and undertows. You'll always design your programs to follow the safe, smooth trade routes . . ."

Sound advice.

But the lessons of the classroom had not been designed for desperate emergencies.

Bey sealed the lid of the tank, stared at the control sequences, and prepared for coming agonies. With this degree of uncertainty, anything might happen. He was using change sequences that he had never employed before—never *heard of* before. They ignored his own teachings, driving an accelerated program that skirted the reefs, risked the whirlpools, and ran the gauntlet of lee shores. It was a guarantee of discomfort and danger, of disaster.

He entered the final command.

The first few minutes were filled with the familiar touch of sensors and catheters, followed by the flicker and swirling rainbow of colors and sounds. Biofeedback was beginning, no different from what it had been a thousand times. Soon it would bypass his eyes and ears to establish direct brain contact. A dozen steps flickered by in a few minutes, the standard preliminary tests as the form-change machine confirmed the parameters of his body.

And then . . . the change.

He sensed a ripple of command, a cold and alien touch through all his being. Strange discomfort touched him—entered him—became a pain that grew as rapidly and irresistibly as a windblown fire, until it burned in every cell. His body shook in surprised agony.

Wrong, totally wrong. Stop it now, while you can.

He thrust away the panic response that rose from the base of his brain. The pain was to be expected, the result of too-rapid change. The shortcuts *were* wrong, but that was by his own design—shape change achieved by deformation and muscular contraction, not by slow and careful rebuilding of body structure. It was a perversion of true form-change. He tried to stay calm as his body's core temperature climbed over twenty degrees. Chemical reactions were running at ten times the normal speed, but still he could understand and follow the processes.

And then pain passed a new threshold, and logic failed.

. . . he was stretched on a rack, seared by internal flames. His body was melting, twitching and writhing against the con-trol straps. A thick layer of mucus squeezed from his skin. Catheter pumps doubled their rate of chemical transfer.

A new change came, more basic and more deadly.

. . . heart pounding an irregular rhythm. Heart stopping. A moment of supreme agony, heart lifeless, a stone in his chest. Lungs collapsed. Kidneys and bowels and bladder, frozen in their action. Blood congealing.

The form-change machine had taken over completely. Only his brain was left, directing the purposive form-change.

The fatal form-change. The change should take weeks, not days. He had underestimated the pain, misjudged the danger. No one could endure such change-speed. It would kill him.

Heartless, lungless, he could neither groan nor scream. He had made a choice—and he was paying the price. Even with the machine's help, body parameters were uncontrollable. A dozen times the monitors in the form-change unit flared their warning signs. Chemical concentrations were wildly far from equilibrium, ion balances at fatal levels, synapses firing spas-tically out of sequence. He had lost awareness of his sur-roundings. The semiconscious body in the tank shuddered and writhed, enduring rates of adaptation beyond all rational limits.

Slow down. Slow down. Reverse the process. Every organ, every cell screamed for relief. And relief was possible. With purposive form-change, the will of the subject always played a central part. The urge to retreat became irresistible.

Stop now, stop now. The fear was no longer deep in his brain. It was rampant surges of pain and terror, invading every hiding place of will and resolve.

Stop. Stop now. He fought against the urge to end it, but the torment was too great. He was in terminal agony, hearing the whimper of protest from every cell. The limit of endurance had arrived; had passed. Pain intensified, sharpened, rose to levels that defied belief . . .

No more. Give in, or die.

And as that thought took firm possession of his mind, the pressure eased.

He sagged in the retaining straps of the tank, unable to move. Every nerve of mind and body was aflame. He sucked the pain deep inside him, grinning in triumph. He could hear his heartbeat.

It was over. No matter what came next, he had won this stage. He had the right final form; he knew it without looking. His tortured body had been cast up, twisted and misshapen, on a strange shore—and it was the destination he had chosen!

Bey Wolf had crossed the form-change ocean.

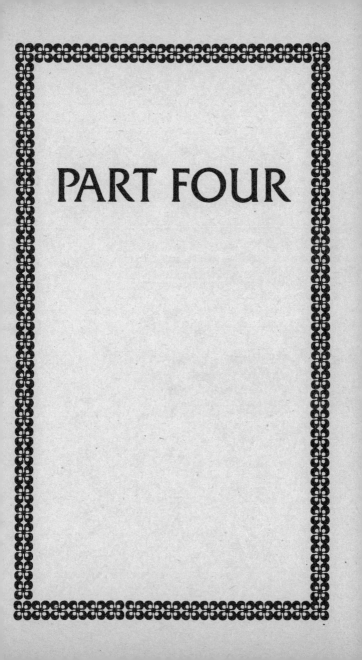

PART FOUR

PART FOUR

CHAPTER 26

Live with a man for years—and then discover that you know nothing at all about him!

Sylvia had been convinced that at the very least Paul would listen to what she had to say. She had clung to that thought, all through the long journey and the docking at Ransome's Hole, and then on through a maze of corridors and slideways that took her and her Roguards deep into the habitat interior. And finally, face to face with him, she realized her mistake.

"It was very foolish for you to come here." His expression was cold, and he stared through her as though she did not exist. He was wearing the same drab uniform as all the others she had seen in Ransome's Hole.

"Paul, I had to. Terrible things have been happening in the Cloud. Thousands of people have died, and all the time—"

"A mistake, and a total waste of time." He turned to the machines standing beside her. "Take her to living quarters K-1-25, level 4."

"Paul!"

But he was already turning, refusing to look her way. "You had your chance to work with us," he said coldly as he walked out. "Ransome is a once-in-a-millennium genius, the best hope for the Solar System. You wouldn't help when we needed it.

Why should anyone listen to you now, when we don't need help?"

And then he was gone. Sylvia tried to run after him and found the Roguards blocking her way. She pushed at them angrily, taking out her frustration on the resilient plastic. Endless weeks of travel to seek Paul Chu's ear—and then dismissed in one minute, without any sign that the two of them had once been lovers and close friends!

It was such an anticlimax, Sylvia was ready to burst with frustration. The machines were moving her back the way they had come, holding her lightly with their jointed arms. She fought them at first, but it was pointless. The gentle touch disguised their strength, but they could apply many tons of force with each flexible limb.

After ten more minutes of slideway travel they brought her to an open door and guided her through it. As it slid closed behind her, she spun around and cursed the silent machines.

"Helps your feelings," said a familiar and cynical voice from behind her. "Don't do much good, though. Better save your breath."

She turned. "Aybee! How in Eden did you get here?"

"Long tale—a long and sad tale, as old Lewie C. puts it. Turns out Ransome doesn't trust me quite as much as I thought." Aybee Smith was sitting cross-legged across a high table, long limbs dangling to each side. "Wait just a minute. I already did this two days ago, but let's make sure nothing has changed." He hopped off the table and circled the room, peering at ventilator grilles and under and on all free surfaces. Finally he nodded. "I'm pretty sure we're safe to talk. No monitoring—or if there is, I can't find it."

He pointed to a chair and returned to sit again on the table. "All right, Sylv, let's play catch up. Who first?"

His scowling face had made Sylvia feel better already. She described everything that had happened since she left the ruined space farm, then heard of Aybee's own zigzag passage from there to Ransome's Hole.

"At least you had no choice," she said. "I'm the stupid one—I set out looking for trouble. And now the whole system's ready to be blown apart, and neither of us can do a thing."

"Not right now. But every day I'm here, I learn more about what makes this place tick." Aybee was prowling the perimeter of the chamber. "They shouldn't have put us together, and they ought to be monitoring us. Ransome is overconfident."

"Overconfident! Right, and with plenty to be overconfident about. We're in a mess. I don't know why you're looking so pleased with yourself."

"Because we finally have a chance to learn what's screwing up the Solar System." Aybee squatted down and wrapped his arms around his crossed legs. "I'll tell you one good thing your friend the Wolfman told me when we were on the space farm. He says you solve problems by getting into the *middle* of 'em. When we were out on the harvesters, we were sitting on the outside edge of things. We only felt Black Ransome's effect at third hand. Now we're right at the heart of his power."

"And we're totally powerless! Aybee, even if we got out of these rooms, I'm not sure we could do anything. Ransome controls everything. We couldn't get a message to Bey Wolf or Cinnabar Baker."

"We might get one to the Wolfman, but it wouldn't help. Last time I saw Ransome he told me Wolf is here, too. He pointed out how convenient it was, all three of us coming to him."

"Bey's in Ransome's Hole? However did he find his way?"

"Same as you and me, I'll bet—a little bad luck and a big lump of stupidity. He came here on one of the superfast ships, same as I did. Ransome is hoping to make Wolf a convert to his cause, like he's trying to convert me. You, too, if you let him."

"Then Baker's our only hope. Aybee, you're the smart one. You have to find a way to let her know where we are."

He was shaking his head. "Sorry, Sylv. It's worse than that. When you said Ransome controls everything, you were closer than you realized. He controls Cinnabar Baker."

"Never! The Cloud is her whole life. She'd never sell out to Ransome."

"That's what I'd have said two weeks ago. But Ransome *showed* me. When you get to meet with him he'll show you, too. He has direct transmissions of meetings from inside Baker's personal quarters. Secret papers and interviews, too, from the Opik and Marsden Harvesters. She must be running a portable recorder during her important meetings and transmitting 'em here by sealed hyperbeam."

"Aybee, I think you're crazy. But if you happen to be right it's an absolute disaster. You tell me that, and still you don't think that Ransome has everything under his control?"

"Maybe he does—for the moment. But he can't have corrupted every person in the Outer System. And he's been winning for too long. It's time for *our* run of luck."

"Aybee, if I said anything like that you'd tell me it's statistical gibberish. According to Paul Chu—damn that man—Ransome has been winning because he's a genius. Are you going to disagree with that, too?"

"Funny you should say that." Aybee stood up and stretched. "I do disagree. I came to Ransome's Hole in a hell of a ship, too advanced to be believed. New drive, new nav system, new technology all over it. First thing I asked when I got here: Who's the genius? Ransome, everybody says. All the ideas come from him. He's the one."

"But you think not?" Sylvia knew Aybee's weaknesses, and evaluating the abilities of others was not one of them.

"Hell, I *know* not. Ransome can snow most people here with physics, maybe all of them. He knows a lot, and he talks a great line. But he's not the real thing."

"How do you know that?"

Aybee gave her a sinister smile. "Because, Sylv, I *am* the real thing. Take it from one who knows; Black Ransome didn't invent that new drive and that new ship. He says he's the Negentropic Man, and something's sure feeding bad information to the Cloud's control system. But Ransome's not the genius who dreamed up the entropy reduction and signal-generation system. No way."

"Then who *is* the inventor? Are you saying Ransome has some supergenius working for him here? And how does the entropy reduction system work?"

"I was afraid you'd ask me that." Aybee smiled more horribly than ever. "You see, Sylv, I don't have the answers. But let me loose for a day or two in this place and I'll get 'em."

"Oh, Aybee." Sylvia slumped down on the chair. "I don't believe in giving up, but be a realist. We'll never get out of here. Black Ransome may not be your supergenius, but he's certainly smart enough not to trust us."

"Speak of the devil." Aybee gestured behind Sylvia. The door had opened, and standing there was Ransome himself, as cold-eyed and commanding as he had been when Sylvia saw that first video message for Paul Chu. He was unarmed and wearing a simple black tunic. His face was pale and showed signs of some unusual strain.

Ransome nodded to Aybee and Sylvia. Behind him stood two of the Roguards. For twenty seconds no one moved.

"You will come with me," Ransome said at last. And then, to the machines, he said, "These two people are now in my personal custody. You are relieved of guard duties until I return them here."

"Where are you taking us?" Sylvia did not like the tone in Ransome's voice. There was a strident edge to it that suggested a man under enormous pressure.

"Wait and see." Ransome lifted his arm and pointed to Aybee. "You first, in front of her. I'll be right behind you."

"Sure." Aybee stepped easily through the door, with a nod at the waiting machines. "Don't wait up for us, we might be back late. Where do you want me to walk, Ransome? You're the one who knows where we are going."

"Follow the gravity vector. Always up."

They started along the left-hand corridor, heading away from the nearest kernels. In forty yards they had reached the first branch and passed a group of armed humans. Everyone nodded respectfully at Ransome and moved to allow the trio to pass on to another segment of passageway. Aybee walked on until he came to a spherical chamber and another fork in the path.

He paused and turned again to Ransome. "I don't know which one of these leads outward. Take your pick."

"Left. Keep going." The voice was gruff, and Aybee could see beads of sweat on the man's face. They moved slowly forward, to a curved part of the corridor screened both ahead of and behind them. An open door leading to an empty maintenance chamber stood on the right-hand side.

"Through there." Ransome nodded his head. "Both of you."

Aybee tensed himself as he went through. Sylvia was between him and Ransome. If he turned to grapple with him, would she be able to get out of the way fast enough?

He had to try. He was spinning around, reaching out his long arms, when the man behind him groaned and sagged forward against the inner wall of the room.

"Aybee! Get him!" Aybee heard Sylvia's shout, but Ransome had fallen forward. His torso flexed itself, then straightened in a painful stretching movement that dropped it to the floor and jerked it two meters into the room.

"Close the door. Keep watch for people," an agonized voice said. "I can't hold any longer."

Then Ransome was twitching on the smooth floor while Aybee and Sylvia looked on in astonishment.

"Ransome. Are you all right?" Sylvia was crouching down next to him.

"Ransome may be fine." The voice was down to a whisper. "But I'm Bey Wolf. Help me, Sylvia. I need five minutes clear."

The body was jerking into violent spasm. The contorted face that looked up at Sylvia was still Black Ransome's, but at the back of the pained eyes she saw something else. "Bey! Is it really you? What's happening?"

The body had uncurled to full extension. It looked nine inches longer than before. The torso shivered. "I did what I told—my classes at Office of Form Control—never to do. Most stupid and dangerous thing in the world. Accelerated form-change, badly defined end-form—programed from scratch—no chance to do parametric variations. I'm outside —region of stability. Size reduction through muscular contraction. Only have partial muscle control." Ransome's face worked to a twisted smile. "Five minutes more."

"Hey, Wolfman, take your time." Aybee looked out along the corridor, and then he slid the door closed. "We're safe here. I'll watch this. Sylv, see if you can help."

"Don't touch me. I'm getting there." An internal crisis had passed, and the twists and jerks in Wolf/Ransome's body were easing. "Aybee, you seem to know your way—around this place. How far—from the main communications center?"

"Half a kilometer. Back along the corridor, and then head out toward the periphery. The place will be guarded, though, and it's not far from Ransome's own quarters. Ransome might be there."

"I don't think so—I think he's been off-habitat. Anyway, we have to take the risk. I have maybe—one hour, before I have to get back to a tank. This form's a *disaster*." Wolf was grunting with pain and effort, forcing his body back to the shorter, more compact shape of Black Ransome. "We should be able to get into the com center. No one here argues with Ransome—not even the Roguards. They told me how to find you without a question. Help me up, Sylvia."

"You look terrible. Take more time."

"We don't have time. We've got to get to the communications center and send a message to the Cloud, saying where we are, before Ransome shows up again. Or someone does a random chromosomal check on me. Or I fall apart. Once the coordinates of this place are known, it doesn't matter so much if we're captured again. Right. Any time."

The tics and twitches were subsiding, and the face had again smoothed to the pale, decisive countenance of Black Ransome. With Aybee leading the way and Sylvia ready to support Wolf if he needed it, they walked quietly on through the habitat and then made a turn outward. The twisting corridors were deserted, allowing Wolf to pause and rest along the way. During the final fifty yards Sylvia felt her face tighten with anticipation and tension and was sure she would be noticed. But the guards at the entrance to the communications facility merely stiffened to attention, stepped back a pace, and saluted as the three passed. Wolf/Ransome stood on the threshold and looked around. The center was empty. He nodded back casually to the guards and closed the door.

"That's the most dangerous part over, at least for the moment." Bey sighed and moved across to the hyperbeam unit. "I knew just what Ransome looked like, even how he moved and sounded—I saw more than enough of the Negentropic Man—but I didn't know his speech patterns or the way he greets people."

"Bey, we got troubles you don't even know about." Aybee held out a hand to prevent Wolf from touching the hyperbeam communication console. "It's not safe to send a message to the Cloud—Ransome has Cinnabar Baker in his pocket. I've seen messages from her."

Wolf shook his head and turned on the communications set. "It's not news to me; I suspected as much. I didn't like the idea when I had it myself, but I knew there was a leak—and I didn't see how it could be anybody but Baker."

"But if we can't trust her, who can we trust?" Sylvia asked.

"We don't trust anyone. We send the message everywhere, spray it across the Inner and Outer Systems. Aybee, can you take over all the communications channels?"

"For a general broadcast?" Aybee glared at the panel for a few seconds, then slowly nodded. "Guess so. Takes a few minutes to set it up—and if I grab 'em all, we'll be noticed. I'll have to push a hundred other users right off the system. Everyone in Ransome's Hole will head this way."

"That's a different worry. Get the com system ready. Sylvia and I will work on the message."

"Give me five. Make me a formatted data set, all ready to send." Aybee bent over the panel and began to work. After a few minutes he swore and looked up. "Problem. System's not set up for general broadcast."

"Can't you jury-rig?" Bey could hear the sound of his own

voice changing, and his hands were starting to tremble. He did not have long to get to a form-change tank.

"I can. But I'll have to sit here and baby it. It's a low data rate, too—I'm going to need half an hour's transmission. But as soon as we start, this whole habitat will start to buzz."

"Agreed." Bey stood up. "Sylvia, you can finish the message. We want everyone in the system to know that Ransome is the cause of control and communications breakdown. Tell them the location data for Ransome's Hole, what he's been doing, all you know about him. Ask help from anyone who can give it. Say we need a hundred ships or a thousand, from anywhere in the system, and while you're at it add a note saying that there's a leak in Cinnabar Baker's office. If it's Baker herself, that takes care of it. If not, she'll do something fast. And you, Aybee, as soon as you're ready, grab the outgoing circuits and send the message."

"What about you?" Sylvia had stood up when Bey did, supporting him as he swayed to his feet.

"I've got to guarantee Aybee his thirty minutes. Hold the fort here. Don't try to leave, even if you finish sending the message. Just lie low until I get back."

"Bey, you look terrible." Sylvia could feel his arm trembling. "I ought to come with you."

"No. You couldn't help me, and sending that message is top priority. Get it ready, then help Aybee send it."

"What are you going to do?"

Bey gave her a wan smile. "I wish I knew. Don't worry, I'll think of something. Aybee, take a ten-second break and tell me how to get to Ransome's personal quarters. Maybe I can cut off our trouble there, right at the top."

Aybee nodded, paused for a moment, then rattled off a series of directions. Then he bent back to his control panel. It was Sylvia who watched unhappily as Bey blundered toward the door. He still resembled Ransome in general appearance, but his body language was subtly wrong. His movements had become jerky, with violent and random twitches of muscle in his arms and legs.

Sylvia kept silent and forced herself to watch him go. Bey thought he had another half hour before he was forced to find a form-change tank. She suspected that was irrelevant. Long before that, Bey would be unable to pass as Black Ransome to anyone with eyes or ears.

CHAPTER 27

"God does not play dice."

—Albert Einstein

"God not only plays dice, but also sometimes throws them where they cannot be seen."

—Stephen Hawking

"God knows what God does."

—Apollo Belvedere Smith

There was silence in the communications center for five minutes after Bey left. Sylvia quickly completed the formatted message and defined a directory reference for it, but then she was reluctant to speak and break Aybee's concentration. He was setting up the master sequence that would take over in one swoop every outgoing message circuit in Ransome's Hole, and it was important to provide no hint of that intention until the moment came for override.

Finally he glanced across to Sylvia and nodded. "Ready as I'll ever be. Where's the message?"

"I put it into a restricted access bank for safety—so no one can take a peek by accident."

"Right idea. Password?"

"'LUCKY.'"

"Yeah. Let's hope." Aybee entered the final call sequence and sat back in his chair. There was a moment's pause, then a flicker of lights across the full display. He nodded. "Okay. We're in business. Now the fun starts—people are being bounced off com circuits all over the habitat."

"Will they know the command came from here?"

"Dunno. Probably. I couldn't see any way to stop it, but I did my best to make 'em freeze. I slapped Ransome's name on everything, so it looks like he's the one grabbing circuits." He stood up. "Keep your eye on that readout. If it goes to zero, yell. It means I'll have to take over. We'll be all done when it hits two eighty. Then we can release the channels."

"What are you going to do?"

"Still don't know. Bey said lie low, but we don't want to just sit here. We need to be useful." Aybee went to the door, opened it a fraction, and peered out. At once he drew back and allowed the door to close.

"What's wrong?"

"Guys outside. Four of 'em."

"Heading this way?"

"No. Not even looking. Just standing there. Bey's doing, for a bet. He sent 'em here to stop anybody getting *in*. But it means we're stuck." Aybee stared around the communications center, then walked across to a horizontal trapdoor set in the curved floor. He lifted it and peered through.

"That won't help." Sylvia had followed his actions. "There's only a kernel down there. The door just gives access to the outside of the shields. You won't be able to get out that way."

"I know. I just want to take a look. I've been itching to get close to a live kernel ever since I arrived here." He paused with the trapdoor half-open. "How's that counter?"

"Up to one seventy."

"Going smooth. Let me take a little peek here." Aybee lay down with his head through the opening of the trapdoor. "It's a live one, all right. Whopping cable for the sensors. Big junction box, too—just like it was on the space farm's ker-

nel." He craned farther into the opening, wriggling his body
forward across the floor until only his hips and legs were
visible to Sylvia. "*And* its own computer console." His voice
was muffled. "Seems like there's a direct link from the kernel
sensors to the habitat's central computer. Now, why do that,
unless . . ." Another eighteen inches of Aybee disappeared
through the trapdoor.

The count in front of Sylvia had been climbing steadily. It
finally reached 280 and froze there, lights blinking softly. A
MESSAGE COMPLETE indicator flashed on. She released all the
com circuits and walked across to the trapdoor. She tapped
Aybee on the thigh.

"What's up?" His body twisted around so he could look at
her.

"Nothing bad, but we're all done with the message. If you
want to go down there, you'll find it easier feet first." She
waited as he turned, then followed him down the narrow ladder until they were both standing on the outer shield of a
kernel. Sylvia stared down at the black, polished surface.

"How do you know this is an active kernel?"

Aybee pointed. "There's the control unit for angular momentum. I've checked a bunch of 'em these last couple of
weeks. Most of them aren't connected to spin-up/spin-down
systems, so they're not ready as energy sources or energy
storage. Matter of fact, I'm not sure just what they *are*
doing." He paused. "This is a live one, though. Hooked up
and active and ready to roll."

The kernel's control panel was a compact unit sitting on the
curved shield surface. Aybee squatted down by it. "So far, so
good. Want first crack at it?"

"I wouldn't know where to start. But if you know a way to
tell what's inside the shields, you can check what Bey suggested to me when we were working on the message. He
thinks there's some new form-change product in there, something that can survive near a kernel. He tried to scan the shield
interior back on the Marsden Harvester, looking for something
unusual, but he didn't find a thing. He wasn't sure he was
doing it right, though. Leo Manx told him to ask you, because

this is your line of work. But you were off having fun on the space farm."

"Yeah. Had a great time there. Real pleasure trip." Aybee was already at the control panel, staring vacantly at its complicated console. "This layout's a strange one for a power kernel console. Too many functions. *And* it's directly linked with the habitat's central computer."

"Can you scan the interior?"

"Dunno." Aybee listed the control function menu and studied it for a few seconds. "Guess I can. Only thing inside the kernel shield—apart from the kernel—should be the radiation monitors. I'll use them to do an interior scan and output it to the screen. We'll pick up an image of anything inside the shields. But I'll bet my butt that we don't find anything in there."

He turned on the display and set the interior monitors to perform a slow scan within the innermost kernel shield. The kernel itself, pouring out gigawatts of radiation and particles, appeared as a tiny, intense point of light on the monitor. The triple shields, reflecting back that sleet of energy, showed on the same monitor as a softer continuous glow.

They both stared at the screen, waiting in vain for any anomalous pattern. When the scan had finished, Sylvia shook her head. "That does Bey in. He was sure there had to be something inside. What now?"

"We gotta use pure logic." Aybee was back at the controls. "One: There's an information source inside the kernel shields. Two: There's nothing inside the shield but the kernel. Therefore—nice clean syllogism—*the kernel must be the information source.* I've been skirting that for weeks, wondering if I'm off my head—but no one would let me get near a kernel and find out!"

"Aybee, let's not get too ridiculous. A kernel is a *power* source. It isn't an *information* source. And how can there be anything inside a kernel? It's only billionths of a centimeter across. And even if there were anything inside, it couldn't ever get a message out. A kernel is a black hole!"

Aybee was shaking his head and changing the scale on the

output display. He had zoomed in to the area around the kernel itself. "Come off it, Sylv. Black holes stopped being black in the 1970s, two hundred and fifty years ago! Hell, you know that —why else do you need shields? You know black holes pump out particles and radiation. Every kernel has its own radiation temperature and its own entropy. Maybe its own *signal*."

"But it's too small! You couldn't possibly pack a signal generator in such a tiny volume."

"We don't know how much space there is *inside*, or what the inside of a kernel is like—no idea at all. The interior has its own geometry, its own space-time signature, probably its own physical laws. Hell, people have been saying for centuries that the inside of a black hole is a 'separate universe,' but we never bother to think through the *implication* of that. If the inside of each kernel is a separate universe, *anything* could be in there—including somebody capable of communication."

"Somebody? You mean something *alive*? How did it get in there?"

"Hey, you'd better define life for me. If you mean something capable of generating nonrandom signals, then, yeah, I mean *alive*. As for how it got there—it's been in there all along."

"But *how*? And what could something inside a kernel possibly want to say?"

"One question at a time, Sylv. Do you want to find out what's going on, or do you want to run a debate? Remember, thermodynamics only tells what's happening on *average* for a kernel's radiation. It doesn't say what gets emitted at any particular moment—so let's take a look at this." Aybee turned on a second screen. "We don't see a thing when we just monitor the total radiation output of the kernel, because the average level is so high. But I can display the time variation of the radiation—the deviation from the average. See that fluctuation? Now, it could be a *signal*. Information, coming from the kernel—from nowhere. Just what Bey was looking for, as bad inputs to the form-change process. And I'll bet this could be responsible for breakdown of communications all through the system. Don't forget there are active kernels in all the important places, everywhere from the harvesters to the space farms. It could be the cause of the snake wrapped around the Kernel Ring, the giant woman walking across the space farm collector, flaming blue swords, giant red space hounds—you name it."

Sylvia was studying the rise and fall of the radiation pattern. "But it doesn't *look* like a signal. It's like pure noise."

"A perfectly efficient signal looks like noise—until you know the rules." Aybee was tracing the circuits leading from the kernel monitors. "Before the signal can be interpreted, it needs to be *decoded*. And that's where the computer systems must come in. See, this signal is fed as an input data stream to the computer—the central computer for Ransome's Hole. Let's have a look at what the computer thinks it is seeing. It starts by—uh oh." He was staring at a new signal on the screen.

"What's wrong?"

"Bad news for Bey." The alert signal vanished and was replaced by a flashing message. "While I was playing with the com system, I took a precaution. I set up a priority interrupt for information about Ransome." Aybee was frowning at the screen. "According to this, Ransome is in two places at once on the habitat. I asked for positional fixes, but all I get as an answer is 'No Defined Location.' Bey might run into the real Ransome."

"Can you do anything about it?"

"Not one thing. We don't even know where he is."

"Then we have to keep going." Sylvia was more intrigued than she had realized. "Let's find out what we've got here. What's the next step?"

Aybee did not answer for a minute or two, then marked a point on the screen with the cursor. "See that trace? It says there's a program on the main computer system, one designed as an interface with this kernel. It ought to be the code/decode algorithm. We can try it. You stay right here, Sylv, and tell me what happens. I'll go to the upper console and execute that module."

Aybee scampered back up the ladder, leaving Sylvia to

wonder what they were hoping to accomplish. It was difficult to see how fiddling with kernels could help them escape from Ransome's Hole. But it was hard to stop Aybee when he had the bit between his teeth—and she did not want to stop any more than he did.

The lighting in the kernel shield chamber was poor, and Sylvia was forced to lean close to see the miniature control display. For another minute or two there was nothing to claim her attention. Then she noticed that the spin-up/spin-down mechanism on the kernel had suddenly been brought into action. It was adding and subtracting tiny bursts of angular momentum, far too little to make sense as power supplies.

"Are you doing that?" she called out.

"Doing what?" Aybee's head appeared at the trapdoor.

"Spin up and spin down. But just little changes. Now it's stopped."

"I've been entering a question about kernel operation. But it shouldn't cause kernel spin change." Aybee was suddenly gone again. "How about that?" his voice called from above.

"Yes. It's doing it again. And now I'm seeing a change in the kernel radiation pattern. What's causing it?"

"I'm not sure, but I've got ideas. Hey!" His voice rose half an octave. "Did you just poke something down there? Touch the sensor leads, maybe?"

"I'm nowhere near them."

"Well, I'm getting something wild on the display here. Come up and look at this."

Sylvia hurried up the stairs and went across to Aybee at the console. The display was flickering with random lights. While they watched, it moved suddenly to a distorted pattern of letters. Sylvia gaped as the screen steadied and an intelligible message began to scroll in.

QUERY . . . QUERY . . . QUERY: ARE YOU READY TO RECEIVE?

"Ready," Aybee said. He added softly to Sylvia, "Let's hope we are."

MESSAGE TRANSFER: DEGREE OF TRANSMITTED SIGNAL REDUNDANCY HAS BEEN REDUCED. ENCODING ENTROPY PER UNIT NOW DIFFERENT FROM ALL PREVIOUS RECEIVED COMMUNICA-

TIONS. DEDUCE PRESENCE OF NEW SIGNAL GENERATOR IN SEND-
ING SYSTEM. QUERY: WHO ARE YOU?

Aybee blinked and stared at the panel. After a moment he shrugged. "My name is Aybee Smith." His voice was suddenly husky and uncertain, and there was a moment's pause before the vocoder could make the adaptation and a transcript of his words appeared on the display screen. "I am special assistant to Cinnabar Baker, general coordinator of the Outer System. I have with me Sylvia Fernald, responsible for control systems in the Cloud. Hey, more to the point. Query: Who the hell are *YOU*?"

CHAPTER 28

"... he felt for the first time the dull and angry helplessness
which is the first warning stroke of the triumph of mutability. Like the poisoned Athulf in the Fool's Tragedy, he
could have cried, 'Oh, I am changing, changing, fearfully
changing.'"

—Dorothy L. Sayers

The interior of Ransome's Hole reminded Bey of a great
cluttered warehouse. Scattered through it, seemingly at random, were hundreds of kernels, each enough to power a
structure twice the total size. The minute singularities were
distributed through the whole structure, held in position by
electromagnetic harnesses and floating within their triple
spherical shields.

With no other masses to provide gravity, the kernels defined the whole internal field of the habitat. Corridors curled
and twisted, following the local horizontal; free-hanging
cables snaked their anfractuous and eye-disturbing paths
across open spaces, bending to follow invisible equipotentials.
The floor of a corridor could veer through a right angle in a
hundred feet and still provide a constant-gravity environment.

In Bey's condition, the journey through the interior was
one episode in a surrealistic nightmare. The spiraling geome-

try around him matched perfectly the reeling condition inside his head. He concentrated his attention on following Aybee's instructions and staggered forward. Fortunately, the interior tunnels were almost deserted. He was beginning to hope that he would reach Ransome's quarters unseen when he saw ahead of him an armed group of four security officers. Two of them were facing his way. There was no way he could avoid their attention, and in any case he knew no other way to his destination.

Bey put all his strength into standing upright and walking smoothly forward. When he was five paces from the group, he gave them a curt nod. "Busy?"

"No, sir." The reply was prompt and respectful. "Not particularly."

"Good. There's an important message going out from Com Central, and I don't want anything to disturb it. I want you to go there and make sure there are no interruptions until I return."

It sounded feeble—*he* sounded feeble. But all he saw was a deferential nodding of heads. As the men moved past him, Bey risked his luck one more time. He reached out to take the hand weapon from the last man's belt. "Let me borrow this. I'll return it to you."

He had gone too far—he was sure of it. But the man did no more than nod, say, "Yes, sir," and hurry along after the others.

Bey stood without moving until they were all out of sight, then allowed himself to sag against the wall of the corridor. Standing erect and talking had been an enormous drain on his energy. He took one step forward and felt in midpace a shock go through his whole body. It was an internal vibration, a tremor of catabolism from every muscle and every nerve. Some inner barrier to destructive change had suddenly crumbled.

He set his mind on the turn in the corridor, twenty meters farther on, and thought of nothing beyond that point. He took one step. His body responded reluctantly and imprecisely to his will—but it moved. Another. One more. One more . . .

He was at the turn. How long had it taken? The next goal was . . . what? A change in color of the corridor, thirty paces away. He had to get to that; there was nothing beyond that. Another step, and then another.

He guided himself along the wall with one outstretched hand. There at last. His eyes sought out and recorded the next objective.

One more effort—twenty steps. Surely he could do that much?

And then one more. Don't think, just move.

On the final approach to Ransome's personal quarters, Bey caught sight of his own reflection in a silvered wall panel. He thought at first that he was facing a distorting mirror. His limbs hung stiff and awkward from his body, his eyes started bloodshot from their sockets, and there was a gray, pasty look to his face. He tried Ransome's confident and commanding smile, and it was a madman's leer.

He stepped closer to the shining surface. It was perfectly smooth and flat, producing no hint of distortion. And the closer he came, the less he looked anything like Black Ransome. He stretched his arms wide and flexed his shoulders. There was the click and crack of frozen joints. His muscles were on fire, and every sign of mobility was leaving him. More and more, he was a poorly made, ungainly scarecrow hung on a misshapen frame. He staggered on.

He had been prepared to bluff, lie, or fight his way into Ransome's quarters. Now he was sure that he had passed the point where he had the strength to do any of those things. Fortunately, they were unnecessary. Perhaps Ransome was so confident of his own power to command loyalty that he scorned protection, or perhaps the area was protected only when Ransome was there; whatever the reason, Bey was able to pass unchallenged through the entrance.

Aybee had told him about the rococo style of the first chamber, with its great water globe filled with exotic fish. Otherwise, Bey would have added that to his growing list of hallucinations. He went on toward the inner suite of rooms. He had no idea how much time had gone by since he had left

Sylvia and Aybee. They needed every minute he could give them. In the back of his mind he still held an unvoiced hope: If somehow he could capture or neutralize Ransome himself, the chance of escape from Ransome's Hole still existed. He knew they could not wait for reinforcements. That would take weeks, even with an instant response to Aybee's signal from the fastest ships of the Inner or Outer System.

At the door of the inner chambers he hesitated for a moment. Surely the message would have been completed. In any case, he dared not wait. He could feel the changes coursing through every part of his body. His long training allowed him to compensate for some of them, but he was close to the limits.

The weapon he was holding was set at the lethal level. He raised it, opened the door, and stepped through—and saw, no more than twenty feet from him, not Ransome but Mary.

Typically, she had ignored the standard dress code of Ransome's Hole. She was wearing a dress of russet velvet with puffed shoulders and a choke collar, and on her head she wore a broad-brimmed green hat. She turned slowly at the sound of the sliding door, an imperious look on her face.

Mary was certainly playing a part—but which one? None that Bey recognized. He lowered the gun so that it was no longer trained on her midriff. Mary ignored it, anyway. She moved right in front of him and reached out to put her hands on his chest.

"Bey!" So much for the idea that he still resembled Ransome. "My poor sweet, what happened to you."

"Where is Ransome?" His voice was failing, curdled in his throat.

"Bey, what are you *doing* here? I wanted to come and see you last week, but I was told you were no longer on the habitat. When did you get back?"

"I never left. Where is Ransome?"

"My poor love." Mary was holding him away from her and inspecting him closely, touching beneath his eyes with a gentle finger. Bey realized for the first time that he was crying. "I don't know what you've been doing to yourself, but I know what you have to do next. You look so sick. We've got to get you to a form-change tank—right this minute."

"Soon. Not yet. Where's Ransome?"

"Bey, you shouldn't even be thinking of Ransome in your condition." She was supporting him, holding him close. "You're shivering all over. I have to look after you."

"Where is Ransome?"

"I don't—" Mary began. She was interrupted.

"If you are so interested in my whereabouts, Mr. Wolf, you might at least look at me." The casual voice came from Bey's left, from a shadowed part of the room. He jerked to face that direction. Ransome was standing there. As Bey raised the gun, the black-clad figure took two steps forward.

"No closer," Bey said. "This is on maximum setting."

"So it is. How very unfriendly." Ransome sounded as calm and rational as ever. "Come now, Mr. Wolf, can we not dispense with these posturings of violence? We are both civilized men, and we have much to talk about."

"Not true. You're a murderer. We have nothing to talk about."

"Let me persuade you otherwise. Do you realize, Mr. Wolf, that this is the third time that I have underestimated you? Really unforgivable on my part. But it makes me more convinced than ever of your value to my operations. You could do wonders for our security systems."

"I'll do nothing for you." Bey waved the gun at Ransome. He was feeling increasingly dizzy and unable to talk. "Move back."

"You will feel differently once you understand my mission." Ransome moved another step closer to Wolf. "You regard the two of us somehow as 'enemies,' people on opposing sides of an argument. But we are not. You will surely admit that you owe no allegiance to the Inner System—they dismissed you after a lifetime's work. As for the Outer System, those people have nothing in common with you. You and I can work together very well. So why not be practical? The old order of the Solar System no longer applies. It will soon be gone forever. Put away that gun and sit down. It is more dangerous to you than it is to me. And you and I must talk."

"I'm past talking."

"No, listen to him, Bey." Mary clutched his arm, but she did not try to interfere with his aim. "He's right. I've followed the reports from the Inner System. It's a total mess there."

"Sure. Because he—" Bey tried to gesture at Ransome and found his arm taking on a spastic movement of its own. "—has been doing his best to *make* it a mess. Can't you see, Mary? He's the *cause* of all the trouble." Bey waved his arm again at Ransome. "I don't have the time or taste for talking to you. Get back up against that wall."

"Don't be silly, Mr. Wolf." Ransome advanced another step. "You escaped from your quarters. An unusual achievement, and one that I am quite willing to recognize. But beyond that you are powerless to influence events. You are in desperate physical shape, and you do not seem to understand reality. I can have a hundred people here to overpower you in a few minutes. So put away that gun."

"Get back! Last warning."

But Ransome was still coming forward, still smiling. And Bey was at the end of his strength.

It was now or never. With shaking hands he pointed the gun squarely at Ransome's head, groaned, and fired.

There was the usual dazzling flash of blue. Bey sagged against the wall. Ransome had given him no choice—too many lives depended on stopping the man—but Bey was sick at what he had done. Would Mary forgive him, understand that he had had to do it?

As the Cherenkov radiation pattern died away, Bey raised his head. Unbelievably, Ransome was still moving. He had walked right through a high-intensity beam. That was totally impossible!

Cherenkov fringes appeared. As Bey watched, Ransome's face turned yellow and began to bubble. The skin evaporated in bursting pockets of light, exposing the wall behind as their color swirls faded.

The bubbles of Ransome's face were bursting in Bey's own

brain. He dropped the gun and sagged against Mary. "Field interference effects—a holograph!"

"Of course." The image of Ransome was beginning to fade, and only his voice seemed to hover clear in the air. "How else could I appear to you when I am far away? And what a simpleton you must be, Wolf, if you imagine that I would not have taken precautions against both death and discovery!"

Ransome's uniform was becoming transparent. His smile showed a black mouth, black teeth, as he turned to face Mary. "Leave this idiot now. He deserves to die. And from the look of it he hasn't long to wait."

He glared at Wolf and shook his head rebukingly, his face filled with contempt.

"I'm afraid I sadly overestimated you, Wolf. You're a fool, no more intelligent than any of the others. Did you seriously believe that I would expose myself to possible death when my life's work is unfinished? If you had agreed to cooperate, I could have saved you. But you tried to kill me—and that means your own death. Your life is finished. For me, and what I am going to do, it is just beginning."

"No." Bey's throat was tightening. He had little time for more words. "You're crazy, Ransome. You're the one who doesn't know reality. *You* are finished. A message was sent from here a few minutes ago. All circuits, to the Inner and Outer Systems. People know where you are, what you are, how many your actions have killed. You're done for, Ransome, even if you don't admit it. No matter where you run to, where you hide, you'll be found and caught and brought to trial."

The distorted image of Ransome's face flared with anger and astonishment. "That was a truly intolerable act. And quite a futile one. I am not finished—I have scarcely started! And I have tools available to me beyond your imagining. I would say wait and see, but you will not live long enough for that. Die now, Wolf. Your time is over."

Was it true? Did Ransome have more secret fortresses, other resources? Bey did not know, and he could no longer attempt analysis. If there were to be new battles with Ransome, others would have to fight them.

Black Ransome, Bey thought distantly. The air around Ransome was turning black. Or was it Bey's own failing consciousness?

"Leave this ignorant fool, Mary, and follow me," a curt voice said. And then even the dark shadow was gone.

Bey struggled to stand upright, to lean away from Mary. She was staring at him, holding him, her eyes wide and her face close to his.

"Bey! Can you hear me?"

Grim, grinning king. Ransome is gone, Ransome is gone. The words drifted through Bey's mind. Ransome's head was dissolved, faded to black. *Fade far away, dissolve, and quite forget* . . . Bey tried to nod, failed, and felt his legs lose all their strength.

"Bey!" The voice was Mary, his Mary, infinitely sorrowful and far away. "I'm here." He could no longer see her. He tried to grip her hand, but as he did so, all feelings withered from his fingertips.

Mary, dressed in white and strewing flowers. *There's rosemary, that's for remembrance.* As he watched, she grew, thinned, paled, became Sylvia, frowned at him in disapproval. *Too little, Bey Wolf, too hairy. Hideous.* Without warning her features flowed and became those of Andromeda Diconis. Her lower lip was full, her face flushed with passion, her red hair —red hair? Mary's hair, Mary's husky voice saying, "There's beggary in the love that can be reckoned," a pale face beneath flowing dark hair and an elaborate headdress. He had seen *that* costume before, many times.

Bey's mind was a chaos of quantum states, transitions without warning or control, words and fragmented images intertwined.

I am dying, Egypt, dying; only I here importune death awhile, until of many thousand kisses the poor last I lay upon thy lips. In his mind he heard Mary speaking, saw again the cotton robe, the dark coiled hair, the tall headdress, and he fought against her grasp. But you're not, Mary. I'm the one that's dying. *I have a rendezvous with death, at midnight on some flaming hill.* But that's not quite right, I'm remembering wrong. And this isn't Earth. I'm dying here, far from Earth. *Far from eve and morning, and yon twelve-winded sky.*

I was always sure that I would die on Earth. In the evening, at the end of some perfect summer's day. *Sunset and evening star, and one clear call for me.*

He felt Mary's arms tightening around him, holding him in the world. Then that sensation too was going. In the end there was nothing left, nothing to hold on to. The whole universe was blinking out of existence.

Thy hand, great Anarch, lets the curtain fall, And universal darkness buries all.

Bey was gone.

CHAPTER 29

"Nothing endures but change."
                        —Heraclitus

Bey had fought hard against it, but the pressure was at last irresistible. He was driven up, reluctantly up—up to life, up to consciousness, up to discomfort, up as firmly and finally as a cork in a tidal wave.

He washed ashore to wakefulness, and for a while he lay with his eyes closed, rejecting the world. But he could not block out the sounds. Close to him was a clogged, asthmatic wheeze, the rattling breath of a human being close to death.

After two minutes Bey could stand it no longer. He allowed his eyes to open and at once came fully awake.

Perched on the open door of the form-change tank, no more than six inches from his face, stood Turpin. The crow's head was tilted to one side, and its beady black eyes glared unblinkingly at Bey. It again produced a dreadful groaning wheeze and followed it with a gurgling cough.

That was echoed by a more distant throat clearing. Ten feet beyond Turpin sat Leo Manx, his face angry and reproachful. When he saw that Bey's eyes were open, he nodded. "At last. Good. I will inform the others."

He stood up and hurried out before Bey could ask the first of his dozens of questions.

Perhaps it was just as well. Bey could not speak. He leaned forward in the tank and coughed his lungs clear of dark, clotted phlegm as Turpin shuffled out of the way with a squawk of rage.

By the time he could breathe, Manx was back with Aybee.

Aybee stared at the spotted floor in front of Bey. "You got me here to see that? Gross, Leo. Extremely gross."

Bey ended a final coughing fit. "How long?" he asked. "How long was I—" He ran out of air.

But he already had some idea of the answer. A trip from the Outer System took weeks. If he and Leo were in the same room, a long time had passed. Even before he saw Leo, Bey knew that he had been in the tank for an extended session. He could feel it in the mutability of every cell.

"Thirty-six days." Aybee looked accusingly at Bey. "Sleeping your head off, Wolfman. *And* you missed all the fun."

"You were in desperate shape," Manx said. "The form-change that you did . . . unmonitored . . . most ill advised—"

"I know. I'm supposed to be dead. You caught Ransome?"

"No." Leo Manx was still looking annoyed. "He got clear away. We have no idea where he went, where he is, what he's doing. Naturally, we're still looking."

"Mary?" Bey's wind had gone again, and he was wheezing. He suddenly realized where Turpin had found the inspiration for that tortured breathing.

"She's here." Aybee paused, then caught the next question in Bey's look. "On Ransome's Hole, I mean. We're still on the habitat." He grinned. "Us and more people than I ever wanted to see in my life. Everybody you ever heard of is here."

"Answering our message?"

"Yeah, and another one I sent a bit later. That one pulled 'em here in droves. Sylvia's about ready to go into hiding. Hey, can you walk better than you talk? If so, you can see for yourself why things are running wild."

"I can walk." Bey considered the prospect. "Maybe."

"Then let's do it. You have to see this for yourself."

Bey stood up, almost toppled over, and realized as he did so that he was back in his old Earth shape. "How the devil . . ."

"Mary Walton," Aybee said. "She didn't really know how to do it, but when you collapsed, she grabbed and stuffed you any-old-how into a form-change tank. Set you up short and hairy—the way she knew best. Just in time, too. Sylvia saw the monitors when she got there. Five more minutes, you'd have been fertilizer."

"That's what I feel like." Bey slowly followed Aybee out of the room, allowing his body to drift along in the low gravity. So Mary was there, and so was Sylvia. Between them they had dragged him back from the edge.

He was glad to be alive. But no one else seemed too pleased.

"What's making Leo so angry?"

"He was locked up for a week. He blames you." Aybee was leading the way into the central communications area. "Cinnabar's even madder. Sit down there."

Bey looked slowly around. He had sat in this chair before. He remembered coming here with Sylvia and Aybee—just. He must have been far gone.

"Why are they mad?"

"They'll tell you." Aybee was not listening. He was at the console, his long body tight with excitement. "Lock in and hold on to your skull. We're going on-line." He spoke into the vocoder. "RINI connect. Identification: Apollo Belvedere Smith. Reference: Anomalous signal generation, defined in session 302. Query: What is status?"

He turned to Bey. "Takes a few seconds. Far as I can see, that's for encoding and decoding at this end. Their replies are instantaneous. Someday we'll know how."

"*Whose* replies?"

Before Bey could get an answer the screen was filling. The words on it echoed through the lock into Bey's ears.

THIS ACCESS POINT CONTINUES. ALL OTHER SIGNAL GENERA-

TION TERMINATED *no equivalent.* QUERY: STATUS OF ANGULAR MOMENTUM CHANGES?

"Computer still can't translate times," Aybee said to Bey. "That's what 'no equivalent' probably means. I'm wondering if the Rinis *have* times in our sense. If not, this next bit won't mean much to them, either." He said to the vocoder, "All angular momentum changes for identified kernels will cease in three more days. Query: Can you confirm we have complete list?"

LIST CONFIRMED. REQUEST INFORMATION ON ALL OTHER KERNELS. MASS, CHARGE, ANGULAR MOMENTUM, *no equivalent* LOCATION YOUR REFERENCE FRAME.

"We will provide. Request that the following message be sent to access point 073. Transfer message begins. 'Cinnabar Baker leaving Ransome's Hole in four hours. Expect arrival at Brouwer Harvester nine days from now.' Transfer message ends."

DESIRED TRANSMISSION PERFORMED. REQUEST: CONTINUED TRANSFER SHOULD PROCEED FROM GENERAL DATA BANKS.

"We will provide all the general data banks." Aybee grimaced at Bey. "Want to say anything? No. All right, let's cut it. Request: Session end."

SESSION END.

"Off-line." Aybee turned away from the vocoder, grinning with mad satisfaction.

"What the hell was that all about?" Bey was feeling angry, but he recognized it as one of the mood swings that accompanied emergence from the tanks. "I assume you're willing to tell me."

"Sure. Just a minute." Aybee set up a control sequence. "Got to give them the data—they want the general system data bank sent through. It's a hell of a job. Going to take months." He leaned back. "You had it half-right, you see. The source of spurious information that was screwing up formchange and everything else is inside the kernel shields."

"But not a changed form, the way I thought it had to be?"

"No. It's something inside the kernels themselves. It—or they—sends out the standard radiation stream, but it's modulated to carry messages. It's your source of negative entropy."

Aybee spoke casually, but he could not hide his excitement. From anyone else, Bey would not even have listened. With Aybee, he had to take it seriously. "You know that what you're saying sounds impossible."

"Sure does. That's why it's so interesting. Wolfman, I keep telling the coordinators, but they still can't grasp the importance of this. Nor could Ransome. Even though he was using the Rinis for his own purposes, he missed the real point."

"He was the one who discovered this."

"Not proven. Somebody in the Kernel Ring stumbled across it, but I'll bet it wasn't Ransome himself. They were spinning up and spinning down kernels. Routine stuff, the usual energy storage and extraction. But the things inside one of the kernels could detect the change in angular momentum. They hated it—it affected their inertial reference frames. But they're *smart*. They figured out the cause and modulated the radiation emission in reply—sent a signal, in effect. After that it was a straight programming job at this end, signal encode and decode. The trick was to spot first that it *was* a signal."

"*Inside* the kernel." Bey stared down at the floor. A billion-ton kernel had an event horizon only a few billionths of a nanometer across. The ultimate hidden signal source. "They call themselves Rinis?"

"No. They don't call themselves anything at all, far as I can tell. That's the code name I gave them. The computer answer to anything I asked at first seemed to be R.I.N.I.—'Received Information Not Interpretable'—so I stuck 'em with it. I'm getting better at questions now, though."

"Who are they, Aybee?"

"Can't give you one answer. Everybody asks me, but I say it's too early for that sort of question. Intelligent, sure. Smarter than us, could be. A species, maybe. But it's more like they're a new universe. A whole cosmos. I'm not ready to worry that. I'm still getting my head around a bit of their science. They gave Ransome a bundle of things—new drives, new communications—but there's a lot more than he realized.

We're going to get some wild theories out of this."

"They're more advanced than we are?"

"Yeah." Aybee paused. "Or maybe I mean maybe. I don't know how to compare. If I wanted to talk fancy like Leo, I'd say it's like their science is *orthogonal* to ours. They move along a completely different axis of understanding. It's easy to use their ideas, and hell to understand 'em. I'm still having trouble with the basics. Like, are the Rinis a single entity or a finite—or an infinite—number of entities? That sounds weird, but from what I can see of their counting it's based on nondenumerable sets instead of integers."

"They can't be a single entity. There has to be at least three of them."

"Why?"

"Because I've seen that many kernels putting out false form-change information."

"That would be true if each kernel were totally separate. We used to think that. Now I'm sure it's wrong. The kernels —at least the kernels involving the Rinis—"

"Isn't that all of them?"

"No. That's why Ransome had to switch kernels on the space farm. He wanted to get one of his special kernels out when it had done its job. But the Rini kernels are connected somehow. What's known by one is known by all of them. At once, no matter how far away. That's what brought so many ships here. I sent a message saying I might have a system for instantaneous communication, across any distance."

"But if they all connect, they're only one object."

"Not to us. We think they're separate objects. But to *them*, their space could still be singly connected. It's like Flatland. To a being living in two dimensions, on a flat floor, each leg of a chair meets the floor separately and must be a separate object. That's the way the kernels seem to us. But in a higher-dimensional world—their world—they are all connected, all parts of one chair."

"But then you shouldn't be able to supply energy and angular momentum to each kernel separately."

"Why not? You can paint one leg of a chair." Aybee turned

to Bey. "Hey, I'm glad you're back in circulation. I've been wanting talks like this for weeks, but nobody seems to care. Cinnabar and Leo and the rest of 'em are all too busy running around talking politics and stopping wars, and there's all this really good stuff needs looking at. Do you know how the drive the Rinis gave Ransome works?"

"No. But it can wait until tomorrow." Bey stood up. "I'm tired now. Don't bother to get up. I can make it out of here on my own."

He was being sarcastic. Aybee had shown no sign of moving. In fact, as soon as Bey had said he was leaving, Aybee had nodded and turned the computer on again.

Bey's feelings were more complicated. Everything that Aybee had said was fascinating, but Bey was getting tired. More than that, he was restless, to the point where sleep was out of the question. Without any conscious plan he set out to follow a familiar path, drifting along the corridors that led from the communications center to Ransome's private quarters.

When he opened the door, he thought that the outer chamber was unoccupied. Then he noticed Sylvia Fernald standing around by the side of the great water globe, staring in at the fish. Next to her was Cinnabar Baker, even thinner than when Bey had last seen her.

They had their backs turned, but Baker somehow sensed his approach and swung around. When she recognized him, she produced a sound somewhere between a snort and a laugh. "At last. I've waited a month to be rude to you."

"You and Leo both." Bey was not getting the praise he had expected. You'd think that when somebody nearly killed himself to make sure an important message got out . . . "I guess you weren't the information leak out of the harvesters."

"Of course I wasn't. But I had quite a time proving it. You made it sound as though the only ones who could be leaking information to Ransome were me or Leo—and then you ruled out Leo."

"That's the way it looked. It had to be somebody close to you, and it had to be someone who moved with you from one harvester to another. And Leo and Aybee were away with us on the space farm."

"True."

"So that means—"

But Cinnabar Baker had spun around and was heading for the door. "Figure it out," she said over her shoulder. "Or if you can't, Sylvia can tell you about it."

Bey stared after her. "She is *mad*. I wouldn't want to argue with her when she's like that."

"She's been furious for weeks. I've never seen her so angry. But not at you. At Ransome. He did the unforgivable thing."

"Worse than trying to take over the system?"

"Much worse, if you're Cinnabar Baker." Sylvia sat down on a long bench by the side of the water globe and patted the seat next to her. "Sit down, before you fall down. You look exhausted."

"What did Ransome do?"

"Baker wouldn't have minded as much if he had done it to her, personally. But Ransome's people got hold of *Turpin*. They put an audiovisual tap into his head. Everything the crow saw and heard was transmitted straight to Ransome, and Baker never went anywhere without Turpin—he even slept in her bedroom. She realized what was happening when she saw the viewing angle of some of the shots. Worst of all, the tap hurt, and the feed for it made poor old Turpin nearly blind and deaf. When Baker found that out, she wanted to wring Ransom's neck with her own hands."

"Where is he?"

"We don't know yet. But we'll track him down."

"I'm not sure of that." Bey finally sat down next to Sylvia. He had become used to being tall, and it was disconcerting to find that his head again came only to her shoulder. His hands were feeling numb, and he rubbed them together. "Ransome was clever enough to make a bolt hole for himself. He's still as charismatic as ever, and he'll always be able to draw people to him."

"I know. Paul thinks Ransome makes the Sun shine. But

next time he tries anything we'll be ready. Ransome's finished, but he doesn't know it yet. I almost feel sorry for him. Mary told me—"

"Where is she? I wanted to thank the two of you for saving me."

Sylvia looked at him and put her hand gently on his shoulder. "She didn't leave a message, Bey? She said she would."

"I didn't check."

"I'm sorry. Mary left Ransome's Hole. Yesterday, and secretly. I knew she was going to do it, and I suppose I should have tried to stop her. But I didn't. She's going to look for Ransome, wherever he is."

The numb feeling was spreading from his hands through his whole body. Mary had gone. Left him again. He accepted the fact instantly. It was something he had sensed when he had entered the chamber and did not find her.

"That's terrible." He took a deep breath. "I thought she really loved me."

"She does; she always will. She told me that, and she had no reason to lie."

"But she prefers Ransome."

"She didn't say that. But she said that Ransome needs her more than you do."

"How can she possibly think that?"

"The last time I talked to Mary, she told me to ask you something."

"She seems to have told you an awful lot."

"She did. But here's her question. 'Before Bey tells you his heart is broken,' she said, 'ask him this: Of all the things that have happened to him since he left Earth, which has been the most exciting and satisfying? And ask him to *think* before he answers.'"

"The most exciting—"

"You're not doing what Mary asked. Think first."

"I *am* thinking."

And he was. *The most exciting*. Was it looking out of the ship for his first sight of a harvester . . . or the strange, perverse pleasure of the first meal with Sylvia . . . the satisfaction when he learned that the Dancing Man was not a dream of his own unstable mind . . . the space farm rescue . . . the giddy time with Andromeda Diconis, sampling the pleasure centers of a hedonistic habitat . . . the thrill of Mary's voice where he had never expected it? Making love to her? Or . . . a memory flooded in, total and satiating. Bright yellow tracers ran again in his mind.

"It was when—" He paused, then the words were wrung out of him reluctantly, one at a time. "It was when I was looking for the reason for the wrong form-changes. And when I realized that the source of the problems must be inside the kernel shields. But I could never describe that feeling to anyone. And there's no way that Mary could have known it."

"Of course not. She doesn't think that way. She didn't know about the form-changes, and she didn't know about the Rinis. But she sensed what *sort* of answer you had to give, if you were truthful. Because she understands you very well. Don't you see it, Bey?" Sylvia put her arms around him. "Mary needs to be needed. When *you* needed her, she saved you—even when you were still back on Earth and didn't *know* you needed her. Ransome wanted to cause chaos and stir up trouble between the Inner and Outer Systems. He knew that form-change equipment would be more sensitive than anything else to the Rini effects on information flow, so trouble would show up there first. Anyone who might understand what was happening had to be dead, insane, or converted, and it seemed easier to drive you crazy than to kill or convert you. But Mary found out what he was doing. She scrambled their signals so that the images you received were distorted and less effective."

"They were almost too much."

"But they weren't. You stayed sane. She would have taken any risk for you. And Ransome needs her now, and she'll take risks for him. You *want* Mary—but Ransome *needs* her."

"I almost died for Mary, back on Earth."

"Did you? Leo told me that you had the Dream Machine on

a medium setting—low enough to break out of it when you decided you wanted to."

Bey stared mindlessly into the great water globe. A small, red-throated fish had come drifting lazily toward them and was poised at the curved transparent wall. It stared goggle-eyed at the two humans, looking at the universe beyond the barrier. That had been Bey before he came out there. Tucked away in his own little fishbowl, safe and warm below a blanket of atmosphere.

Earth. Suddenly he had a great longing to be back there, to see blue sky and drifting clouds.

"I'm going back, Sylvia. My job here is finished. The Rinis are interesting, and they're going to change our whole universe, but they will be Aybee's lifework, not mine."

"I know." Sylvia was still holding Bey. "Aybee's going to miss you. He'd never say it, but you're his idol, you know."

"Hard luck for Aybee."

"He could do a lot worse. Mary told me one other thing. She said that when you met her out in the Halo you talked a lot about me. She didn't speculate why, but I think you were trying to make her bring you here."

"I was. It was the only way I could think of to do it. I wanted to make her jealous, so she would want to bring me along and see I preferred her to you. I don't mean that I *do* prefer her to you, but . . ."

Sylvia was shaking her head. "Bey, when I hear you say things like that, I wonder if you know anything about women at all. If Mary had been the least jealous, or thought for a moment that you were interested in me, the last thing she'd do is encourage a meeting."

"But that's exactly what she did."

"Do you need it written out for you? You didn't talk Mary into bringing you with her to Ransome's Hole—she was intending to do that all along!"

"But you said there was no way she would—"

"Not so you could see if you liked Mary better than me." Sylvia's voice was warm. "You hairy, self-centered little ape. Mary did it for *her* purposes, not yours. She wanted to see if she liked you better than Ransome. But after she heard you talk about me, she said she felt less guilty about leaving to follow him."

Bey sat for a few seconds in silence, staring into the blue-green depths of the water. He was feeling tired but not the slightest bit heartbroken. Even the revelation of Mary's motives did not upset him.

"I'm a total idiot, you know," he said at last.

"We're all idiots."

"I'm the worst. I thought I was being so clever with Mary. I'm going back, Sylvia. Back to Earth, back to something I'm good at. To the Office of Form Control again, if they'll have me. But I'm really going to miss you and Aybee and Leo. I'm even going to miss Cinnabar and old Turpin, but I'll miss you most of all. Would you come and visit me—see the Inner System for yourself?"

"Among all those little hairy Sunhuggers?" He knew she was laughing at him. "What do you think I am?"

"I think you're a big, heartless skeleton that pretends to be a woman. Earth's not as bad as you think. I think you'd like it. Will you do it? Come and visit?"

"I'm not sure." She ran her finger along the hair on his wrist and refused to look at him. "No promises. But we'll see."

Bey nodded. It was all the answer he could expect, but it was enough.

He looked again into the water globe. The little red-throated fish was up against the wall, and it was still staring out at him. It had no eyelids, but Bey felt sure that it was trying to wink.

ABOUT THE AUTHOR

Charles Sheffield is Chief Scientist of Earth Satellite Corporation. He is a past-president of the Science Fiction Writers of America and of the American Astronautical Society, a Distinguished Lecturer of the American Institute of Aeronautics and Astronautics, and a Board Member of the National Space Society. Born and educated in England, he holds bachelor's and master's degrees in mathematics and a doctorate in theoretical physics (general relativity and gravitation). He now lives in Bethesda, Maryland.

DEL REY BOOKS

JAMES P. HOGAN

The man who is putting science back into science fiction!